Behind Shadows

Netta Newbound

Junction Publishing
New Zealand

Copyright © 2014 by Netta Newbound.

All rights reserved. No part of this publication may be reproduced, distributed or transmitted in any form or by any means, including photocopying, recording, or other electronic or mechanical methods, without the prior written permission of the publisher, except in the case of brief quotations embodied in critical reviews and certain other noncommercial uses permitted by copyright law. For permission requests, write to the publisher, addressed "Attention: Permissions Coordinator," at the address below.

Netta Newbound/Junction Publishing
Waihi 3610
New Zealand
nettanewbound@hotmail.com
www.nettanewbound.com

Publisher's Note: This is a work of fiction. Names, characters, places, and incidents are a product of the author's imagination. Locales and public names are sometimes used for atmospheric purposes. Any resemblance to actual people, living or dead, or to businesses, companies, events, institutions, or locales is completely coincidental.

Book Layout & Design ©2013 - BookDesignTemplates.com

Ordering Information:
Quantity sales. Special discounts are available on quantity purchases by corporations, associations, and others. For details, contact the "Special Sales Department" at the email address above.

Behind Shadows/ Netta Newbound. -- 1st ed.
ISBN 978-1503217102

For my gran—forever in my heart

No trait is more justified than revenge
in the right time and place.
—Meir Kehane

Chapter 1

Amanda

I stood in the doorway, staring at my sorry excuse for a husband.

Michael was sitting on the lid of the toilet, his back against the cistern, jeans around his ankles and the buttons of his blue-and-white striped shirt open to his chest. He had his hands twisted in the red hair of a woman kneeling in front of him, her head bobbing up and down in his lap.

Eyes rolling in ecstasy, he caught sight of me standing there. He stared blankly for a few seconds, the colour draining from his face. He jumped to his feet, knocking the woman to the floor in a sprawling heap. His penis went from rock hard to flaccid in an instant.

I could hear stifled laughter and whispers as a crowd of fellow-guests gathered behind me.

My heart pounding in my chest, I turned and hurried down the stairs—the gawking audience parting for me, sending the odd pitying glance my way.

I reached the front door and heard a commotion behind me. Over my shoulder I saw Michael was charging down the stairs, still buttoning his shirt.

"Wait, Amanda. Let me explain."

I ran into the street, ignoring the demands and excuses pouring from his lying mouth. A strong gust of wind blew my pink cotton jacket open, the fabric flapping violently. I pulled it tight and fastened the large black buttons.

I raced along the street, heading where was anybody's guess, but I needed to put as much distance between us as possible.

I couldn't believe he could do this to me. So what if we'd been arguing quite a bit lately—every couple has their rocky patches, but to do this! To humiliate me like this!

Hot tears began to coat my cheeks and made it difficult to see where I was going. I stopped and leaned against a high wooden fence to catch my breath and wipe my eyes. I almost shot out of my skin as something heavy smacked into the fence behind me and a dog began barking ferociously.

I set off running again, but was gaining little ground with the squally wind hammering into me.

I knew I should have stayed at home with the children. At least I'd be certain they were safe and tucked up in bed—not left with a young girl we hardly knew.

As I reached the bottom of the road, another gust of wind almost blew me over, making me stagger backwards. A McDonald's bag swirled in front of me and its greasy contents fell into the gutter.

I had no idea where the hell I was heading. This suburb of London was unfamiliar to me. The taxi journey had taken twenty minutes from my home in Pinevale. I fished the phone from my jeans' pocket. 'No Network Coverage' flashed across the screen. A fresh bout of tears filled my eyes.

Without a phone signal, I didn't know which direction to head in. I pulled the collar up on my thin jacket, shoved my hands in the pockets, and turned to the left—at least that way the wind would be to my back.

My blond hair whipped around my face. A huge raindrop hit me on the shoulder, another landed in front of me on the pavement.

There was a squeal of brakes as a black cab stopped beside me. I sighed as relief flooded through me and I reached for the door handle. Just then, the window wound down and Michael stuck his head out. My stomach clenched as I stifled a scream.

I snatched my hand away as though I'd just been burned and spun away from the cab, continuing along the road. The raindrops were now gaining momentum, I was seconds away from being soaked to the skin.

"Get in, Amanda. We need to talk." The howling wind absorbed most of his voice, but not enough for my liking. I'd have preferred to not hear him at all.

I ignored him.

Michael jumped out of the cab and fell in step beside me. "Come on, get in. It's dangerous around here at this time of night."

His whining voice irritated me.

"Piss off, Michael! Leave me alone. I'll come home when I'm good and ready." A thick wad of hair blew into my mouth. I gagged as I picked it out, and then pushed the mess off my face with both hands.

"Don't you wanna check on the kids?"

My stomach flipped. That stopped me in my tracks. I didn't want to give him the satisfaction of being right, but I did need to check the children were safe. Especially after the uneasy feelings I'd had recently.

That had been the cause of an on-going argument and Michael accusing me of paranoia, but I didn't care what he thought anymore. Somebody was watching me, and I knew it.

With a weighty sigh and an equally weighty heart, I got into the taxi. Sitting sideways on the seat, I faced the window with my back to Michael.

The rain, heavier now, pelted the windows and the wind buffeted the sides of the cab. The metallic, twanging sound of the recorded Indian music filled the awkward silence.

The cab stank of smoke. A pine tree shaped air-freshener hanging from the rear-view mirror gave off no scent at all. To be fair, a full-sized pine tree on the passenger seat would struggle to mask the stale stench.

My stomach churned, and my mouth filled up with saliva. I prayed I wouldn't throw up. The driver was deluded if he thought we wouldn't notice the stench. Any fool could work out he must have a sneaky puff when he was alone. He didn't even have the sense to hide his cigarettes and lighter, they sat on the dashboard in plain sight.

Michael reached for my hand. A feeling, similar to an electric current, zapped up my arm. I tore my hand away. "Get off!" I hissed.

A sharp intake of breath was the only sound he made. He moved to the other end of the seat, no doubt planning his next move.

We pulled up outside the house. I got out of the taxi and left Michael paying the driver. The rain had settled to a fine mist yet seemed wetter than regular rain. I ran up the concrete path and searched out anything unfamiliar looming in the garden shadows.

Every shape looked different and seemed more sinister in the dark. The squally wind and rain fuelled my imagination and I shuddered as the hair stood up on the back of my neck. The feeling of being watched was stronger than ever.

I tapped on the lounge window and sensed movement behind the curtain. A couple of seconds later the front door opened.

"Charlotte, I thought I made myself clear. Check who it is before you open the door!" I hurried inside and stood in the hallway, shivering. My breath escaped in short, noisy gasps and blows. I struggled to ignore the urge to lock and double lock the door and leave Michael on the other side of it.

"I'm sorry, Mrs Flynn. I forgot," she said as she backed into the lounge.

"You forgot? I shook my head. "Great—just great. So if a mad axe man burst in and chopped you all up into little pieces that would be okay, hey? Because you forgot." I knew I was over-reacting, but I couldn't help myself.

Her huge brown eyes stared at me, and her mouth turned down at the corners, quivering.

"It's okay, Charlotte," Michael said as he stepped inside. "Get your coat—I'll walk you home."

Charlotte lived on the next street, it would take all of five minutes to get her home but we were responsible for getting her there safe and sound.

I glared at Michael, my face flushed with anger at him for not backing me up. Taking a deep breath, I exhaled in a controlled blow, forcing myself to calm down. I didn't want to lose it in front of Charlotte. Her mother was the local gossip and anything I said would be twisted in triplicate and all over the estate by morning.

"How have the children been?" I asked when she came back from the kitchen, her bag and coat over her arm.

"Jacob didn't stir at all and Emma fell asleep after the first story." Her tone was more clipped than usual. I guessed she wouldn't babysit again, which suited me fine.

Once they'd gone, I went into the lounge. After almost five years of living in a dated, seventies time warp, we'd begun modernising. This was my favourite room. It was normally immaculate and the kids didn't come in here very often. We used it at night once they were in bed.

Charlotte had flung the expensive, lime-green cushions onto the floor, but not before smearing one in melted chocolate. I threw it back down angrily before picking the rest up and placing them onto the sofa, then sat down, hugging the dirty cushion to my chest. I was more upset over a chocolate covered cushion than my husband's indiscretions.

I knew most people would be hysterical by now. They would be throwing their own, or their partner's, belongings into a suitcase and talking divorce and child custody. But numbness had kicked in with me instead. Doctor Freda always said I didn't process things like normal people do. She explained my reactions were understandable considering what I'd been through. But I didn't think it was a problem, who wanted to have emotional displays every two minutes? I know I didn't. I'd had a cry and now I would deal with the situation my way.

Still clutching the cushion, I checked the windows, making sure they were locked with the key, and then went through to the kitchen-dining room. We used this room most of the time. There was a small sofa at one end as well as a dining table and chairs. It had a cosy, lived-in feel. The children's toys covered the rug in front of the gas fire.

I placed the cushion on the sink and then checked and double-checked the back door and windows before heading upstairs.

In the light from the landing, I could make out Emma's beautiful curls tumbling over the pillow and my heart contracted in my chest. I bent to kiss her cheek, my nostrils filling with the unique scent of my daughter.

Princesses, crowns and flouncy fabric filled the shocking-pink room—a total contrast to the bedroom I'd had growing up, which wasn't that hard to achieve. My children would never have to experience a cold hard mattress and grimy threadbare blankets.

I picked up a lifelike baby doll from the floor and placed the ugly thing next to Emma on the bed. Emma took her thumb from her mouth and cuddled the doll protectively. I perched one knee on the window seat and checked the window was secure, glancing out into the shadows of the back garden. I shuddered again and closed the curtains.

In the room across the landing, I bobbed my head to miss the giant, luminous stars hanging from the ceiling. I detested them. They were tacky and didn't go with the Noah's ark theme I'd designed. However, Michael's parents had bought them for Jacob and he loved them.

Jacob's duvet was off and scrunched up underneath him. One fat little leg stuck through the bars of his cot. Being extra careful, so as not to wake him, I squeezed it back through, then pulled his duvet out and covered him up. Noah and Mrs Noah adorned the duvet's centre, and numerous pairs of animals and birds surrounded them.

I checked the window, then sighed as I closed the bedroom door.

Once in the bathroom, I slid the bolt in place and switched on the shower. I took off my brown, leather boots, followed by my jeans, T-shirt and underwear, leaving them in a pile in the corner. I stepped under the hot jets of water, praying it would wash away the images of my cheating husband, but instead it had the opposite effect.

Silent tears fell and mixed with the shower water. I rubbed my eyes, then my face. My hands moved from my neck and chest, and cupped my small, round breasts. I picked up the sponge and began scrubbing my skin, starting at my neck and moving further down.

Short gasps escaped from my parted lips.

I was ashamed at the way my body betrayed me. The more I thought about Michael with that woman, the more aroused I became and the harder I scrubbed myself with the sponge—as though I was punishing myself.

My skin raw, sobs mixing with pants, I let the roughness of the sponge rub between my thighs, not able to shake the images of Michael and his tart.

It was over in seconds. I dropped the sponge then slid to the tiles, sobbing out loud.

What the hell was wrong with me? I couldn't understand how the evening's events had me feeling like this. It wasn't normal.

I wasn't normal.

Downstairs the door banged, followed by the sound of the TV. He was home.

I got out of the shower, swiped my hand across the fogged up mirror, then applied moisturiser to my bright-red cheeks, calming the tell-tale flush of my orgasm.

My pale-blue eyes had a dull lifelessness to them that I hadn't seen in a long, long time. It was no surprise that Michael had gone for the redhead. The mass of strawberry curls he'd had twisted in his hands looked sexy and wanton compared to my fine, lank and colourless tresses and that wasn't the only notable difference. My boyish body was no comparison to her voluptuous curves.

I pulled my comfortable, Cookie Monster nightie on, then crept onto the landing and padded down the stairs. I knew Michael wouldn't have secured the dead bolt on the front door and I'd get no sleep tonight if I didn't do it.

I placed my cupped hand on top of my keys on the hall table and scooped them up, gripping them in my fist to stop them jangling. I wasn't in the mood for another argument—not tonight.

Suddenly, the volume went up on the TV and the football commentator's yell made my feet leave the floor. I twirled around, locked the front door and ran back up the stairs.

In the bedroom, I slid the flimsy bolt into place, more as a statement than for protection. No way was he going to sleep in my bed.

My legs were fidgety and I couldn't get comfortable. One minute they were out of the duvet, the next back in. I thought about tonight, unable to understand why Michael had insisted I go with him, only to ignore and humiliate me. Five years of marriage must mean something to him—or maybe not. Too hot again, I sprawled out onto the cool sheets on Michael's side.

Startled by a loud bang, I shot off the bed, my heart in my mouth. Disorientated, I realised I must have fallen asleep after all.

Michael was shaking and banging the door. "Amanda!" he yelled.

"Leave me alone, Michael," I said, moving to stand inches away from him, my fingers on the handle.

"Open the door or I'll kick it in," he slurred. He must have been at the whisky downstairs. He'd had a few drinks at the party, but he hadn't seemed drunk, not like now.

I opened it slightly. "Shush!" I nodded towards the children's rooms. "Not tonight, Michael—we'll talk in the morning." My lips trembled.

"Open the fucking door. Now!"

"Be quiet!" I realised it was pointless. "Fine, come in. I'll get in bed with Emma."

I stepped back and he slammed the door into me, knocking me off balance. I fell backwards onto the bed and he pounced on top of me in an instant. The look in his eyes warned me not to mess with him. Blood surged through my veins, and my stomach churned.

"Michael, wh-what are you doing?" I didn't think he would hurt me, but I'd never seen him this angry before.

"Shut up, bitch! You're so high and fucking mighty, aren't you? Snooty Amanda, never does anything wrong. Now you have the excuse you've been waiting for to get rid of me," he said as he gripped both of my wrists.

I tried to resist, but it was useless.

"What the hell do you expect me to do? I caught the woman sucking your cock, for Christ's sake!" My voice sounded much stronger than I felt.

"Maybe if you paid me some attention, I wouldn't be tempted. I have women falling at my feet. But you—my own wife, you never even notice me." He yanked my arms above my head and trapped them in one of his.

His hardness pressing against my belly alerted me to his arousal. That was all I needed. I tried to wriggle out from under him, but he was too heavy.

With his free hand, he yanked my nightie up, shoving his knee in between my legs.

"Michael, you're hurting me!" My voice now quivered.

I was transported to another place and time. Being pinned down, the dark shape over me, and the stench of alcohol—all scarily similar, yet vastly different.

Petrifying fear gripped me as I remembered a cold, dank room, and a grimy, bare mattress. I knew these images weren't real. But the fear was real, and the anger bubbling deep within me most definitely real.

I opened my mouth to scream but instead a roar escaped from deep within me. Accompanying the roar was a sudden burst of strength that enabled me to yank my hands free. In quick succession, I grabbed his hair, pulled his head towards me and sank my teeth into his face.

The salty taste turned metallic.

Michael screamed and leapt to his feet.

I got upright just as fast, surprised by the strength I'd found.

He howled like a baby, hopping from foot to foot, his hands pressed against his cheek. I raised myself to my tiptoes and hissed into his ear. "Now, leave me the fuck alone!"

I closed the door behind me.

***

I lay snuggled next to my daughter's tiny body all night. The steady rise and fall of her breathing soothed me, and God knows I needed soothing. My stomach was in knots, and uncontrollable tears soaked the pillow proving Doctor Freda didn't know what the hell she was talking about. I did have emotions, but I'd just learned to hide them from an early age. However, the events of last night had been too much even for me to ignore.

What had happened with Michael was bad enough, but the memories that had surfaced horrified me the most. Memories I'd blocked for such a long time.

The birds in the garden began their morning song and I knew the children would wake soon.

I heard the toilet flush, followed by the squeak of floorboards on the landing.

I slid out of bed and crept downstairs.

Michael stood at the kitchen sink filling the kettle, dressed in a tight fitting grey t-shirt and pyjama bottoms. His body tensed as I entered the room.

"We need to talk, Michael," I said.

As he turned around, the breath caught in my throat. A deep cut under his right eye appeared swollen and inflamed.

"Oh shit! I didn't mean ..." I put my hand to my mouth to stop myself from crying.

His cheeks coloured. "I'm pretty sure I deserved everything," he said, unable to look me in the eye. "What do you wanna do now?" Wiping his hands on his pyjamas, he leaned back against the bench, his shoulders stooped and his chin almost touching his chest.

I shrugged and shook my head. "I don't know," I said. "I just can't think straight at the moment." I pulled a chair out from under the table and sat down heavily.

We'd met in Italy, almost six years ago now. I was twenty-one, Michael a little older at twenty-four.

My interior design course had finished and I was lucky enough to score some work from a builder, giving me hands-on decorating experience.

After three years in Italy I was used to vain, flirtatious men. Michael, just another in a long line, loved himself more than he could ever love anyone else.

There was no denying he was handsome. With his tall, athletic build and broad, shoulders, clothes hung from his body to perfection, no matter what he wore. His bright blue eyes—the first thing I noticed about him—stood out against his olive complexion. Natural golden glints shone in his brown, stylishly messy hair. He was always preening himself in front of the mirror. However, good looks wear thin I'd found.

It began with a one-night stand, as I guess many relationships do. I'd never been happier in my life at that stage, or as free. I wasn't interested in anything more serious than a quick fumble, perhaps a drink or two, maybe dinner.

Michael had other ideas, and he pursued me until I relented. Maybe because he wasn't used to rejection, who knows? For the first six months, I couldn't have asked for a better, more doting and affectionate man. Then as soon as I got pregnant, and we married, everything seemed to change.

They were subtle changes at first, he was less attentive and more critical and I began to withdraw into myself more and more. But we'd got by, learned to live with each other's quirks and oddities. We had a relatively good marriage.

At first, we'd juggled the children between us since we were both self-employed. That was until his building work began to dry up and my interior-design business began to soar.

It was a no-brainer that Michael should stay at home with the children while I was the breadwinner—which seemed to stick in his craw. He hated admitting to his friends that he was a house husband.

He also hated how overprotective I was, and said I interfered too much. He accused me of being paranoid because I wouldn't let him leave the kids alone in day-care.

Things had become worse recently though. The fact that we weren't having sex was the main problem—I'd lost my libido since Jacob was born. I knew Michael was frustrated, but I couldn't help myself.

Then the arguments began. It was obvious that something was very wrong, but I'd ignored it, hoping things would settle down again.

Now I knew the reason for his attitude, and I can't say I was too surprised.

Just last night, before we left home, Michael called me an embarrassment, because I'd refused to change out of my jeans. If dinner or a dance—the theatre even—had been our destination, then fair enough. But we were going to a house party, for Christ's sake, not a bloody fashion show.

In the cab on the way there, he'd sulked like a spoiled brat and continued to be horrible until we arrived at his friend's house. Then, as though someone had flipped a switch, my moody husband turned into Prince Charming once again.

Most women he met hung off his every word. To think that those same tired old lines had hooked me once upon a time—not anymore though.

His smarmy, cheesy patter worked a treat, especially on women of a certain age, but he'd always insisted flirting was as far as he ever went. And although I'd had my suspicions in the past, I'd never thought he would have the gall to do it right under my nose.

"Who was she?" I asked, a twinge of hurt making me wince and I closed my eyes and took a deep breath.

He shrugged. "I met her at the party. I was stupid," he said as he fiddled with the corner of the tea-towel in his hands.

"Don't worry. I'll move out."

I gasped and took another deep breath and held it until I felt light headed. Once I'd composed myself, I looked at him. "Do you want to move out?"

"It's not about what I want anymore, is it?" He whispered.

"Things can't stay as they have been, Michael, that's for sure."

I was no saint. During the three years I'd spent in Italy, I'd been promiscuous and lost count how many sexual partners I'd had. I was always searching for something to fill the emptiness I felt and I was well aware of how sex could be an entirely meaningless act.

But once I met Michael I thought I'd made it. He was handsome, funny and easy to get along with. But I still sometimes yearned for the excitement of my old ways.

Watching Michael having raw, exciting sex on a toilet seat with a stranger had got me going. Last night's shower performance was proof of that.

I knew I wasn't the easiest person to get along with. The only emotion I showed was directed towards the children. But I loved him in my own twisted and dysfunctional way. I was hurt by his actions but understood why he'd done it. He needed more of a physical relationship than I'd been capable of giving him.

"I don't want you to move out," I said.

He grabbed the bench top to steady himself. "You mean ...? Oh, Amanda, you won't regret it, I swear to you," he said as he walked towards me. He held out a hand and grasped mine, squeezing tight. His hand trembled and his beautiful blue eyes brimmed with tears.

He bent to hug me, but I held up my hand and shook my head. "It's not over—not just like that," I said. "You need to prove yourself to me, Michael. I need to know I can trust you and that you'll never humiliate me like that ever again."

"I promise, Mand. I love you, and I will make it better."

"We'll see, but if you ever pull another stunt like you did last night you will regret it, I promise you. And I don't just mean because of a tiny nip on your cheek either."

Chapter 2

Amanda

The following Saturday was a beautiful day, unusually warm for mid-October. Michael suggested we make the most of the weather and take the children to the zoo.

It had been ages since we'd been out as a family. I contemplated refusing to go, but Emma was so excited that I shrugged and said, "Why not?"

I set about packing for every eventuality: nappies, wipes, changes of clothes, snacks and drinks.

Emma had chosen her own outfit and dressed herself this morning. She looked cute in her navy-blue leggings and a pink roll neck jumper, her golden curls held back with a purple, butterfly headband. Both the children had been blessed with Michael's full-bodied curls, but my colouring and although I hated my pale complexion and the colour of my hair, it was lovely on them.

Emma had her own bag and followed me around the house packing. I laughed as she peered into the fridge—the concentration on her face was priceless.

She tucked her favourite blanket into the top of her bag. "I'm weddy, Mummy."

I knew I'd have to start correcting her speech soon, but she sounded adorable. She'd always been advanced for her age in many ways except for her childlike pronunciations.

The drive to the local train station took ten minutes. It made good sense to travel into the zoo on the train, cutting out all the parking issues.

The kids were so excited. They'd never been on a train before. Emma didn't stop chattering for a second. The bag on her back was almost bursting at the seams—I didn't think she would carry it for too long.

Michael and I sat together.

Every time I looked at him, an image of him with that brazen hussy flashed before my eyes and it made my heart break a little bit more. Not that he'd have guessed how I was feeling. If asked he'd have probably said that things were back to normal with us, but it was far from normal for me.

He reached for my hand and held it the whole journey. He'd been making a huge effort all week, but I still felt cold to his touch.

The children were sitting across the aisle from us. Every time we went round a bend Emma squealed with delight, grabbing hold of Jacob, who laughed hysterically at his big sister. Everyone in the entire carriage cracked up laughing at them too.

We walked from the train station at Camden Town. The wind had picked up a bit, but it was still warm. By the time we arrived at the zoo's entrance, in Regents Park, we were sweltering hot.

We got in a queue behind a busload of Japanese tourists. Michael groaned, rolled his eyes, and looked at his watch. But the well-organised tour guides cleared the crowds, getting us through the gates and in front of the reptile house within a few minutes.

The one and only time I'd been to the zoo was as a schoolgirl with my class. I could still remember my excitement at seeing all the fantastic wild animals I'd only read about in books.

"Okay, where to first?" I asked.

"How 'bout we go in the opposite direction to everyone else?" Michael said, nodding at the throng of tourists just ahead of us. "The aquarium's right here."

"Good thinking, Batman, the aquarium it is then," I said.

Emma was trying to undo my grip on her arm with her free hand, her eyes darting everywhere.

"Emma, would you please stop doing that?"

I pulled her to the side of the walkway and crouched down in front of her. "Right, before we do anything, Emma, you need to listen to me."

"Wook, Mummy, monkeys," she said, paying no attention to me whatsoever.

"Emma, are you listening to me?" I shook her arm which seemed to do the trick.

"Yes," she said, startled.

"You have got to keep close to me and hold my hand at all times, do you hear me?"

"Okay, Mummy, can we see the monkeys?"

"Later. We'll go to the aquarium first." I laughed, feeling exhausted already.

Michael led the way with Jacob in his pushchair, and I held on to Emma for dear life.

I'd always hated crowds and noise, but I didn't want to spoil the day so I fixed a smile on my face.

The seahorses, one little yellow one in particular, had Emma mesmerised. I couldn't tear her away from the tank.

"Come on, sweetie, there are a lot more animals to visit yet," I coaxed.

"Five minutes, five minutes, Mummy, pwease." Her face almost touched the glass.

"She is pretty, isn't she?" I said, kneeling beside Emma in front of the tank.

"Can I take her home, Mummy?" She gazed at the tiny creature longingly.

"No, honey. They need to stay at the zoo."

We finally made our way to the exit. Michael and Jacob were sitting outside the door, waiting for us.

"Thank goodness! I was about to send out a search party, you've been ages," Michael said standing up.

"Emma fell in love with a seahorse. She wanted to take it home with us." I raised my eyebrows at him and smiled.

"Mummy pwomised to get me one fwom the shop," Emma said. Her big blue eyes sparkled.

Michael cocked his head to one side, his eyebrows mimicking mine. "Oh, she did, did she?"

"Not a real one." I laughed. "I had to say something, or we'd have been in there all day."

"Well let's hope we can find one then, if Mummy promised." He smiled at Emma.

Our next stop was the gorillas.

Jacob went berserk and almost screamed the place down, he held himself rigid with fear while Michael struggled to release the clasp of the pushchair.

Once he was in his daddy's arms, his screams calmed to sobs. Michael wafted his hand in front of his nose, telling me Jacob needed changing.

We weren't getting very far at all.

At the Oasis café, I ordered drinks and got a map of the zoo while Michael took Jacob into the bathroom. Emma and I sat down at a table studying the map.

"Oh wook, Mummy, they is penguins and a dwagon."

"A dragon? Are you sure?" I couldn't imagine what she'd seen. "Show me."

She handed me the booklet and there certainly was a dragon.

"Ahh, a Komodo dragon. You are right, Miss Emma—and yes, we can go later."

"Go where?" Michael said as he pulled out a chair.

"A dwagon! Wook, Daddy, wook, Jake, a dwagon."

I pushed a mug of coffee across the wobbly, plastic table to Michael, and emptied a bottle of juice into Jacobs's cup. "Someone smells sweeter—don't you, baby?" I said handing Jacob his drink and a piece of apple.

Refreshed, recharged, and eager to continue on our way, the penguins were the next stop—followed by the butterflies, pelicans and parrots. By the time we got to the big cats Jacob was sound asleep.

"Aw, Michael, I wanted him to see the lions," I grumbled. Though I had to admit his flushed, chubby little cheeks and his cherry lips, pursed into a continual kiss, was just too cute. I bent and kissed him several times in the hope he might wake up, but he was spark out.

"Let him have half an hour and we'll wake him up. You take Emma into the bugs. I'll wait here for you."

I glanced across the path and noticed the giant wooden, creepy crawlies on the roof of a cabin and a B.U.G.S sign emblazoned above the entrance.

"You scaredy cat." I laughed. "How about you go in, and I'll stay here with Jacob?"

"Piss off!" Michael's smile lit up his cheeky eyes as he plonked himself down on the bench and crossed one denim-clad leg over the other.

"Aw, Daddy, you sweared." Emma scowled at Michael, her arms folded across her chest.

"I'm sorry, sweetheart. Mummy knows I don't like spiders." He shuddered.

"Michael, you're gonna frighten her. We have to go in now if only to show her there's nothing to be scared of and that you're a mardy bum. Hey, Em, is daddy a mardy bum?"

She giggled. "Yeah, Daddy, you're a mardy bum."

"You're right, but ask me if I care." He laughed, giving me a glimpse of the fun-loving, easy-going man I married. My heart fluttered. Maybe there was a chance of salvaging something from this train-wreck of a marriage after all.

"Come on, Mummy, wet's go." Emma tugged on my arm.

"Okay, if I must." I didn't want Emma growing up with the same irrational fear as her father, but even so, the thought of coming face to face with hundreds of bugs made me squirm.

The entrance was dimly lit and creepy. I'm not sure if the bugs preferred it this way or if the staff got a kick out of giving everyone the heebie-jeebies, but less than two minutes in and I itched all over.

Emma, not at all bothered, stood on a platform with one of the guides looking at a red-kneed, bird-eating spider. "Wook, Mummy, his name's Bowis, come and see!" Her face beamed.

I shuddered, more than a little freaked out. "I'm okay thanks, sweetie, you carry on." I kept my distance and left Emma to run back and forth in awe of the horrid, crawly things. Large glass tanks featured a whole host of bugs. There were hissing cockroaches, huge beetles, crickets, and praying mantises to name but a few.

My phone rang. I dug in my handbag while a guide explained to Emma what was happening inside an anthill. I found my phone and walked back towards the entrance.

"Hello, Amanda speaking."

"Good morning, Amanda," a woman's voice said. "My name is Judy. I got your number from a mutual friend. I believe you're an interior designer?"

The lady sounded middle-aged, her voice so light and whispery I was having difficulty hearing her. I glanced at Emma, still engrossed in the ants, and walked a bit further towards the entrance.

"Yes, that's right. How can I help you?" I pressed the phone tight against my ear, putting a finger in my other ear.

"I need a quote for some work on a house in Kingsley. Does this sound like something you'd be interested in?"

"Yes, I'm sure I would," I said, punching the air excitedly.

"The thing is—" She cleared her throat. "—I don't live in London and I'm not very well at the moment, so I won't be able to make the trip for some time. I need somebody to help me get the place shipshape, but ..."

I braced myself for the 'but'.

"I'll require you to work alone. We'd be in close contact via email. How does this sound?"

"I ... er ... yeah, sounds okay, I guess. Depending on what you want done of course. Do you know if any building work is needed?" I tried to keep a professional tone to my voice, but I could hear the smile in my voice. I leaned my bottom against the frame of a blacked-out window.

"There shouldn't be too much, but I believe your husband is a builder, isn't he?"

"Gosh, you have done your homework Mrs ... oh, I'm sorry—I didn't catch your name."

"Call me Judy, and yes I did do my homework. The house is full to the gunnels with antiques so I need somebody I can trust. My sources tell me I can rely on you, which suits me. Do you think you'd like to take the job on?"

"Yes, it sounds interesting, Judy. Could I give you a call later to get a few more details?" I switched hands and wiped my sweaty palm on my trousers.

"I have your email address, Amanda. I'll send everything you'll need. I look forward to working with you, dear."

The phone went dead in my ear.

I'd been short of real design work. With the recession, most of the jobs that I'd taken on had been small and I'd sub-contracted a lot of the actual work out. This was better than turning anything down, and instead, meant I could take on more jobs and cream a nice commission off the top without killing myself.

This sounded perfect for me. Properties in Kingsley were ultra-expensive. Maybe this was just the job I'd been waiting for to get my name known.

I practically bounced over to where I'd left Emma.

A crowd of children surrounded the ants, but she wasn't among them. I walked a bit further, past the dung beetles and stick insects. There was still no sign of my daughter.

"Emma?" Although not loud, the urgency in my voice made the kids and some adults stop and stare at me.

I reached the exit and began to shake. My legs felt as though they were going to buckle underneath me. I steadied myself before re-tracing my steps back inside.

A young woman approached me dressed in the zoo's uniform. Her name was Jane, according to the badge she wore.

"Is everything all right, madam?"

"Have you seen my little girl? She's four years old, with blond curly hair?"

"I'm sorry, madam, but you've just described almost half the room. Can you tell me what she's wearing?"

My chest was getting tighter by the second. It was as though all the oxygen had been sucked out of the air. "She's blond, pink jacket, huge backpack ..."

"Do you mean the little girl you left with a few moments ago?"

I felt as though I'd just been slammed into an invisible wall, knocking every ounce of air from my lungs. "What do you mean? I never left with her." I reached and grasped at the woman's arm to steady myself. "I didn't go anywhere! I was standing over there on the phone," I said, my voice taking on a shrill tone.

The woman's eyebrows knitted, confusion flashing across her face. "I don't know how to say this, but I just saw a woman I would swear was you leave with the little girl you described, not five minutes ago."

***

I couldn't believe what she was telling me and I felt my legs buckle.

Jane gripped my arm and I leaned against her. "I'll make some calls and alert everyone she's missing. In the meantime, you need to go over to the information centre at the zoo's entrance. I'll make sure they're expecting you," she said. "I'd take you myself but I'll have to wait for somebody to relieve me."

"No, no. That's fine. Thanks for all your help." I raced back to Michael, unsure how my legs still held me upright. The tightness in my chest made it hard to breathe.

Michael was chatting on his phone. When he noticed me, he ended the call.

"Michael, Michael, Emma's gone!" The words left me in a breathy rush.

"Calm down, Amanda!" He jumped to his feet, grabbed me by the upper arms and shook me roughly.

Our raised voices woke Jacob, who began to scream, which he always did if woken too soon.

"I can't f-f-find Emma. The girl said a woman took her."

"What do you mean 'took her'? Was she crying?"
"No, no. I don't think so. She didn't say Emma was upset."
"Okay, let's not panic. I'm sure she'll be okay. Now, tell me again, what happened?" Michael's face had drained of all colour.
"We have to go to the information centre first, I'll tell you on the way."

I told him everything, all the while running towards the zoo's entrance. I had my eyes peeled for a blond woman in a bright red jacket. The knot in my stomach was so big it felt like a ton weight.
I couldn't believe this was happening. I'd always prided myself on being vigilant when it came to my kids. I never let them out of my sight. I cursed myself for answering the bloody phone in the first place.
By the time we reached the information centre, I felt like a nervous wreck.
Michael spoke to the woman at the counter who was, as Jane had said, expecting us. She wrote down some details before getting on the walkie-talkie and giving a description of our beautiful little girl.
An older lady with short blond hair led me into a small room at the back of the office. She made me a cup of sweet tea, as though this kind of thing happened all the time.

"She'll be fine, love. They get so excited that they don't even think to check you're still beside them. Before long she'll realise you're not there and start to cry and then a member of staff will locate her. You'll see." She placed the cup on the desk in front of me. "There you go, sweetie, now get that down you."

I hoped and prayed she was right. Just then, a voice came over the walkie-talkie confirming they'd found a little girl answering Emma's description in the aquarium. Relief flooded through me. I held on to the arms of the chair to steady myself, taking deep breaths, tears pooled in my eyes again.

Emma's cries reached my ears as soon as I entered the aquarium. Michael was close behind me, pushing Jacob.

"Mummy," she squealed, running to me.

I dropped to the floor and hugged her, both of us sobbing. My breathing was rapid and harsh.

"Naughty, Mummy!" she scolded.

"I'm sorry, sweetheart, I didn't mean to lose you. I was on the phone." I wiped her eyes and straightened her hair. "Come on, let's go home."

Michael stood at the entrance looking over at us, the relief was evident on his face. I smiled at him and he nodded his head and gave me a tight-lipped half smile.

I hugged the attendant who had found her. "Thank you so much. I imagined all kinds of things had happened to her."

"Don't worry." The middle-aged woman hugged me back. "It happens all the time. It's easily done with all the crowds."

"Did you see anybody with her?" I asked, dropping my voice so Emma couldn't hear.

She shook her head. "No. She was alone, crying for her mummy. Why do you ask?"

My stomach dropped to the floor at the thought of my daughter wandering around calling for me. "The girl in the insect house said she left with a woman who was dressed the same as me!"

She shook her head, her face screwed up in a 'no-I-don't-think-so' way. "She was probably just mistaken. Maybe she noticed the two of you together earlier and got confused. Don't worry, your daughter's safe now, and I don't think she'll wander off again anytime soon."

We walked back to the station subdued. Emma, her bag now hanging on the pushchair, dragged her little legs, scuffing her feet on the ground.

"Don't do that, Em. You'll ruin your new shoes."

She lifted her feet higher but continued walking in a lazy way as if the fright had zapped all her energy.

Once we were back on the tube, and we'd all calmed down, I decided to have a chat with Emma about the dangers of wandering off.

"But I didn't, Mummy. You did."

"I told you, darling. I stepped to the side of the room to answer my phone. I wasn't away for long and when I came back, you'd gone."

"I fowwowed you. You wunned away. Naughty, Mummy." She began to cry again.

I looked up at Michael. His eyes had narrowed and he had a strange expression on his face. "What?" I snapped.

"Nothing," he said, his voice was flat and he turned to face the window.

"Michael, of course I didn't run away from her. You were outside waiting for me, for goodness sake. She's confused that's all." I shook my head, feeling my face flush even though I didn't have anything to be guilty for.

***

Instead of going straight home, we took the children to the ballpark where we spent a couple of hours before going on to McDonalds for dinner.

Emma seemed to have recovered from her ordeal and both she and Michael were soon back to normal.

I was glad to be home. I kicked my boots off, slipped my poor aching feet into my slippers and groaned.

Michael had taken the children upstairs to run them a bath. I opened a bottle of merlot and filled two glasses. I half-emptied my glass in one swallow then topped it up again.

I tidied the mess from the front-door mat, putting the shoes into the wicker basket and hanging coats up on the hooks. I took the bags through to the kitchen and set about unpacking.

I screwed a plastic carrier bag up and opened the drawer to shove it in. It was as though the contents of the drawer sprang to life and hundreds of plastic bags seemed to double in size and come up to meet me.

"Woah," I said. Shoving them back down, I slammed the drawer. "Bloody hell, that needs sorting out," I said to myself.

Emma's backpack was crammed full. I shook my head as I pulled out a half-eaten sandwich stuck to her favourite pink, crocheted blanket.

I threw the sandwich into the bin and reached for the dishcloth to wipe off the gooey mess.

As I placed the blanket on the bench top, I noticed a clunk. I shook it and a small silver item fell to the floor. Picking it up, I was surprised to see a tiny seahorse brooch. Now where the heck did that come from? Goosebumps covered my entire body.

Upstairs, I found Michael chasing the children from room to room with a towel on his head. He was pretending to be a monster and roaring at the top of his voice. Emma was squealing and almost running on the spot. I thought she might pee herself. Jacob belly-laughed at them both.

"Hey, hey, calm down now, come on," I said as I pulled Jacob into my arms.

"Again, Daddy, 'gain," he cried.

"No more, darling, it's bedtime. Daddy will read to you instead—won't you, Daddy?" I mock-glared at Michael and smiled.

He shrugged and winked at me. "Sorry, squirt, your mummy's right, it's bedtime."

"Aw, Mummy, you spoiled-ed it." Emma stomped off to her bedroom.

I waited until I'd tucked Emma up in bed, before pulling out the seahorse from my pocket. "Emma, where did you get this from?"

Her eyes lit up. "A horsey! Can I keep him?" She snatched the tiny trinket from me.

"I found it in your bag, darling. Do you know how it got there?"

"No," she said as she inspected the brooch.

"Tell the truth, love—you won't be in trouble," I said, sitting down on the edge of the bed.

"I don't know!" she said.

"Give it back to me." I held my hand out. "Now, please."

She began to cry. I took a deep breath and exhaled slowly. I was so exhausted, I just wanted to get back to my glass of wine and unwind.

Having put Jacob to bed, Michael came into Emma's room. I explained to him about the brooch.

"She's had a rough day, Mand. Maybe she could keep hold of it till the morning?"

"I s'pose," I sighed, willing to agree to anything for a quiet life.

Michael pinned the pretty brooch to the top corner of Emma's pillow and she stopped crying right away. I left them reading a story.

Back in the kitchen, glass in hand, I spied Michael's phone charging on the docking station. I remembered his hurried call at the zoo. I went to the bottom of the stairs and listened. He was still reading to Em.

My heart racing in my chest and all my nerves jangling, I unlocked his phone. He used the same number for everything. My clumsy fingers could have been sausages for all the use they were.

I opened the inbox. Empty.

The call log showed one name, numerous times—someone called Toni. A sick feeling settled in the pit of my stomach. I prayed he wasn't at it again. My head was in a whirl. There must be some other explanation. He'd sworn to me it had been a one-off.

When Michael came downstairs, I was topping up my wine for the third time. I handed him his glass and sat down next to him on the sofa.

"Where do you think the seahorse came from, Amanda?" he asked.

I shrugged.

"We'll get to the bottom of it, don't worry."

"We will indeed," I said, looking at my cheating husband out of the corner of my eye. "We will indeed," I repeated.

Chapter 3

Dennis

"Gotcha, you stupid bitch!" Dennis muttered to the computer screen, a smile spreading across his face. Taking that computer course had been the best thing he'd ever done. His typing was still very slow, but getting faster every day. He wondered how he ever managed without the internet.

Sophie03	Where do you want to meet?
Dannyfitz	Somewhere private. I'm married and will need to be discreet.
Sophie03	My grandmother is away and I have the key to her house.

Dannyfitz   Perfect. What time and where?

"Fuck! That was easy," he said aloud, signing off from the chat room. Young girls had changed a lot in the ten years he'd been away. He'd made it clear to Sophie03 that he expected sex and the fifteen-year-old had been eager to meet up.

Luckily she had a place they could use. He looked around his squalid room with its ripped wallpaper and dingy furniture. This place made his skin crawl. It was no place for a young girl. He'd told her he was thirty-nine and owned a big house in Richmond.

Standing up, he checked himself out in the tarnished mirror above the bed. He was in good shape for almost sixty years old. He had a small paunch and his hair had gone quite grey, but that made him look distinguished, he thought.

"Not bad. Not bad at all," he said to his reflection.

***

As Dennis parked the car, he was surprised by a feeling of impending doom. He almost gave in to it and raced out of there.

Instead, he forced himself to calm down and think about it rationally. Perhaps it was the guilt that was getting to him, or could the rehabilitation classes be having some effect? Possible, but unlikely.

He couldn't see anything wrong with what he was about to do. If the girl wanted it—and she obviously did—what was the problem? He thought about his probation officer and laughed. She would piss her monstrous pants if she knew.

Taking one last glance at his reflection in the rear-view mirror, his cold grey eyes looked back at him. He raked his fingers through his hair. After breathing into his hand, he inhaled deeply through his nose. Satisfied, he picked up the box of chocolates and a bottle of cheap wine from the passenger seat, and got out of the car.

The door to the house stood ajar. After knocking for the second time, he pushed it open a little further with his boot and stuck his head inside.

"Hello? Sophie, can you hear me?"

Still nothing, but he could hear a sound coming from inside like a vacuum cleaner or something electrical. He felt uneasy once again.

He glanced back at the battered old navy-blue Ford parked on the street and wondered if he should follow his instincts and get the hell out of the place? But the itch in his pants was too great to ignore.

He crept into the hallway with slow, uncertain steps, all his senses wired.

The place smelled musty as though it had been shut up for some time. He followed the sound that was coming from the back of the house, his heart racing.

"Hello-o, Sophie?"

He reached the kitchen and realised he'd gone too far as the sound was now behind him. He backtracked and came to a door under the stairs. When he opened the door, the noise was louder.

"Sophie?" he called down the stairs.

"Oh, is that you, Dennis?" The soft voice came from deep within the cellar. "I'm trying to get the heater to work so we can have a bath. Can you help me, please?"

The girl's voice made his hard-on twitch. It had been more than ten years since he had stroked, caressed or tasted a nubile young body. All his senses were telling him to turn and run—the last thing he wanted was to be banged up for another ten years. However, he couldn't ignore the painful urge in his groin.

A bare bulb hung from the centre of the ceiling, casting dark shadows to the outer reaches of the room. He descended the rickety wooden steps, taking care to place his feet in fear of falling.

Sophie was at the back of the cellar, bending over the boiler. She was perfect from behind in the skin-tight, faded jeans. He was in danger of coming in his pants if he wasn't careful. He grabbed the end of his cock through the fabric of his trousers and gave it a sharp pinch.

Her long blond hair hid her face. He walked up to her, put his hands on either side of her hips, and rubbed his hardness against her. "Look what I have for you, my dear."

"Oooh," she giggled, standing upright and arching her back. She was tall, as tall as he was.

Her head tilted backwards, resting on his shoulder. The scent of soap and shampoo, mixed with her excitement, filled his nostrils. She pushed against him with her exquisite tight bottom and groaned.

He could barely control himself. He placed his hands on her upper arms and tried to turn her to face him, but she shrugged his hands off.

"No, wait! It's sexier this way. Close your eyes," she whispered.

He did as she asked, anticipation surging through his veins. She was right—it was erotic not seeing her.

She pushed herself provocatively against his engorged hardness, deliberately replacing her bottom with her hand, she rubbed at it with continual strokes, like a masseuse. Her touch grew more tantalising and urgent as she turned around and crouched in front of him, then with the other hand she unbuckled his belt. He felt her pull his trousers down around his ankles, his breath catching in his throat as his heavy penis sprang free.

Sophie wasted no time. Her cold hands added an extra sensation to the red-hot silky skin of his huge, throbbing cock.

"Oh yeah, good girl, yeah," he groaned as he wrapped one of his hands in her hair; with the other he steadied himself on the boiler.

Sophie roughly pulled at him, making his breath hitch.

"Steady, girl, take it easy," he moaned. Her breath was so close, teasing and driving him wild. He put the roughness down to inexperience which excited him all the more.

The next sensation was unexpected, although not altogether unpleasant. Sophie, moving quite fast, grabbed at his testicles. He felt himself lifted briefly. A confused grunt stuck in his throat.

A feeling of warm liquid running down his legs and splattering the floor, made him think he'd urinated. He groped for his penis, but his fingers sank into a squelching, empty space where it should be.

He felt the cellar walls move in and out. He was dizzy and confused. It couldn't be what he thought. There would be pain. Someone was playing a cruel trick on him.

Sophie had stepped away into the shadows.

In his panic, he tried to get under the light where he could see, but his trousers, still around his ankles, made him stagger before he crashed backwards to the icy floor.

As he hit the ground, Sophie took a step forward into the light, and the shock hit him like a freight train. Tightness in his chest prevented him from taking a full breath. Hot lava-like bile filled his throat and mouth. He swallowed it back down. His mouth opened and closed, but no sound came out.

"Still the same, I see. Prison didn't make a blind bit of difference to you, did it?" she said as she continued walking towards him. Blood covered the front of her pink blouse and had spattered down her jeans.

He shook his head, his wide eyes blinking rapidly. "You," he managed to utter. As he scrambled backwards, his right hand still deep in his groin, pressing into the gaping, bloody hole where his penis and testicles should be.

Hitting the far wall, he could go no further. Blood spurted from his crotch in terrifying amounts. He felt the life draining from him with every beat of his heart.

He welcomed the darkness when it came.

Chapter 4

Amanda

"Can we watch it again pwease, Mummy?" Emma said, still hugging the Toy Story DVD case.

I glanced at Jacob who asleep on Michael's knee. "Aren't you tired of it yet, Em? We've watched it four times already. I almost know it word for word."

She shook her head.

Michael disentangled himself from Jacob and lay him down on the sofa. "I'm going for some fresh air," he said for the third time this afternoon. I noticed him check his jeans pocket for his phone before heading for the door.

He'd also been sending and receiving numerous texts. When I asked who they were from, he fobbed me off with some story about a mate of his. I could tell he was lying by the way he avoided my eyes.

"Don't be long then, I was going to order pizza for dinner."

"Yay!" Emma said.

***

The bright blue numbers on the clock rolled over to 4:00am. Michael's droning snores were normally a comfort but tonight they irritated the shit out of me. I sat up and hugged the pillow to my chest, feeling so betrayed and let down. I was tempted to press it down over his mouth and nose, to smother every lying, cheating breath from him.

It had taken all my energy to keep quiet earlier, to act normal. There wasn't any point in accusing him without evidence. He'd only deny it and turn it around on me like he always did. But I'd be damned if I'd allow him to get away with it. Not this time.

Feeling fidgety and fractious, I got out of bed and headed downstairs. My eyes were drawn to the silver-framed photo on the hallstand. It showed a different couple, smiling and loved up, taken soon after we'd met.

I leaned against the wall and poked my fingers into the corners of my eyes, trying to prevent the tears from forming. This was such a mess. I knew I shouldn't have given him another chance. It was pointless, he couldn't change.

The fact that he was having an affair hurt like hell, but didn't bother me as much as the lies and deceit. The accusations of paranoia, and the blatant way he sent and received his secret texts as if I no longer mattered—or maybe he thought I was too stupid to notice.

I can't say I was surprised. From personal experience, I knew the old saying of money makes the world go round was a load of old bull. It was sex—sex made the world go round and men were like wild animals when it came to having to get their end away.

Michael was no different than most, but I'd had enough.

I spun away from the wall and over to his phone. I yanked it out of the docking station and punched in his pin. The screen yielded. Typical Michael, any other guy wouldn't let their phone out of their sight, but not him. The cocky bastard hadn't even bothered to change his password.

My heart thumped in my ears and my breathing felt forced. My trembling fingers trawled through his contacts until I came to Toni. Before I could think about what I was doing, I'd pressed edit and changed the number for my own.

The maddening buzz of the alarm clock woke me. Thankfully I'd managed to get a couple of hours sleep. I was bog-eyed and could have stayed in bed for a while longer, but I had to go to Kingsley to check out the house belonging to the mysterious Judy.

I'd had an email from her last night, and it was as vague as the phone call had been, giving me an address on the other side of the city and a key code. There was also a brief message asking me for a full report on the condition of the property, including photographs, to be emailed back to her as soon as possible.

Ordinarily, I would have been over the moon, but instead I felt emotionally flat.

I thought of the way I'd felt after the phone call on Saturday— so excited I'd almost danced back to the spot where I'd left Emma. Then I remembered the complete crash back to earth once I'd discovered she'd vanished.

It seemed every time I allowed myself to be happy some unseen hand dealt a crippling blow.

I was in the bathroom when I heard Michael and the children up and about.

Emma and Jacob were still dressed in their pyjamas and were already munching cereal by the time I reached the kitchen.

"Good morning, my babies," I said, kissing them both and dodging the spoon Jacob foisted in my face in an attempt to feed me soggy cereal. "No thanks, sweetie—you eat it."

We were lucky to have a huge kitchen that could fit a small sofa and our full-sized dining table and six chairs with room to spare. An old-style portable TV sat on a shelf in the corner and was blaring with unnecessary noise. I reached for the remote and turned it down.

"Hey, missus, I'm watching that," Michael said. He placed a cup of coffee in front of me and bending to kiss my cheek.

"Thanks, Michael, I need this, I've got a splitting headache—I didn't sleep very well."

"Tell me about it. You were tossing and turning for hours," he said.

"I suppose I kept you awake, did I?" I looked at him, head cocked to the side, eyes wide, waiting for his answer.

"Yeah, you did," he nodded, smiling.

"So the snoring was just you heavy breathing then was it?"

"Ah..." He seemed to think about it for a moment and puckered his lips. "Okay, maybe you didn't keep me awake, but I was aware of you tossing and turning." He laughed.

"Yeah, thought not. You could sleep standing up," I grumbled.

Emma laughed, "Daddy, can you sweep standink up?"

"Quite possibly, Em, although I've never actually tried it." He rubbed Emma's hair.

I noticed the time—almost 8.30am. I swigged the last of my coffee and jumped to my feet. "Oh, well, best be off. See you guys later." I kissed them all goodbye before leaving.

In the cold light of day, I was feeling a bit stupid. There was no reason to suspect Toni was a woman just because of the spelling—maybe Michael had just spelled it wrong. He was right. I was paranoid.

As I drove out of the street, my phone beeped—a message.

Heart racing, I pulled over to the side of the road. I reached into my handbag for my phone and held it tightly in my hand, just staring at it. Did I want to do this? If it was what I thought—how would I deal with it? It would change everything.

For the first time, I understood why some women turned a blind eye to their husband's extramarital antics; it was much easier than having to deal with such a messy situation. Anyway, the message was on my phone now—it wasn't as if I could ignore it. Taking a deep breath, I opened the flip.

1 new message

I exhaled through pursed lips. My thumb wavered then hit the view button.

Hot Deals on Gift Ideas + Furniture Clear Out! Starts 10am TODAY!

Relief flooded me—a sale! Not Michael.
I laughed out loud, reached for the gear stick and pressed my foot on the brake, but before I could change gear my phone beeped again.

1 new message

Once again I pressed the button, but this time I was still smiling.

Hey sexy—mrs has gone—what u doin today?

Oh my God! I was right after all—the low-down lying cheat. Even though I'd suspected him, I was unprepared for the feeling of sheer devastation that enveloped me and the tears fell freely. I had a crushing feeling in my ribcage that was like a physical pain.
The phone beeped for a third time, but I wasn't as quick to check it. My mind was still reeling and

trying to process my thoughts. I rubbed my face in my hands to wipe away the tears and pushed my hair back.

Back in control, I sighed and picked up the phone from my lap where it had fallen.

1 New Message

I hit the button.

He doesn't deserve you. Get rid of him.

How strange. The message had been sent from a private number. Surely it wasn't a coincidence. But what other explanation could there be?

***

I slowed the car along the tree-lined street, looking for number seventy-nine. My eyes almost popped out of my head as I pulled into the drive of the elegant, detached Edwardian house.

From the first glance, I could tell the grand old lady had been neglected. The gutters on the side of the building hung loose and the brickwork needed pointing. A huge ivy plant was growing out of control across the upstairs windows. But it was still a stunning property.

I got out of the car. Michael and the text business were forgotten, for the moment at least.

Old houses were my passion and my excitement returned. I couldn't wait to get inside.

The double-bay frontage looked as fabulous today as it would have done a hundred years ago. Solid, painted-brick handrails edged the wide concrete steps. I slowly climbed them, taking in every detail.

Stained glass adorned the beautiful leaded windows on either side of the front door. A rare, copper turn-key doorbell sat in the centre, though a tacky keypad door lock stuck out like a sore thumb next to the original fittings.

I took the printed email from my bag and punched in the four-digit number. The door opened against a huge pile of newspapers that had already been shoved aside against the wall.

Musty unused air hit my nostrils like a sledgehammer. I rummaged through the pile of papers, surprised that the earliest date was more than six years ago.

The spacious hallway was as grand as I'd imagined it would be.

A large fireplace stretched along the wall to the right while an ornate office desk was on the left, with an old-fashioned typewriter in its centre. I swiped my hand across the keys and looked at my fingers, then clapped my hands to remove the dust, wiping the remainder on my jeans.

A sweeping staircase ran up the left-hand side of the hall, the banister continuing across the landing at the top. A doorway to the right led to a formal lounge. The architecture oozed old-English charm, with high ceilings, moulded architraves, and a picture rail adorning each wall.

An elegant chandelier hung from the centre of the ceiling. The large, wide fireplace, back to back with the one in the hall, had built-in, cushioned benches in the alcoves on either side.

Heavy curtains covered the windows. I pulled them aside and the light poured in. Houses of this type were built for the light with deep bay windows.

The air was thick with dust from the curtains. It looked as though thousands of tiny fairies danced in the sunlight. My eyes stung. Blinking rapidly, I pulled my scarf over my mouth to stop myself from choking.

The dowdy, mustard-coloured wallpaper needed replacing. However the Axminster carpet, although old-fashioned, was in great condition and suited the house to perfection. Some basic cosmetic changes would make a world of difference.

Across the hall, I discovered a room almost the mirror image of the first, except for the fireplace being smaller.

I wandered through to the back of the house and into a large kitchen. The heels of my boots were making a loud, clomping noise on the tiled floor and sounded like an intrusion in the still silence of this empty old house.

Windows covered most of the left-hand wall. This room had been extended, but not in recent years. The curtains and curtain pole had fallen down from over the French doors, which led to a long, narrow back garden.

Apart from the dust, the owner could have just popped out to the shops. The hair stood up on the back of my neck. Dishes were piled high on the draining board, with a dishcloth over the tap, and two cups and saucers sat on the bench top by the kettle. The oak table in the centre of the room was set for two and seemed eerily sad. I wondered what had happened here.

I tried to imagine the room as it would have been years ago. The original coal range would have cooked all the family meals. This would have been the heart of the place. As it was now, the poor old house had no soul. It needed a family, laughter, and lots and lots of love.

Back through to the entrance hall. The grand staircase wouldn't have been out of place in *Gone With The Wind*—well, maybe it wasn't quite as grand as that, but along the same lines. Climbing them, I appraised each hand-turned spindle and wondered how many bottoms had slid down the well-worn banister over the years.

There were four large bedrooms on the first floor. Each of them had the previous occupants' belongings scattered through them, as if one day they had just up and left, leaving everything in its place. I understood furniture still being in there, but the personal effects were a mystery. I'd have to find out what Judy wanted done with them before I could do anything else.

Another flight of stairs led to a massive attic. Easels and old canvases filled the room. One wall was lined with shelving, crammed full with paints and other art supplies. It must have been used as an art studio once upon a time.

Back downstairs, I got my camera and Dictaphone to begin taking notes for the report. During the process, I discovered there was a door next to the kitchen that I hadn't noticed earlier.

The handle was stiff, but after several attempts it opened. The skin on my face met with damp, cold air, vastly different to the rest of the house. I could tell by the smell of earth this was the cellar.

I shuddered and slammed the door shut, leaning my back against it while I caught my breath. No way would I be stepping foot down there.

Once I had finished, I closed the curtains and packed my things into the car ready to head home. I was still unsure of what I would do about Michael. I was glad I'd given myself chance to calm down, instead of racing home all guns blazing and shooting him through the head at point blank range—or something to that effect.

As I locked the front door, tell-tale prickles on the back of my neck caused a shudder. I walked to the end of the drive and onto the street, peering around. I couldn't see anybody, yet I couldn't shake the feeling off—someone was definitely watching me.

I got in the car. My phone flashed with even more texts from Michael.

- Very quiet today baby, normally hear from you before now x.

- She's gone out, but I should get away later x.

- Miss you x what's wrong? x.

- Kids asleep—I'm lying here thinking about you, guess what I'm doing x.

There were also seven missed calls and two voice messages. Luckily I hadn't set my voicemail up with a personal message, so Michael still wouldn't know whose mailbox he'd reached.

I felt sick. It was my own fault for snooping, any other woman would still be oblivious. Now I knew for sure I didn't have a clue what I was going to do about it, so I decided to do nothing for now.

The strange text message from earlier bothered me, though. It had been sent from a withheld number and didn't make any sense. At first I thought it had, but that was just my confusion filling in the gaps.

Thinking about it now, I knew that it couldn't have been related to my situation it must have been sent to me by mistake.

Chapter 5

Amanda

"Goodbye, babies, I'll be here when you get back." I kissed them both as I fastened their coats. "Michael, you will keep an eye on them won't you?"

"I always do, Amanda," he snapped.

"I know you do—keep your hair on! I'm only asking." I couldn't help but fuss. "And keep your hats and gloves on, you two—it's freezing today." Maybe freezing was an exaggeration, but as soon as the sun hid behind a cloud there was a cold undertone.

"Awight, Mummy," Emma said.

I walked them out to the street and watched until they turned the corner. Looking up and down the street I couldn't see anybody, but I knew someone was there. The familiar prickles, much stronger than usual, felt like invisible ice fingers gripping the back of my neck.

"Piss off!" I shouted into the road, turning on the spot. "Just leave me the hell alone!"

The curtains twitched across the road. Mrs Corless didn't miss much.

"Nosy old biddy," I muttered as I walked back into the house and slammed the door.

I rarely got the house to myself and was glad of the peace and quiet. I had lots of work to do. And after my usual ritual of making sure all the windows and doors were secure, I made a cup of tea and put away the bread and milk Michael had just brought home. Then I screwed the plastic bag up and opened the drawer to try to stuff it in but was stopped in my tracks. The usually chaotic and messy drawer had been cleaned out, the plastic bags had been reduced and the remainder tied in individual little balls. This was something that I had been meaning to do, but hadn't got around to—or had I? I knew for a fact that Michael wouldn't have done it, he wasn't that domesticated.

Puzzled, I picked up my tea and made my way upstairs to the spare bedroom that doubled as my office and storeroom.

It wasn't meant to be a storeroom, except for the vacuum cleaner in the corner and the ironing board behind the door, but Michael always dumped everything else just inside the door.

Today I had to climb over a box of old clothes, a basket of ironing and an acoustic guitar before I could get anywhere near my desk. Not a lot really, but the tiny room was already full to bursting with the desk and office furniture. I tidied it into some kind of order, creating a path to get in and out.

I sat in my comfy, faded-blue, swivel chair. The ancient computer took a few moments before making sounds of life. I'd had it for years, a faithful old thing, but it was much too slow now. I'd been planning to get myself a laptop but there was always something more urgent we needed to buy.

The computer opened on the last viewed page and as I read it, I broke out from head to toe in goosebumps. Finding a UK Divorce Lawyers website was bad enough but the half completed question on the website had my mind reeling.

My husband is having an affair—and I need to know a legal way to get him to leave the family home. We have two small children ...

"What the ..." I said aloud. I didn't remember searching for this information, but who else could it have been. There was no way Michael would have done it, leaving incriminating evidence like this for me to find. Plus, nobody knew I was even aware of the affair.

Returning home the other day, I'd changed the numbers back in his phone and Michael had been none the wiser. Except maybe for being a bit confused as to why Toni never received any of his messages.

After the initial shock and upset had worn off that day, everything was back to normal—worryingly so.

Maybe I needed a trip to my shrink, Doctor Freda. I'd not been to see her for months, but I knew what she'd say when I told her about everything that had been happening.

The way I could switch off my feelings and emotions was a built-in safety valve as far as I was concerned. But Dr Freda had different ideas. She blamed it on some disorder stemming from my childhood trauma.

I hit the back button on the computer and scrolled through page after page of family law sites and several more search engines regarding infidelity and the custody of children.

I knew it had to have been me, but I had no memory of it at all. First the tidied out drawer and now this, I must be cracking up. I was grateful that Michael hadn't come across it instead of me.

I closed down all the pages and erased the history before checking my emails. There were several in my inbox but nothing worth reading. I was waiting for a message from Judy with the plan of action for her property.

I got down to the business in hand—my six monthly VAT returns and paperwork for the accountant. Something I always put off until the last possible moment, and absolutely dreaded.

I'm ultra-organised in most aspects of my life, but seem to have a mental block where the financials are concerned. I never put receipts together in one place like any normal person. Instead, I have to ferret through handbags, the car, drawers, pockets and even email. And then painstakingly go through each one, putting them in date order before writing each item down.

When I heard the excited chatter of Michael and the children, I looked at my watch, surprised it was five o'clock already. I finished the last of the expenses log and rushed downstairs.

Emma and Jacob were in the hallway, Jacob still in his pushchair. The black bubble coat made his arms stick out to his sides reminding me of the

Michelin Man. Michael stood outside the front door, talking to the neighbour.

"Hello, my darlings. Did you have a good time at the park?" I bent to kiss them both.

"Mummy, Mummy, we fed the ducks and a boy felled off the swing and his pants was wipped and his knee was all blood." Emma's bright blue eyes sparkled with excitement, a big smile on her cold, red face.

"Ripped darling, his pants were ripped," I corrected, undoing her pink coat and slipping it off her shoulders.

Emma's nose wrinkled as she tilted her head to one side. "How do you know?"

I laughed. "Because you told me, sweetheart. Did he cry?"

"Yes he cwied and so did his mummy, and a man in a big ambuance taked him away."

"Oh, the poor boy. You certainly did have an exciting afternoon." I unbuckled Jacob from his pushchair, removed his hat and coat and lifted him into my arms.

"Yes, and daddy boughted us an ice wolly but Jacob dwopped his on the floor."

"Lolly, darling. Daddy bought you an ice lolly," I said as I hung the coats up then walked through to the kitchen.

"I said wolly," she said irritably.

"Aw poor, Jakey, did you drop your lolly?" I said, squeezing the little lump, still in my arms.

"Din't matter," Emma said behind me. "Cos Daddy's fwiend boughted him a new one. She's nice."

My stomach did a twirl. Out of the mouths of babes, as the saying goes.

A movement caught my eye. Michael was standing in the kitchen doorway, squirming. His eyes wide open and his lips apart, he shook his head from side to side ever so slightly, as if trying to think of a way to deny everything.

No avoiding it now; his dirty little secret had to be dealt with. I didn't even care anymore. I flashed him a look I hoped dripped with contempt and he recoiled. How dare he take my kids to meet his slut of a girlfriend?

I jumped as a knock at the door brought me back to earth. I handed Jacob to Michael and followed Emma as she ran down the hall.

A tall, dark-haired man dressed in a black overcoat, grey woollen suit, white shirt and funky blue tie stood on the doorstep. "Hello there, I'm looking for a Miss Amanda Flynn," he said in a broad northern accent.

"That's me," I said, my mouth suddenly parched. "How can I help you?"

Emma stepped towards me, her arms raised up around my waist and she buried her face in my cardigan. I placed a protective hand on her head.

The man reached into his overcoat pocket and pulled out his ID. "Detective Inspector Stanley, is there somewhere we can have a little chat please, Miss?"

"It's Mrs, but you can call me Amanda. What's all this about?" My mind was working overtime, imagining all kinds of things.

"If I could come in for a minute and I'll explain."

Holding the door open, I ushered him into the living room.

Michael, who had been loitering in the kitchen doorway, now came in behind us, with Jacob still in his arms.

"Michael, this is Detective Stanley. Detective, this is my husband, Michael."

"Hello, Mr Flynn," he said shaking Michael's hand. "I just need a word with your wife—shouldn't take more than a few minutes.

"Can you take the children through to the kitchen please, Michael?" I unwrapped Emma's arms from around my waist and pushed her towards her dad. She made a few disgruntled sounds but grabbed on to the hand he offered.

I knew Michael hated the police. For some reason he was scared of them, even though he'd never been in trouble in his life. People in authority freaked him out and it was obvious he couldn't get out of the room fast enough. Some support he was.

The door closed, we stood awkwardly in the middle of the room.

"So what can I do for you, Detective?" I was eager to find out what the heck he wanted.

"Mrs Flynn-"

"Amanda," I interrupted.

"Amanda. I need to ask a few questions regarding a missing person's case I'm working on."

The hair stood up on the back of my neck. "Fire away," I said, trying to sound nonchalant.

"When was the last time you had any contact from your father?"

As his words hit home, it felt like my legs were about to give out on me. Staggering backwards, I steadied myself on the arm of the sofa before collapsing onto the seat.

"Mrs Flynn ... Amanda? Are you all right?"

I heard him, but it sounded as though my head was under water. Pressure built up in my ears as though they were going to pop and my mouth filled with saliva.

"I'll get you a drink."

He left the room and returned moments later, glass in hand. With Michael and the children in tow. I tried to pull myself together and sipped at the glass of water offered.

"What did you do to her?" Michael's high-pitched voice sounded irate.

"I simply asked her a question that has obviously disturbed her, Mr Flynn."

"I think you should leave!" Michael said. The children started crying.

"Not until I've spoken to your wife, sir." The detective's no-nonsense manner had the desired effect and Michael backed off.

"I'm okay, Michael. Take the children, please." I sat up and placed the glass on the coffee table, taking a deep breath.

Michael stared at me, his eyebrows raised and head cocked to the side in an unspoken question.

I nodded. "Go on. I'm fine now."

They left the room. Detective Stanley raised his eyebrows and pointed to the armchair opposite me.

"Yes, of course—sit down," I said, noticing for the first time how ruggedly handsome he was, the v-shaped scar below his right eye intrigued me. I attempted a smile. "I'm sorry, detective. I haven't thought about my father in years. Why isn't he still in prison?"

"He was released six weeks ago, Amanda. Were you not informed?"

"No! But he got twenty years. How can he be out already?"

"I'm not sure, Amanda. And I can only apologise that you weren't contacted," he said with a half-smile and half shrug.

"Six weeks, you said?" My mind raced, and my eyes probed his face for answers.

"Yeah, almost." His eyebrows knitted together. "Why?"

"I knew it! I knew someone was watching me. Michael accused me of being paranoid, but I knew." I slapped my palm against my leg.

"What do you mean, someone watching you—has someone been hanging around?" His eyebrows puckered, and one dark brown eye closed slightly.

"I haven't seen a soul—I've just had this overwhelming feeling. Like I said, Michael thought I was paranoid." I raised my eyes to the ceiling and back to him and sighed.

"Have you received any strange phone calls?"

I cast my mind back to the past few weeks and shook my head. "No, nothing. Oh, except there was the seahorse ..." Ice-cold shivers ran up and down my spine as I told him about the strange day at the zoo, about Emma vanishing and the seahorse that had appeared in her backpack.

"Emma said that I'd been the one she'd followed though, and the girl in the insect house also said she left with a woman dressed like me. Not a man—not my father," I said, shaking my head.

"Chances are it has nothing at all to do with him, but considering his history we can't rule it out. Maybe he had an accomplice and is up to his old tricks." He looked at me intently, his mouth a firm line.

"When did he go missing?" My head was in a whirl and I had a weakness in my limbs. The very thought that Emma's disappearance had something to do with my father made my soul quake.

"He didn't show up for his probation appointment, which is one of the conditions of his early release. He's supposed to report, in person, once a week for the first three months. He also needs to sign onto the sex offenders register at the local police station every three days. This is as much for his safety as for the safety of the public."

I couldn't concentrate. My mind was still reeling. I rubbed my face with both hands.

"He was diligent for the first five weeks but vanished over five days ago now. All his things are still at the hostel and nobody's seen him there for almost a week."

The detective sat forward on the chair, his trouser legs riding up and giving me a glimpse of a mass of dark hair above his grey socks. My stomach muscles clenched and I cleared my throat—trying to pull myself together. What the hell was wrong with me?

I tore my eyes away and shook my head, a sudden thought occurring to me. "What about his ex-wife? You must know she was also charged and I know she was released three years ago. Maybe they hooked up again." A strange jittery feeling encompassed my whole body, as though my nerve endings had been hard-wired to the mains.

"We have officers trying to locate her as we speak. It shouldn't be difficult—we monitor paedophiles closely. We need to know where they're living at all times."

He stood up and extended his hand to me.

As our hands touched, I could no longer ignore how utterly masculine this guy was. My nostrils filled with the scent of his aftershave and I suddenly visualised leaning in to him and chewing on his delectable bottom lip. However, he seemed oblivious to the effect he was having on me.

"Try not to worry too much, but it won't hurt if you're extra careful for the time being. I'll keep you informed of any news. In the meantime, if you hear from him or have any more strange episodes, please call me." He dug in his jacket pocket and produced a business card, placing it on the coffee table.

I followed him out to the door and watched as he walked down the path and got into a charcoal-coloured car. I closed the door, then sat at the bottom of the stairs. What the heck had just happened? My thoughts should have been consumed with the devastating news I'd just received, not imagining snogging the face off the detective.

It had been months since my libido upped and left and I couldn't have been more shocked at its inappropriate re-appearance, but I guessed it must have something to do with the shock I'd just had.

I needed to pull myself together before facing Michael and the fifty thousand questions I was sure awaited me in the kitchen.

Chapter 6

Michael

"What the hell's going on?" Michael mumbled, pressing his ear to the kitchen door. The kids were making too much noise with their incessant chatter; he couldn't hear a thing.

Amanda was in the lounge and looked dreadful, being questioned by a detective who sounded as though he'd just walked out of an episode of Coronation Street! What the fuck was that about?

She had been driving him berserk lately, being paranoid and grumpy. She couldn't stand the kids out of her sight. But then she'd lost Emma at the zoo. If he'd have lost their daughter he'd be hung, drawn and quartered by now.

He was sick and tired of her and their shitty life together. The only reason he was still there was because he loved his kids so much, and the thought of leaving them tore his heart out.

But he had tried his very best to make things work.

When they met, she was a challenge—she had been the first woman to reject him and had really got under his skin. She was sexy and beautiful in a natural way. She didn't have to rely on lotions and potions to accentuate her features like most women did.

She fell pregnant very early in the relationship and so he did the right thing and popped the question.

She wasn't a bad wife at first, and although not very adventurous in the bedroom, she had been willing and would try anything he suggested without complaint.

Recently though, she was uninterested in him. They never had sex anymore and it was pointless even trying. Then, to top it all, she'd caught him with Toni in a very compromising position and he thought he'd blown it, big time. But she'd given him a second chance.

Now, thanks to Emma, she knew he'd been at it again. He'd need some fancy talking to get himself out of this one. If indeed he could be bothered at all.

He heard the lounge door open and he went back to sit with the children.

Paper and crayons covered the entire dining table. Emma sat colouring a large flower, her tongue sticking out of the corner of her mouth in total concentration. Jacob had rubbed green crayon all over the wipeable plastic tablecloth instead of the picture of a fire engine in front of him.

"Jacob, love, you're supposed to draw on the paper, not the table." Michael picked up Jacob's hand and placed it onto the paper. "Em, that's beautiful—you're so good at staying inside the lines now," he said, his ears still tuned in to what was happening on the other side of the door.

He heard the front door shut, and then nothing.

After a few minutes, he got up to investigate and found Amanda sitting on the stairs with her head in her hands.

"Mand, what is it? What's wrong?" He sat next to her, pulling her into his arms and she began to sob. He positioned her in a way to avoid getting her tears and snot all over his Armani shirt. Michael was surprised. He'd never seen her so broken and vulnerable before.

After a few minutes, Jacob, sick of being stuck in his highchair, started to cry.

Amanda sat up straight and wiped her face on her sleeve before going into the kitchen. She lifted Jacob from his chair and placed him on the rug and emptied the contents of his toy box in front of him; dolls, cars, blocks and farm animals covered the floor.

Michael followed her. Standing in the doorway, he raised his eyebrows and shrugged at her as she started to prepare dinner.

"Not now, Michael. We'll talk later." She flashed him a warning look.

Gone was the softness of a few moments ago. Back in its place was the tough, no-nonsense, impenetrable exterior. Any other man would give her a slap for the way she spoke to him. He wasn't a violent man, but she'd been pushing his buttons lately.

With a shake of his head he went into the lounge to watch the news, but switched the television off after a few minutes. He couldn't concentrate.

His thoughts returned to his wife. He had loved her, maybe still did in a way, but she frustrated the hell out of him.

He'd tried his best to be faithful, but it wasn't easy. Amanda was every red-blooded man's dream with her tall figure that was on the skinny side of slim—natural blonde hair and pretty face. But emotionally, he always found himself on the outside with no chance of getting in.

There had been the odd bit on the side over the years—nothing more than most men got up to. But then he met up with Toni four months ago. He'd known her from school, but they hadn't seen each other in years. He found her in the supermarket car park shaken up and crying—she'd been attacked by a hooded youth who'd snatched her bag.

Michael stayed with her while she waited for the police to arrive. Afterwards, he took her for coffee and waited with her until she calmed down.

They'd been seeing each other ever since—and not just for sex, although she was a minx in the bedroom—or bathroom as Amanda had discovered. In the beginning, they'd meet several times a week at the park or playground. Initially, it was just for a chat, but after a while they began having wild, sexy romps every Tuesday and Thursday at Toni's house.

He would drop the children off at the day-care—another thing Amanda would go stark staring mad about. She expected him to stay there with them when all the other parents dropped their kids off, but he'd felt like a weirdo hanging about the nursery.

Now a detective had turned up on their doorstep, for whatever reason, and it had knocked her for six. What the fuck had she been up to?

After making sure the children were sound asleep, Michael poured two glasses of wine.

He was wary about confronting Amanda, knowing she'd want her own answers about Toni. However, the desperation to find out what had been going on with his ordinarily boring wife overshadowed everything else.

Amanda was sitting with her feet curled underneath her on the sofa. She wore white pyjama bottoms and a purple T-shirt with a large white smiley face across the front. She seemed miles away.

"Here you go, Mand, get this down you, love," he said as he handed her the wine and sat down next to her.

"Thank you." She took the glass from him and placed it on the coffee table without taking a sip.

"Right, Mand, are you gonna tell me what the police wanted?" The suspense was driving him mad.

She turned towards him as if seeing him for the first time. "They're looking for someone...someone from my past," her voice seemed very far away.

"Who?" He sat staring at her, waiting for her reply. He was about to ask the question again when she shuddered and looked at him.

"Does it matter who?"

"Yes, of course it does," he said.

"It's just someone I haven't thought about in a long time and never intended to think about again." She gave a huge sigh. "I couldn't help the detective so let's just forget it, shall we?" Her hands shook as she reached for her glass.

"You're obviously still upset. What could be so terrible you can't tell me? I won't let you come to any harm, Manda. Who is it?" he urged. He couldn't begin to imagine what had got her this worried.

"My dad," she whispered.

He shook his head in confusion. "Who? Did you say your *dad*?" His voice had gone up a few octaves.

She nodded.

"You said your dad was dead along with the rest of your family." He pushed himself back on the sofa, wanting to put some distance between them. "What the hell's going on, Amanda? Why would you say something like that?"

"Because I wished he *was* dead, that's why," she said. "He's a horrible, sick man who's been in prison for the past ten years. I found out today that they released him six weeks ago." She slammed her glass down onto the table, the wine sloshing everywhere.

She turned to face him again, her large blue eyes fixed on his. "I *told* you I was being watched but you wouldn't believe me."

"It's not that I didn't believe you, Amanda, but I couldn't imagine why somebody would want to watch you—it didn't make sense—it still doesn't."

He stared at the woman in front of him—the woman who had shared his life for so long—the woman who had given birth to his children. But all he saw was a stranger.

"I need to get the kids away from here—he knows where I am, and I don't want him anywhere near them." She was shaking so much her teeth chattered. Tears filled her eyes and then great racking sobs shook her body.

He pulled her into his arms. "It's all right. I won't let anything happen to you or the kids, I promise," he said.

"Don't you see? It already has. He somehow got to Emma at the zoo. What about the seahorse he put in her bag?" Huge tears spilled from her lovely big eyes.

"Now you're being daft," he snapped. "Emma said she followed *you*. Nobody took her, and she probably just found the brooch," he said as he forced himself to soothe her.

"You don't know him, Michael. I do. I know how his sick mind works, trust me. I also know he won't be happy until he punishes me."

Alarm bells started ringing in his head. "For what? Come on, Amanda, I think it's time you told me everything."

"I testified against him. I was the one who had him locked up." Her voice was no more than a whisper, and large silent tears streamed down her face.

"What did that monster do to you? Tell me—it's all right." He pulled her head to his shoulder, stroking her silky blond hair.

"He ... he raped me."

***

Maybe I shouldn't have blurted it out like that, but I needed him to take me seriously for once in his life. Plus, if I'm honest, I also wanted to hurt him for a host of reasons, though none of them—apart from carrying on with another woman—were even his fault.

The expression on his face, once I'd told him, reminded me of the time a seagull crapped on his shoulder in Blackpool. He was disgusted. Just another reason for him to think of me as damaged stock. Now I was the woman who'd slept with her father in his eyes, regardless of the circumstances.

Michael had gone out soon afterwards, making some excuse about needing fresh air and clearing his head. Forgotten was the grand speech of being there to protect us. Two hours had passed already, and it didn't take a genius to work out where he'd gone.

My heart contracted in my chest and I bit back the tears. I knew it was over. Had known all week since the texts but I wasn't sure what I was going to do about it. Now the decision was out of my hands–it had been obvious by his reaction.

I wondered what he'd do once he knew the whole truth. The watered down version had freaked him out enough.

I understood why he'd find it difficult to comprehend. His had been an overindulged childhood. His parents had spoiled him rotten and he was their world. It would be impossible for him to imagine his father abusing him in any way. Even now he only had to click his fingers and they would come running.

And yes, I had lied to him when we first met, telling him my family were dead. But no-one in their right mind would tell the whole sorry truth straight off and I never found the right time afterwards.

The police and courts protected me when the story first hit the papers. I didn't have to face people looking at me the way Michael had tonight—like it was somehow my fault.

He'd go mad when he found out my mum was also still alive. She left us when I was four or five years old and I didn't hear from her again until I tracked her down when I was seventeen years old.

I remember being stunned by how much I looked like her—golden blond hair, slim features, pale blue-grey eyes, full lips and a slight frame. But that was where the similarity ended. She was a self-centred woman and a god-awful mother.

After she had left my dad she shacked up with a man living in a council house in Scotland. Once I found her again, we met up a couple of times when she came to Pinevale, but things had been very strained between us. I could never understand why she left—especially now, after having babies of my own. There was no way on this earth would I ever leave them.

My brother Andrew disappeared when he was fifteen. His suffering had been even worse than mine—as well as the sexual abuse, Dad also beat him regularly. The police tried to find him but came up with nothing. For years I'd thought Mum must have come back for him, but once I found her, I knew she hadn't. I now suspect my dad was behind Andrew's disappearance.

Pouring yet another glass of wine, I put the cork in the bottle and took what remained to the kitchen. I was afraid I'd drink the lot.

I intended going to Judy's house in the morning to start planning her job. Work would have to be the drug I used to distract myself.

I'd received an email from her earlier asking me to choose the wallpaper and soft furnishings. Her deadline gave me plenty of time if I started straight away. I should be pleased, but instead I felt nothing.

I would be able to do most of the work on the house myself. The place was basically sound and just needed a lift. Though I'd have to employ some gardeners and get a builder to sort the exterior masonry and guttering.

When a car pulled up outside, I got up to peer through the window. I wasn't expecting it to be Michael as he had gone out on foot.

A small, light-coloured car was parked at the end of the path, and I watched as Michael uncurled himself from the passenger seat—then leaned back in to kiss the driver.

A cry escaped my lips and I held my breath, my hand covering my open mouth.

It was one thing knowing what he was getting up to, but having my face rubbed into it this way just blew my mind.

Shocked by his blatant disregard of my feelings, I still hadn't moved when he let himself in.

"Oh, I didn't think you'd still be up," he said, avoiding my gaze.

"You don't say!" I pursed my lips, walking into the hall. My heart felt as though it was going to burst from my chest, and I knew the tears were itching to fall, but I held them back, refusing to let him see.

"Meaning?"

"Forget it, Michael. If you don't know, I won't waste my breath," I said, totally dejected.

My head held high, I started up the stairs. "I'll be sleeping in Emma's bed. Oh, and for the record, I couldn't go to bed until you got home—the door needs to be deadlocked. In case you've forgotten, there's a nutcase out there. Remember?"

"Amanda," he called as I reached the top of the stairs.

"What, Michael?" My breath came out in a huge sigh.

"Sorry."

I watched as he walked into the lounge. So that was it. The end of our not-so-wonderful marriage. I felt an immense sadness.

Chapter 7

Annie

"If you keep harassing my customers, Annie, you'll be straight out that door." The barman threw a towel over his shoulder and glared at her, pointing a thick sausage-finger towards the double doors.

"Aw, c'mon, Joe, I'm doin' no 'arm. Thish ish me 'ole buddy, aincha pal?"

She had pounced on the man as soon as he entered the bar, trying to hit him up for a drink. She was certain he'd be good for it.

She'd become an expert at picking the weak and gullible ones out of the crowd, they tended to avoid her gaze, often agreeing to anything if she would just leave them alone. She'd almost succeeded with this one too until Joe stuck his fucking big nose in.

The elderly gentleman squirmed in his seat. "Um, er," he stuttered, his watery old eyes pleading with the barman.

Annie pushed herself off the stool and shoved the man in the shoulder. "Be like that then, Grandpa." She swayed, falling sideways.

Experienced with drunks, Joe had seen it coming and reached out, grabbing her by the arm.

"Gerroffme!" she roared, the sound coming from the pit of her stomach. Yanking her arm from his grip caused her to fall off balance in the opposite direction. Her arm flew up smacking the old man in his large, bulbous nose.

Sprawled out, face down on the sticky, booze-soaked carpet, she felt herself being yanked backwards. Here we go again, she thought.

Several of the locals had jumped forward to assist Joe in evicting the screaming, stinking drunk out of the bar. They carried her through the double swing doors and dumped her on a seat in front of the old stone wall.

The cold night air hit her like a sack of spuds. She lay quietly for a moment or two.

"What ya shtaring at, shupid bitch?" she shouted to a girl standing at the bus stop. Annie was used to people looking down their nose at her and she normally ignored them, but she was too angry tonight and she needed to lash out at somebody.

The girl said nothing. She continued eating from a paper parcel, not attempting to turn away.

"Cat got ya tongue?"

"Erm, no, not really. I was going to ask you if you want a chip." She stepped forward, holding out the delicious smelling package.

Annie's stomach growled. She realised she hadn't eaten anything all day, and couldn't remember if she'd had anything yesterday either. She hesitated, before putting her hand in and pulling out several fat, juicy looking chips.

"Fanks. Do-a know ya?" Annie looked her up and down, one eye closed, the other squinting. The girl's long, blond hair shone in the moonlight.

"I don't think so. Here, you may as well finish these off," she said, handing over the rest of the chips.

Annie knew the reason the girl had had enough all of a sudden. She was aware of the offensive smell that emanated from her—she often turned people off their food. Snatching the parcel greedily, she began stuffing chips into her mouth.

Once finished, she licked the salt and vinegar off the greaseproof paper and licked each grubby finger in turn. She rolled the paper into a ball then dropped it to the ground.

Annie stood up, taking a couple of seconds to get her balance while holding on to the wall. Hunched over, she staggered up the street towards town.

"Fanks for the chipsh," she called to the girl who was once again standing at the bus stop.

"You're welcome. Goodnight."

After a few steps, Annie felt an odd slapping feeling coming from her left foot. She stopped and bent forward to investigate. As she lifted her foot up she noticed the sole of her old boot had come loose. Before having the chance to right herself, she lost her balance and found herself face first in the gutter.

With neither the energy nor the inclination to get up, she closed her eyes, allowing herself to drift off into a booze-addled slumber.

Moments later she felt a hand on her shoulder. Annie shrugged it off, a scowl on her face.

"Are you okay? Are you hurt?"

The gentle voice was close to her ear. Annie struggled to open her heavy eyelids.

"Leave me 'lone!" Once again, she shrugged at the hand that was back on her shoulder.

"Let me help you. Where do you live?" the girl persisted.

"Not goin' 'ome—need a drink firsht." Annie's eyes were now open and she tried to sit up.

"Gosh, don't you think you've had enough? Come on, let me help you get home." The girl assisted her into a sitting position.

"Told ya, need a drink."

"What if I buy you one to take home? Will you let me help you then?"

"S'pose," Annie said looking at the girl and waiting for the catch.

"Right, sit there—I'll be back in two ticks," the girl said as she grabbed her large grey handbag off the road beside Annie and ran in the direction of the off-license. She returned a few minutes later with a plastic bag at her side.

"What did ya get?" Annie was now sitting on the kerb, her feet in the road.

"Vodka, but you're not having it till I get you home," the girl said as she put her arm under Annie's elbow and lifted her to her feet. "Right—lead the way?"

Annie's flat was the last in a row of run-down, single-storey flats. They walked around the back of the building, through the overgrown garden that resembled a rubbish dump. There was an old broken toilet that lay on its side at the back door and blocked half the entrance. They had to manoeuvre themselves around it and in through the wide-open kitchen door.

"Don't you lock the door?" The girl walked in behind Annie, carefully placing her feet on the filthy, torn oilcloth.

"Na! No key."

Annie flopped herself down on the threadbare, floral chair by the window.

The only other seat in the sparsely furnished room was a rickety, wooden dining chair and the girl perched on the edge of it.

Bottles, pizza boxes and old newspapers covered the carpet from wall to wall.

Annie wasted no time. She opened the bottle of vodka and chugged on the neck of it. After a few mouthfuls, she noticed the way the girl was eyeing up the mess. "Watsh up wiv ya face, snootytoots?" she snarled, her top lip pulled back from her teeth like a vicious, growling dog. "I washnt always like thish ya know? I 'ad a good job an' nice cloves jusht like you."

The girl said nothing as she took her bag from over her shoulder and hugged it to her chest. Her heels were off the floor, and her legs nervously bounced up and down.

"I don't need you judging me. Go on—pish off!" Annie motioned for the girl to leave, sloshing vodka all over the floor as she did so.

"I'm not judging you. I want to help you."

Annie, who had spent years conning every ounce of help from anybody and everybody she could, saw a meal ticket with this girl and decided to milk it for all it was worth. It didn't matter that she was drunk—survival was foremost on her mind. Getting tomorrow's liquid fix was essential.

"Sorry. Not used t' people bein' kind t' me."

"Why don't you tell me about it?"

"Wha'?" Annie screwed up her face again.

"You know, your life, before this," the girl said as she waved a hand at the room, shaking her head. "How did you end up here?" Her voice was quiet, barely more than a whisper. She had a faraway look in her eyes.

"It washn't my fault," Annie said and glanced around the room, as if seeing the state of it for the first time, and for a split second she was embarrassed. "I wasa shchool teacher 'nd a good one. I teached English...tauched...taught English." She ran a hand through her grey, matted hair. "Yeah you 'eard right—English. I loved it, but it was shtolen from me."

"So you did nothing wrong? It was all taken from you and you did nothing to deserve it?"

"I said so, din't I?" She looked at the girl with a puzzled expression on her face. "Are ya sure I don't know yer?"

"I don't know, Annie. Why? Do you recognise me?"

The girl stood up and was above Annie now.

Annie had to lean all the way back in her chair in order to look at the girl's face. She did seem a bit familiar, but Annie couldn't place her.

Her heart was pounding in her throat, confusion washed over her, and she chewed her bottom lip. "I din't tell you ma name. W-who are yer? What's this all about?" She was beginning to feel a little uneasy, even with the effects of the vodka. "Did I teach yer? Is that it? Tell me, girl," she shouted.

"Oh, you taught me all right, but not in the classroom."

The calm quiet of the girl's voice made Annie shudder. "Now ya bein' shtupid. How else could I teach yer?"

The girl stepped away from Annie and picked her way around the room, kicking at the rubbish with her high-heeled, brown boots. "Well, let me see. You taught me in lots of different ways, Annie." She stopped and glanced back at her. "You taught me how to be quiet, for starters. Little children should be seen but not heard. Isn't that right, Annie?" the girl said, her pale blue eyes wide open, her eyebrows raised as she waited for Annie's answer.

"What the..." Annie couldn't continue. Her mind was racing, making her giddy.

"You taught me how to muffle my cries while your beast of a husband stuck his cock into me. You taught me how to allow your sick mates to rape me time after time, without ever complaining. Yes, Annie, you taught me all right. You taught me how to hate somebody so much, I can taste it. I guess you could say I was your number one student." The girl had made her way back to Annie's chair as she spoke.

The realisation dawned on a suddenly sober Annie. "Oh my God!" she said in a whisper. "It wasn't my fault. He forced me to."

"You should have protected us," the girl said. "Children are innocent and helpless. I needed you to protect me."

Annie, rigid with fear, felt a warm sensation as she pissed herself.

The girl grabbed hold of Annie's coarse grey hair. Then she knelt on top of her, pinning her to the seat, her knee in Annie's chest. She yanked the hair back until Annie let out a blood-curdling scream.

***

This was what the girl had been waiting for. She shoved a large object the size of her fist into Annie's open mouth, stuffing it as far down her throat as she could.

Annie tried to struggle, muffled cries escaping as she thrashed about, but the girl was much stronger than a wasted, weakened drunk.

She held Annie's mouth and nose closed until her body sagged. Then she reached down and picked up the half-full bottle of vodka and smashed it onto the edge of the windowsill. She rammed the jagged glass into Annie's upturned face, twisting and turning, in and out.

The girl smiled at the sickening, squelching sounds.

Chapter 8

Amanda

My nose tickled. I swiped the back of my hand across my face.

More tickling.

I opened my eyes to find Emma and Jacob standing at the side of the bed, giggling.

The sun poured in the window making me squint. I held my hand to my forehead, to block out the light.

"What's so funny? You little rascals," I said, reaching to catch hold of them and causing another bout of giggles.

"You was snorwing, Mummy." Emma laughed.

Jacob added his garbled opinion and also laughed.

"No, I wasn't."

"Oh, yes, you was."

We'd played this game a lot since the pantomime last Christmas. I knew not to continue or else we'd be there all day. "Where's daddy?"

"I'm right here, Amanda." Michael stepped into the room.

I'd been sleeping in Emma's bed since last week, leaving Michael in our room. He'd stayed out two nights, obviously with his trollop, but at least he had the decency to call so I could dead bolt the door.

"Oh hi. Sorry I got back so late last night." I knew I must have spoiled his plans, especially with it being Halloween—Michael and his mates always did something on Halloween.

"That's okay. Right, you two give Mummy a kiss and let's get you ready for day-care.

After a mad five minutes involving lots of tickling and laughing, the children left.

I wanted to stay in bed, exhausted after a full day at Judy's. Once I'd packed away all the personal things into boxes, I'd painted the front door step with some paint left over from another job, and I'd begun stripping the wallpaper in the kitchen. I'd also contacted a local plumber because the drains stink, and arranged to meet him next week.

Our house was in darkness when I had arrived home. I'd phoned Michael earlier in the evening and told him I would be late. Nine-thirty seemed a bit early for him to have gone to bed, but I was relieved not to have to see him.

He'd left a plate of food on the stove—cottage pie and vegetables. I heated the food up and devoured it with a cup of tea before having an early night myself.

I dragged my weary body out of bed and headed for the bathroom. It was the next room on our list to modernise. The yucky green bath had a permanent tidemark that wouldn't budge no matter what I used. As I stepped into the ugly, brown-plastic shower, somebody knocked on the bathroom door.

"Yes?" I stuck my head out of the cubicle.

"Manda, are you okay?" Michael said.

"What do you mean? Of course I am—you saw me not five minutes ago. Why?"

"I found your sweatshirt in the bin. It's covered in blood."

"I spilled some paint," I said, shaking my head.

"Not blood?"

"Not blood," I confirmed.

"Are you sure?"

"Of course I'm sure, Michael." I slammed the shower door. "Idiot," I said under my breath.

I got out of the bathroom to an empty house. I was tempted by the silence to crawl back to bed for an hour, but I had an appointment with Doctor Freda and she was a stickler for punctuality.

***

I'd been seeing Dr Freda for almost eleven years. Not that we always got along—there had been some humdinger fights between us. Still, she was the only constant person in my life other than Michael and the kids. We gave each other lots of attitude, but there was a mutual respect.

The receptionist was talking on the phone and waved at me as I entered. I sat down on one of the two beige leather sofas and chose a couple of magazines from the neat pile on the coffee table.

The receptionist hung up the phone. "You can go through, Amanda. She's waiting for you."

"Thanks, Monika. You're looking very bronzed. Have you been on holiday?" I appraised her slender figure. She wore red knee length skirt and feminine cream blouse, meant for much warmer weather than our autumn climate.

"Got home from Greece last week. I'm already planning my next trip—I loved it."

"Ooh, lucky you." I stood up and placed the magazines back on top of the pile. "Is she in a good mood today?" I nodded in the direction of Dr Freda's office.

"You know what she's like—she doesn't do good moods." Monika laughed.

"I heard that, Monika, thank you. Amanda, come on through." Dr Freda was standing in the doorway glaring at us, and shaking her head, though a slight smile played behind her amber-coloured eyes. She was dressed in a black trouser suit and black blouse. Her jet-black hair was scraped back into a severe bun, a complete contrast to her pale, almost translucent skin. She would have made a great bride of Dracula, but she was a day late—Halloween was yesterday.

I glanced back at Monika, gave an exaggerated wince, and then smiled. Wiggling my fingers at her, I mouthed, *see you later.*

Monika had been the receptionist longer than I'd been a patient. She was also Dr Freda's mother.

Dr Freda was back behind her desk when I entered her office. I closed the door behind me and sat opposite her on the formal wooden chair. The light, airy room always relaxed me. The golden pine furniture was modern yet classy and uncluttered. I couldn't have designed it any better myself.

"It's been a while, Amanda." The doctor smiled, her face softening. "I'm glad you called. Are you okay on the chair? Or would you prefer ...?" She indicated the two leather sofas, exact replicas of the ones in reception.

"No, I'm fine here thanks," I said, taking a deep breath. "I've been good actually, Doc. Until a few weeks ago, that is." I knew how fast the hour would fly by, so I wanted to get straight down to business.

"What happened a few weeks ago?" Freda said, in her uninterested way. Her eyes were expressionless.

"I felt sure someone was watching me all the time. Michael and I started fighting about it—he thinks I'm paranoid, like you do."

She ignored my dig.

"What happened around that time to cause these feelings?" Her elbows rested on the desk and her fingers were steepled under her chin.

"Lots happened at around the same time. I caught Michael with another woman." I waited for her reaction—there wasn't one. "Oh, and Emma went missing at the zoo. The attendant saw a woman who looked like me leave with her. Once we found her, Emma said she'd followed me. Plus, somebody had put a seahorse brooch in Emma's bag while she was gone—after we'd promised to buy her one."

"Odd. So where were you when this occurred?" She glanced at me over the top of her frameless glasses.

I recognised her expression. "Hold on a minute, Doc—don't start all that crap again. *I didn't do it.*" I clenched and unclenched my teeth.

"I didn't say anything, Amanda."

"Yet!"

Once again, she ignored my sarcastic comment.

"What else happened?"

"For weeks I felt as though I was being watched. I'd even begun questioning myself and wondered whether I was paranoid after all."

Doctor Freda raised her eyebrows as she tapped a pen on the side of her chin.

"Until I had a visit from a detective. They said my dad had been released from prison six weeks earlier, which was the exact time the sensation of being watched began."

Freda's professional façade almost slipped. She shuffled in her seat, moved a couple of pens around her desk and cleared her throat. "How has it affected you—this news?" she asked, back in control.

"I'm scared. I preferred thinking I was paranoid. Now he's in hiding, which terrifies me. I have no idea where he is, or what's going on in his head." I leaned back into the chair, stretching my shoulders and arching my back.

Her head cocked to the side. "In hiding?"

"Yeah—that's reason the detective came round. He'd stopped checking in with them and he hasn't been home. He could be anywhere." I shrugged.

"How are you in yourself?" she asked as she steepled her fingers on the desk again.

"Fine," I said. My voice sounded flat.

"You mentioned you caught Michael with another woman."

"Yeah, at a party. She was giving him a blowjob in the bathroom. I walked in on them." I bounced in the chair, fidgeting.

"How did it make you feel—seeing him like that?"

"Upset and angry at first."

"And afterwards?"

"Horny. It turned me on thinking about it."

"So what happened?"

"He said they'd just met, and that he was sorry. He lied though—he's still seeing her."

"How do you know?" Her eyebrows arched.

"I changed her number in his phone for mine. I received loads of raunchy texts, not intended for me."

She smiled, her eyes softening again. "Ingenious, Amanda. Upsetting though?"

"No, I don't care. Once he found out about my dad our relationship was over anyway." I shrugged again.

"And you're not bothered?" Her eyes narrowed.

"I was, but not now."

She nodded, her lips pursed.

"What?" I asked.

"I know you don't want to hear this, Amanda. But you're showing classic symptoms of Dissociative Identity Disorder. Understandable, after all you suffered."

"I'm sorry, Doc, I disagree. I googled it after our last meeting and I don't have multiple personalities." I took a deep breath and tipped my head back as far as I could to stare at the ceiling. I exhaled deeply.

"That can be a part of it, yes, but not in the way you're thinking. There are different degrees, like with everything. For instance, did you ever drive somewhere, and arrive at your destination with no recollection of the journey?"

"Yeah, but doesn't everyone?"

"Exactly. Now cast your mind back to something you didn't want to do. How did you feel?"

"I dunno—scared." I pinched an aching spot between my eyes.

"How scared? Think—quickly. How scared, Amanda?"

"*Scared!* All right! For God's sake!" I snapped.

"Good. Now think about doing that thing. How did you feel?"

"I don't know!" I shrugged again. My chest tightening, I placed my fist on the spot between my breasts.

"Think. Can you remember?" she demanded.

"Kind of." I was agitated, my legs bouncing up and down irritably.

"So you remember being scared, really scared, leading up to the actual event?"

I nodded.

"But you can't remember how you felt during the event?"

I shook my head. "No," I said, puzzled. She was right. I could remember the fear from before, but not during. It didn't make sense. It should have been much, much worse. "Why not, Doc?"

"It's because you dissociated. You would have learned to do this as a child, to enable you to deal with what was happening to you."

"So you're saying I'm crazy?" My legs, still twitching, now felt weak. I chewed my bottom lip.

"No, I am not. There are some severe cases—but as I said earlier, you're not that bad."

"So what other symptoms should I look for?" I rubbed my forehead, not sure I could cope with much more.

"Promiscuity, sexual repression, depression, paranoia, inability to make friends."

I thought about the feelings I'd had towards DS Adam Stanley. In fact, I had all of these symptoms bar depression.

"You had a lot of these symptoms in your past. There's also your reaction to catching Michael with his pants down, pardon the pun. Not to mention Emma going missing, and finding the brooch."

"You think that was me?" I was horrified. How could she think I would do that? My blood pumped noisily in my ears.

"Maybe, maybe not, but we can't rule it out. Also, blackouts—do you ever lose time?"

I shook my head.

"You need to be aware of the symptoms, and make a note of any unexplained or blank moments."

My mind flitted to the messages on the computer screen and the tidied up drawer. There had been lots of unexplained occurrences over the past few weeks when I thought about it, but I wasn't ready to share this information with her.

I took my shoes off and placed my feet on the seat in front of me, my arms wrapped around my knees.

"What are you thinking about?" she asked.

"Just thinking about the time I did black out years ago—remember? Do you think that was connected?"

She nodded. "Possibly."

"So what can I do? Take medication?"

She shook her head. "There is no medication, except for treatment of some of the symptoms—for instance depression and things like that. But accepting you have a problem is the first step and working closely with me. I can help you train yourself to understand and recognise the symptoms, and how to deal with them. They may never get any worse than these mild symptoms."

"I'm not depressed though," I said, shaking my head.

"No, and that's good." She looked at her watch. "Can I see you again next week, Amanda? I've got another client due, but I know you still have a lot of questions."

My heart jumped in my chest. She was dead right, I had questions. Shocked that my session had finished already, I put my shoes back on and numbly walked to the door.

"Goodbye, Amanda. Book your next appointment with Monika on your way out. Oh, and by the way, that was a good session. Well done."

I wanted to scream, *you cold bitch!* But I didn't.

***

Once home I typed Dissociative Identity Disorder into Google again. The first time Freda had suggested it, I'd been horrified. We'd been talking about Sandra and Peter at the time, my foster parents, and the reason I'd removed myself from their lives. To my mind I was protecting myself. I needed to avoid risking their rejection.

Another classic symptom, Dr Freda had said.

In my last internet search, I hadn't been able to get past the multiple personalities. Reading it now, I was surprised how many of the symptoms I had. I knew I had better not tell Michael. In his perfect world, mental illness was not acceptable. He'd have me locked up in a nuthouse if it was up to him.

My foster mother, Sandra, had been on my mind a lot recently. I'd lived with her and Peter for three and a half years—the only normal school-aged years of my life. Peter died when I was away in Italy.

I kept in touch with Sandra for a while. She always treated me as her long-lost daughter when I made an effort to visit. But I hadn't been able to handle the feelings she evoked in me. My own mother had never cared enough, yet this woman couldn't care more if she tried.

Maybe it was self-preservation—if I kept my distance, I wouldn't be let down. Anyway, for whatever reason, I stopped visiting. I hadn't seen her since I was pregnant with Jacob. I wasn't even sure if she'd want to hear from me after all this time.

I needed to think about things a while longer.

***

I stared at the TV screen, numb with shock. I couldn't get the image of that woman's face out of my head. Reaching for the phone, I dialled Michael's number, but it went straight to voicemail.

"Michael," I said calmly. "You need to come home as soon as possible. I need to go somewhere urgently—please call."

I ran upstairs and changed from my nightdress back into my jeans and T-shirt, still reeling from what I'd seen on the ten o'clock news. I knew I had no choice but to face this right away.

Back in the lounge, I began pacing a groove into the carpet. I'd seen very little of Michael over the past couple of days, I'd been busy at work, and he avoided me when I got home, hanging around long enough to hand over the children. He wasn't even trying to disguise his affair anymore, and I was past caring.

I heard a key in the lock and Michael rushed in, out of breath. "What is it, Mand, what's wrong?"

"I need to go out. Please stay with the children and deadbolt the door. I'll call you when I'm on my way home."

"Why? What is it? What's happened? Wh ..."

"Later, Michael," I interrupted. "I'll tell you later."

I parked my car next to the only other vehicle in the car park. I'd expected it to be much busier for a Friday night.

The sergeant on the desk looked as though he was about to nod off and jumped to his feet when I entered. "Yes, Miss, what can I do for you?"

"Good evening, Officer. I need to speak to DS Stanley, please."

"I'm sure he's already left for the evening. Can I get the duty officer for you?"

"No. I'm sorry to be a nuisance, but it has to be DS Stanley. He gave me his card, but I've misplaced it. He said I could contact him at any time." My voice sounded shaky.

"I'll call him for you—can I say what it's regarding?"

"It's about the murder in Peckham. Tell him I know who did it."

He did a double take at me before writing down my details, and then he went into the back office to make a call.

The officer came back through and called me to the desk. "He had left for the night, Miss, but he's on his way back. You may have a little wait though. Are you sure you wouldn't like to talk to the duty officer?"

"No. I'll wait, thank you."

A short while later Detective Stanley breezed into the waiting area. He was dressed in grey slacks and a white t-shirt that showed off his well-built chest to perfection. Unfortunately, the casual black jacket he wore over the top restricted my view.

"Mrs Flynn, it's nice to see you again."

He bent towards me with his hand outstretched, and I suddenly felt claustrophobic, pushing myself into the chair as far as I could. I hadn't realised how huge he was.

I shook his hand and felt that same zing of electricity that I'd felt the last time we met. I was relieved when he stepped back, giving me space to stand up.

"I'm sorry to bother you so late, but this couldn't wait till the morning."

"Follow me," he said. "We'll go somewhere a little more private, shall we?" He indicated the group of young lads who had just piled through the door—one of them gushing blood from his nose, all of them talking at once.

The sergeant on the desk pressed a button opening a door to the side of the desk and Detective Stanley led me down a corridor and through to an interview room.

"Please, take a seat," he said, holding his hand out towards the two chairs and a small table that filled the tiny room.

I sat on the chair furthest from the door.

"Can I get you a cup of tea or anything? The canteen is limited and not very nice, but the tea's wet and warm," he said.

"No, thank you. I just need to speak to you about my father. Have you located him yet?"

He pulled out the other chair and sat down, sighing heavily. His size overpowered the cramped little room. "We've had no word of his whereabouts since I last spoke to you. In fact, we've come up against a brick wall. His laptop's missing, and his car too, but his clothes and other personal effects were left behind."

He scratched his fingers through his short black hair, which promptly stuck up above his right ear.

I had to make a conscious effort to stop myself from patting it down.

"Mrs Flynn, you could have telephoned me for this. I came back here tonight because the desk sergeant said something about a murder."

"Yes. Do you know about the woman on the news tonight—the one beaten to death in Peckham."

"Vaguely. What about her?"

"She was my step-mother, Annie. I think my dad killed her." Once I'd said the words out loud my heart pounded in my throat, making breathing difficult.

"Let's not get carried away with ourselves yet, Amanda. I know it does seem like a coincidence, however that might be all it is."

"But she testified against him, too. She said he made her do those awful things and she even got a lighter sentence because of it. My dad threatened her in the court in front of everyone. He promised to make her pay, and now he has."

"I'll check with homicide, see if I can find out a bit more. Do you mind waiting for a few minutes?"

"Of course I don't mind waiting, he's probably coming for me next."

Chapter 9

Adam

It had been three months since Adam had transferred from Manchester to Pinevale. He'd found it hectic at first and was certain he'd made a huge mistake, but he was beginning to settle.

His colleagues were okay. Nevertheless, he chose to keep himself to himself. Tonight they'd invited him to the local pub after their shift had finished, but Adam opted to go home for an early night instead. It was much too soon for socialising. Shit, he felt guilty enough being able to wake up every morning and face a brand-new day. He couldn't imagine partying. Maybe it would eventually happen, but not yet.

He'd arrived home to half a dozen voicemail messages from his old mum. He loved his mum dearly, but she drove him bonkers. Since his move to Pinevale, she worried about him more than ever. She seemed to forget he was a grown man and would panic if she didn't hear from him every second day. She also had a habit of leaving a message and instead of waiting for him to get back to her; she would just keep calling his home and then his mobile, leaving a fresh message every time.

He returned her call and ate his fish and chip supper while chatting with her. She seemed in good spirits when he hung up. After a quick shower, he headed off to bed.

In typical sods-law fashion, the phone rang as soon as he closed his eyes.

He didn't hesitate when the desk sergeant explained the reason for his call. He was concerned for Amanda Flynn. The file on Dennis Kidd had sickened him.

Not only had he sexually abused his own children for years, he was also the instigator of a paedophile ring. His children had been passed around at parties to satisfy the depraved urges of the guests. Dennis had also supplied photographs and video footage of them to a seedy sex shop in Soho, making a good income for himself.

However, the police had made very few arrests. Dennis had kept the information close to his chest and the only names he'd given them were of people already dead.

Annie had been more co-operative, although she didn't have any real information. She had pointed the finger at some influential men but offered no real proof. The investigation had more holes than his grandmother's lace tablecloth.

Adam suspected a number of palms had been greased. He detested corrupt cops more than anything, but he knew it happened in every profession the world over. He also knew most people were honest. A small minority were not. People just found it more shocking somehow when the police were the bad guys.

Dennis had also been under suspicion for the disappearance of his son, but he had never been charged in connection with it. The evidence had pointed to Andrew running away, and who could blame the lad?

Once in his office Adam called Kate King, the detective in charge of the murder, but she said she wasn't able to interview Amanda until the morning. Kate told him that Annie had lots of enemies; most people they had spoken to detested her. Her neighbours said she brought the area down with her repeated drunken behaviour. He could imagine the uproar there'd be when they found out she was a convicted paedophile to boot.

Back outside the interview room, he looked at Amanda through the glass. Her shoulders were stooped and worry etched across her face. Adam wondered about her husband. Why would he leave her to deal with this alone, especially with a potential lunatic after her?

He thought of his own lovely wife and how he'd have been glued to her side if this had happened to her. Unexpected thoughts of Sarah brought a fresh lump to his throat. His face flushed, and the familiar palpitations in his chest were stronger than ever. He wondered if it would get any easier.

He gave himself a mental shake as he walked back into the room.

"Okay, Amanda, I'm afraid we can do no more this evening," he said, sitting down opposite her. "DI Kate King wants to see you tomorrow morning if possible; she's the homicide detective in charge of the case."

"Can't I just speak to you? Tell you what I know?"

"I'm sorry, Amanda, but I work in missing persons—this is homicide."

"Can't you be there too? Please, it's still about my dad and he's still missing. Please?" She eyed him imploringly.

Adam stood up and pushed the chair under the table. "I'll see what I can do. Now you need be here first thing in the morning."

His initial instincts were to run and hide, this wasn't his case and he no longer worked homicide, his choice.

But something about this woman tore at his heart—she seemed so vulnerable, like a frightened little girl. Her large grey-blue cat-like eyes were the most haunting eyes he'd ever seen. But when she smiled, they lit up her entire face.

He knew he should stay away, but he was inexplicably drawn to her.

He also knew that no matter what, he would be there tomorrow.

Chapter 10

Amanda

I couldn't face going home right away. I called Michael, who answered on the first ring.

"Hi, I'm going to be a little longer, is everything all right there?" I asked.

"Yes fine. What's going on?"

"I'll tell you later, it's a long story. Is the door properly locked? Have you checked on the children?"

"You're beginning to frighten me now, Amanda. Is all this connected with your dad?"

"I'll be home in a couple of hours, I'll explain everything then," I said, hanging up. I knew he'd freak out once he knew and I didn't need that right now. I'd prefer to tell him in person later.

I deviated to the Kingsley house. I needed to occupy my mind for a while.

***

The house gave me an immense feeling of foreboding. Streetlights threw menacing shadows that hung about under the trees. I was grateful for the tiny torch on my key ring.

With trembling fingers, I punched in the numbers on the keypad—relieved when the hall light illuminated the deserted front garden.

I gagged at the smell from the drains, it was putrid, unbearable. I couldn't get a plumber there until Monday because it wasn't deemed as urgent with everything still working.

I had hoped to finish stripping the wallpaper in the kitchen, but I could barely breathe. When I was there during the day I opened all the windows and doors, however I couldn't do that at night. So I gave up and headed home.

The door was locked. Dead bolted from the inside as I'd insisted.

I tapped on the living-room window and heard a kerfuffle behind the door—someone was whispering and rushing around. Alarmed, I began hammering on the door.

"Michael! Michael!" I yelled. "Open the door. Michael!"

The door was opened by a rather shifty looking Michael. I pushed my way inside and was shocked to see his girlfriend in the hall.

"The fucking nerve of you, Michael. Get out of my house now! Get out, get out! Both of you—now!"

"But-"

"Get out! NO buts—just fuck off! The pair of you—go!"

I was vaguely aware of the kids crying but I was too angry to care. I shoved Michael and his tart out of the door and slammed it shut.

***

Waking up in my bed, with the children on either side of me, the memory of last night hit me. I couldn't get over Michael bringing his girlfriend to my house.

I didn't know how I was going to make it to the police station with the children in tow. Detective Stanley had said he'd be present when I met with the homicide detective. I didn't want the children with me, but I had nobody I could call for help.

Once again, I found myself thinking about Sandra. I couldn't just contact her after all this time. What would I say? "Hey, Sandra, it's me. I'm in a spot of bother. Oh and by the way, can you have my kids for the day?"

No, I needed to think this one through for a while longer.

After breakfast, I tried to tackle Emma's unruly locks, and she almost screamed the place down. In the middle of our battle, there was a knock at the front door. It was Michael.

Emma squealed and ran to him. "Naughty mummy hurted me, Daddy."

He bent and put his arms around her, scowling at me.

"She didn't want me to brush her hair, that's all," I said, shaking my head. "What are you doing here anyway?" I glared at him, not wanting a fight in front of the children.

"I came to take the kids to the park. Aren't you going to work?"

"I'm going to the police station."

He cocked his head, squinting at me with a confused expression. "What for?"

"I'd have told you last night, but you were otherwise engaged," I said, grabbing my bag I walked to the front door.

He followed. "Tell me now."

Outside, I stopped on the path, making sure the children couldn't hear. "It's about the murdered woman."

"The drunk? It's all over the news. What could you possibly know about her?"

"She was my stepmother. Oh, and by the way, Michael—if you let that fucking woman in my house again, that won't be the only murder all over the news."

***

DS Stanley met me at the front desk as promised. He looked distinguished in his dark-grey woollen suit. Again, I was surprised at his sheer presence. He was easily 6'5" and the span of his shoulders was huge. There weren't many men I'd met that could make me feel small and protected the way he did.

After ushering me into the same interview room, he organised coffee to be brought to us.

A few minutes later a short, overweight blonde limped into the room, seeming flustered and distracted. DS Stanley introduced her as DI Kate King and pulled a chair out for her. She was nothing at all like I'd expected.

DI King didn't waste any time getting down to business.

"Mrs Flynn—"

"Call me Amanda."

"Amanda. Could you tell us in your own words about your relationship with Annie Duncan?"

"She used to be my stepmother. Annie Kidd I knew her as, she must have gone back to her maiden name."

"What kind of relationship did you have?"

"I'm sure you already know, Sergeant. She was an evil, twisted human being. She deserves to be dead."

DI King looked at me, seeming very interested suddenly. "So you're not sorry she's been murdered?" she said.

"No."

"You told Detective Stanley you knew who killed her."

"Yes—my father, Dennis."

"What makes you think that? I was told you hadn't seen him in a number of years."

"It doesn't take a genius to work it out," I said impatiently. "He's been locked up for years, and as soon as he's released he goes off the radar. Then the woman who was his partner in crime and who testified against him is murdered. Of course it's connected."

"At this stage, I agree it might be connected, but how—I'm still unsure," DI King said.

"I also testified against him. He'll be after me next, and I'm terrified for my children."

"I understand that, Amanda, and we'll do everything we can to protect you. But I must ask—where were you on Wednesday night?"

"I worked late. I'm restoring a house in Kingsley and I lost track of the time."

"Was anybody with you?"

"No, I work alone."

"Did you see anybody? Maybe you stopped for petrol on the way home?"

"I saw a handful of trick-or-treater's. They knocked on the door, but I don't know who they were. I waved to their parents at the bottom of the drive. Hold on a minute—why are you asking me all these questions? Surely you don't think I had anything to do with it?"

DS Stanley was quick to reassure me. "Of course we don't, Amanda, but we do need to ask nonetheless."

"I didn't see anyone. No-one can vouch for me—I didn't get home until late, and my husband was already in bed," I shrugged. "So now what?"

The door opened. Another plain clothed detective came into the room and handed DI King a piece of paper. She read it, then passed it to DS Stanley before she made her apologies and left the room.

"What was that all about?" I asked, getting worried now. I'd come here today to help them, and suddenly they were treating me like a criminal.

"I'm not sure. I'll just go to check, I won't be long."

And he also left.

Chapter 11

Adam

Adam glanced down at the piece of paper Kate had thrust into his hand before rushing from the room and tried to keep the surprise from his face. He then made his excuses and followed, hot on her tail.

Michael Flynn was in another interview room, alleging Amanda had something to do with the murder.

As Adam entered the room, he nodded his head at Amanda's creep of a husband before sitting down next to Kate. He couldn't understand how any decent man could accuse his wife of such a thing? Obviously, there was no love lost between them, but even so—she was the mother of his children for God's sake!

Michael told them Amanda hadn't got home until very late on Wednesday evening; he was in bed already.

"So why do you think she had something to do with the murder of Annie Duncan, Mr Flynn?" Kate said.

"Her sweatshirt." He sat up straighter, a slight smile playing at the corners of his mouth. "I found it the next morning. She'd put it in a plastic bag in the bin. It was covered in blood."

Kate gave a small gasp. Her feet shuffled under the table and she leaned forward, licking her lips.

Adam had already heard the rumours about her. She was nicknamed Rottie because she could be like a Rottweiler with a ragdoll if she got the mere whiff of a result. He wondered if he'd led Amanda into the lion's den.

"Did you ask your wife about the blood?" Kate asked.

"Yeah. She tried to tell me it was paint, but I knew it was blood straight off," he said. The side of his mouth lifted in a sneer. "I must admit though, I never thought she was capable of something like this."

Kate glanced at Adam and raised her eyebrows before turning back to Michael. "Maybe you should explain, Mr Flynn."

Michael shook his head and glanced down at his hands. "She's been acting strange lately, and things have been strained with us. She even bit my face a couple of weeks ago, look at this scar." He moved his hair away from the side of his eye and showed a discoloured area with a scab in the middle.

"Has she ever been violent before?" Kate said, almost on the edge of her seat. The more she heard, the more her eyes sparkled.

"Not really, but this time she just snapped like a woman possessed. She frightened me. I don't know what's wrong with her. You know, she never even told me about her family—I thought she was an orphan all these years. Imagine the shock when I found out her dirty little secret."

"Maybe she had good reason to keep it to herself," Adam said, feeling he needed to defend Amanda. She had nobody else to, if her own husband was ready to see her hang. "Sometimes it's best to leave the past in the past and focus on the future instead, Mr Flynn. Unfortunately for your wife the past seems to be back to haunt her."

Michael shrugged. "Well, you can let her know I'm taking the kids at least until this mess is over. Even if she's got nothing to do with the murder, there's still a nut-case out there with a sick taste for kids and I'm not gonna let him anywhere near mine."

The shrill sound of Kate's mobile had her up on her feet and in the corridor. When she returned a couple of minutes later, she was eager to wrap up with Michael, dismissing him in no time at all.

On their way back to Amanda, Kate turned to Adam. "She did it! She was seen buying vodka on Wednesday night, and a number of people have given her description as the woman who helped Annie get home."

Adam's stomach did a flip. He hadn't seen this coming. He'd not sensed anything off about Amanda at all. "So what now?" he asked.

"We turn up the heat."

He followed her into the interview room.

Chapter 12

Amanda

I sat staring at the back of the door for a while before deciding to check if it was unlocked. It was.

Popping my head into the corridor, I came face to face with the uniformed officer who'd brought in the coffee earlier.

"Can I help you, Ma'am?"

"I...'erm...I need to use the toilet," I stuttered.

"Of course. Follow me."

He led me to a room down the corridor and waited outside for me. Then he walked me back to the interview room.

"Where did the detectives go? I need to get back for my children."

"They shouldn't be much longer. Can I get you another coffee while you wait?"

"No, thank you. But please let them know I need to get going."

When the detectives returned thirty minutes later, I was fuming.

"About bloody time! Didn't you get my message? I need to go home to my children."

"That won't be possible right now, Amanda. We still have a few questions to ask." DI King limped over to take the chair she'd vacated earlier.

"I've told you all I know and it's getting late. Can I come back tomorrow?"

"Your husband has been in to see us," she said. "He said to tell you he will be taking the children away for a few days."

"What the fuck!" I couldn't believe my ears. "He can't do that. Where's he taking them?" I felt distraught at the thought of my children being taken to God only knows where.

"Don't worry, Amanda, I'm sure they'll be okay. He was just concerned for their safety," DS Stanley explained, but I noticed he couldn't meet my eyes. "Okay, Amanda."

DI King snapped my attention back to her.

"Where were you on Wednesday night?"

"We've already done all this. I told you earlier."

"Just answer the question, please." Her tone was more formal than before.

"Working. In Kingsley."

"When did you last go to Peckham?"

"What's happening here?" I said glancing at DS Stanley, but he was still trying to avoid my eyes.

"We've had some further information that we need to check out," he said. "Please co-operate, Amanda. We shouldn't take too long."

Kate King asked again, "When were you last in Peckham?"

"I already told you—never!" I began to panic. "What makes you think I've ever been there?

"Someone fitting your description was seen walking Annie home the night she was murdered," Kate said.

"That's impossible. It wasn't me." My head was in a spin.

"Also, we have reason to believe you disposed of an item of clothing that was covered in blood."

"It was paint! Check for yourself. I don't believe this is happening. I came here to help you, and now I'm your number-one suspect."

"We have a team of officers going over to your place now to check your rubbish. In the meantime, we need to arrange for an identity parade. It looks as though you'll be with us for a while longer."

Chapter 13

Adam

"We have to release her," Adam said. "There's nothing to hold her on."

"We have officers checking the dump as we speak. They shouldn't take much longer—they know where it should be." Kate was hanging on by a thread and they both knew it.

The identity parade had been a waste of time. Three people saw the girl with Annie, yet all three chose a different person from the line-up, and not one of them chose Amanda.

"It doesn't ring true, Kate. Why would she kill Annie now? She could have done it at any time."

"It's all we have to go on at the moment."

"That doesn't mean she's guilty, just because you have no more leads," he said, shaking his head.

"I know that," she spat.

"You're gonna have to release her—for now at least. I'll go and tell her."

Adam couldn't believe Kate. She'd been a detective for years and should know better than to focus on one lead of enquiry. Maybe it was the pain she was in that was clouding her judgement.

He was relieved that Amanda had begged him to attend the interview now, Lord knows what would have happened if he hadn't been there.

His plan had been to leave Kate to her case and get back to his own work, but how could he? Kate would have Amanda tied up like a trussed kipper if he wasn't there to make her see sense.

Amanda lay in a foetal position on the wooden bench of the stark white cell and she sat up when he entered. "Have you come for another round of interrogation?"

"No, quite the opposite. You're free to go."

"About bloody time. What happened? Hold on, let me guess. Nobody recognised me? Well, well, what a surprise—considering it wasn't even me."

Adam shrugged and bobbed his head. He knew better than to antagonise an angry woman.

She stood in front of him, looking up to meet his eyes. "I'll tell you something for nothing though: I'm glad she's dead. Somebody did the world a favour that's for sure. She was a nasty, sick human being." Her eyes filled, and as she blinked, two large tears ran down her cheeks.

"I wouldn't let DI King hear you—she'll keep you in another night." He awkwardly patted her arm and smiled.

"She wouldn't. And besides, what about the sweatshirt? She must know by now it was paint."

"The rubbish had already been collected. She's still searching the dump for it."

Amanda shook her head and smiled. "This could only happen to me. I was the one abused for years, yet I'm treated like a criminal. You wouldn't believe what Dennis and Annie did to me."

"I read the file, Amanda, and I sympathise, but you must understand we need to check out all avenues. You've gotta admit, you have a very good reason to want them both dead."

"But I didn't do it! You've got to believe me."

"For what it's worth, I do. Now come on, let's get you home."

He walked Amanda to the exit before going back to his office, puzzled by the effects she was having on him. He considered himself a decent detective—he always worked by the book, with excellent intuition and he was sure of Amanda's innocence even though the evidence was piling up against her.

Maybe he'd lost his edge.

Her childhood had been horrific. That would have been obvious to him, even without reading the file.

As a victim of child abuse himself, he could identify with her, could feel her fear.

His abuse had been physical, not sexual. Even so, he knew the helplessness a child felt when their carers—the people supposed to love them, to protect them—were the ones who terrified them the most.

Adam's stepfather had been a hard man, ex-army, and would take no-nonsense. The worst part of it for Adam had been the way his beloved mum had turned a blind eye to his abuse of her only son.

She had never been a very strong woman, but after Adam's dad died she withdrew into herself. By the time she met Vernon at the local church she'd been a widow for four years and was grateful for his attention.

Vernon was a God fearing, religious man with very definite ideas of how a household should run and how a twelve-year-old boy should behave.

His mum had made excuses for the way he treated Adam, believing it was for his own good. But as Adam got older, the abuse became much worse and went from physical beatings to the withholding of food and basic human needs.

Vernon was smart though and withheld just enough to cause Adam maximum discomfort but not enough for anyone on the outside to notice. Adam began stealing food from his school mates and was getting a name for himself. When Adams form teacher, Mrs Brady, noticed something wasn't quite right and took him under her wing, he eventually confided in her.

Vernon was never charged with anything. However, he left the family home and divorced Adam's mum, who had been distraught and had still not recovered from the humiliation. This was one of the reasons Adam felt so responsible for her to this day.

However, his abuse hadn't been a patch on Amanda's.

It had shocked him to learn that, at fourteen years of age, she had given birth to a baby. Paternity testing couldn't prove Dennis was the father as it was just as likely to have been Andrew.

Amanda's labour had started in her bedroom when her stepmother Annie was the only other person home. Dennis had never allowed Amanda to see a midwife or a doctor. He'd insisted they would deliver the baby themselves, but Annie panicked and instead called an ambulance. This gave Amanda her chance to escape.

She told the midwife everything, and after her Caesarean birth the premature baby was given up for adoption. Amanda never laid eyes on it and for the next six weeks she remained in a trance-like state.

He'd told Amanda he'd read the file but hadn't mentioned that he knew all this. Kate mustn't have read it or she would have been in for the kill—vicious cow that she was.

He poured himself a coffee from the pot. It was hot and wet—he didn't care that it tasted burnt.

Sitting down at his desk, he opened up the missing person file. The rugged yet handsome face of Dennis Kidd looked back at him.

"Where are you?" he said aloud. He rubbed his chin, the rasping sound of stubble reminding him he'd missed his shave this morning.

He couldn't understand what made a man do the kind of things Dennis had done to his children. No matter how many times he read similar cases it never got any easier. Now this monster was out there somewhere—doing what, was anybody's guess.

His phone rang.

The desk sergeant told him Amanda was asking for him. He stuffed the file into his drawer, switched off the light and closed his office door on the way out.

His stomach did a little lurch when he saw her sitting in reception. She looked done in, elbows on her knees and her head in her hands.

"Amanda, I'd have thought you'd be home and in bed by now."

"I would have been but my car won't start."

"I'm about to leave myself. Come on, I'll drop you off at home. The car can wait till tomorrow."

"Are you sure? I don't want to put you out, but I didn't know what else to do. My phone's dead," she shrugged, smiling sheepishly. But the smile didn't reach her sad blue eyes.

"No problem at all. Let's go."

They drove the first few minutes in silence, Amanda seemed deep in thought. He wished he could console her in some way–assure her that they'd catch her father and everything would be alright. But he wasn't sure they could.

He didn't trust Kate to do the right thing, and he wasn't sure how much help he'd be. It would be best all round if he were to go back and bury his head into the missing person files, leaving Kate and her team to investigate this case.

But although that was what he'd prefer to do—deep inside him was a bloody good detective, one who had been a bit battered and bruised of late but he was still there. He knew he had no choice. Amanda needed an ally and unlikely as he was, he was all she had.

"How long have you been here?"

Her voice surprised him from his own thoughts.

"Sorry?"

"You're obviously from up north. How long have you been in Pinevale?"

"Oh—er ... not long, a couple of months."

"You're accent is very strong. I guessed it must be recent." She smiled. "What made you come here? I'm not sure London would be my choice."

The sky was suddenly lit up by fireworks, giving Adam a few moments to gather his thoughts. He didn't know what to tell her. He rarely spoke about his private life and especially not with a stranger and a suspect at that, but something about her made him want to spill his guts.

"I'm sorry—none of my business," she said.

"No—it's not that. It's just difficult to talk about. You see, my wife died and I had to get away. Here was as good a place as any."

"I'm sorry—I had no idea."

"Why would you? It's okay, honest."

He turned onto her street. The house was in darkness as he pulled the car along the curb.

"He's actually taken them," she whispered. Her gaunt expression was illuminated by the feeble street light.

"I'm sure it's just for their safety. He's concerned there's a murderer on the loose."

"He's not concerned about me though," she whispered.

"I take it things are not right between the two of you?"

Amanda shook her head. "No. They haven't been for ages, but all this has freaked him out."

"Is there anyone that would come and stay with you for a few days?"

She shook her head. "No, there's nobody."

Once again, Adam was surprised at the sudden jolt of tenderness he felt towards her. He wished he could comfort her, pull her into his arms and calm her fears, but he couldn't, he needed to keep his professional distance.

"He knows how I feel about the children. I can't remember a night we haven't spent under the same roof." She shook her head, poking at the corners of her eyes in an attempt to halt the flow of tears. She opened the door and stepped out onto the street.

Adam asked, "Do you want me to come over to take you for the car in the morning?"

"Would you? Thanks so much." Her face lit up at his suggestion.

"Call me just as soon as you're ready—it's no problem."

Adam waited until she was inside the house, and then felt compelled to wait a little longer. After a few minutes, he saw the lights go out downstairs and the front upstairs light go on. Amanda appeared at the window and closed the curtains.

"Come on Adam, you're no better than a peeping Tom," he muttered.

He started the car and drove to the end of the street, discovering it was a dead end. He did a U-turn, slowing down as he passed the house again.

A movement in Amanda's garden caught his eye and his stomach lurched. A man dressed in black with a dark hood covering his face, was standing at the side of the path underneath the trees. He was looking up at Amanda's bedroom window.

Adam's headlights caught the prowler's attention and made him turn to face Adam before he ran through the garden down the side of the house.

In the time it took Adam to park the car and get out, the guy was long gone. After searching the back garden, he returned to the street. In two minds whether to contact Amanda or not, he decided on the latter. Instead, he rang through to the station requesting a patrol car to keep an eye on her house.

Chapter 14

Brian

"It's almost ready, sweetheart," Brian said as he placed one of the frozen meals into the microwave. Since he'd retired six months ago this had become a daily routine. Barbara made the lunch most days, she always had more energy earlier in the day, but dinner was now his responsibility.

The microwave dinged, and he replaced the piping hot lasagne package with the frozen one and reset the clock.

He had tried to cook a meal from scratch several times, but it never turned out right. Cooking wasn't his forte.

Barbara had spoiled him when he was working; she always had his dinner on the table when he'd arrived home. Recently though, she'd been tired, and everything was a huge effort for her.

Brian, happy to share the load, now did all the household chores. All except for the laundry—he'd ruined too many garments so Barbara insisted on doing that herself.

He transferred the lasagne to a white, gold-rimmed plate, added a few lettuce leaves and some slices of tomato and cucumber. "Voila," he said, pleased with the results and then put the plate onto a tray and buttered two slices of bread.

He shuffled through to the lounge. "There you go, sweetheart," he said, placing the tray onto her knee. Another bad habit, but they didn't see the point setting the table for just the two of them. It was different when the children came to visit. Then the tablecloth and best crockery would make an appearance. Otherwise, they preferred to eat in front of the goggle box.

"Thank you, love," Barbara said her husky voice raspier than usual.

The doctor insisted she should give up the cigarettes, but there was no way she would. She'd been extra breathless the past few weeks though, and the inhalers didn't seem to make any difference.

"You feeling okay, Barbs?" He handed her a knife and fork, his forehead puckered.

"So-so," she croaked, before a bout of hacking coughs tore through her.

He gazed at his poor wife. Her grey, recently set curls bounced as she coughed, and her slitty eyes watered down her fat cheeks.

She'd been such a looker when they met, almost forty years ago now. Bizarrely, the smoking was one of the things that had attracted him to her; he'd thought she was sophisticated back then. He'd loved her so much.

He still loved her, adored her even, and he was terrified of losing her.

She glared up at him, her lips pursed, slight annoyance tinging her weary face.

He realised he was still staring at her.

"What now? Don't start again, Brian. I couldn't stand another bloody lecture. Go and get your dinner." She wheezed and placed one hand on the arm of the tray and the other on her chest as she began to cough again.

"Nothing—don't worry, I won't say another thing," he said and returned to the kitchen.

After they had eaten, he switched channels for the news, another of their routines. It seemed all their activities revolved around the TV. They never ventured very far. He used to have a couple of pints in the local after work, but now it was too much of an effort.

He was half listening when an image came onto the screen that had him choking on his cup of tea.

"Hey, Bri, isn't that the teacher you were friendly with?" Barbara rasped.

"Be quiet!" he snapped. "I worked with her. I wasn't friendly with her. I got sick of your insinuations the last time around."

"Sshhh, we're missing it. I wonder what she's been up to this time," she said.

...and according to police reports, the woman was found dead in her Peckham home from what appeared to be a savage beating. The officer in charge of the investigation, Detective Inspector Kate King, says her team are working to piece together the circumstances surrounding the death. Witnesses have placed her outside the Retro Bar on Peckham High Street at around seven-thirty on Wednesday evening. She was last seen walking towards her home with another woman. Police have not released any more information. The victim's body is now with the County Medical Examiner's office for an autopsy. The police are also trying to locate the victim's ex-husband, Dennis Kidd, who has been missing for the past two weeks ...

The image on the screen changed, but in its place was another familiar image. Brian felt light-headed. His breathing caught in his throat, and he struggled to bring it back to a normal rhythm. Perspiration dripped down his face and into his mouth—he was vaguely aware of its saltiness. He needed to pull himself together. He couldn't let Barbara notice how this was affecting him.

"Hmmnn, that's interesting hey, Bri? She's dead. I wonder who did it. I wonder if it *was* Dennis or one of their poor molested victims. Bri, Bri, are you listening to me?"

"I ... I'm sorry Barb, I think I'll go out to the shed for an hour or so—I'm sick of sitting in front of the telly night after night." He needed to get out and clear his head.

It was just past six o'clock, but it was already very dark outside. There was no moonlight or stars. He had to take shuffling, baby steps to cross the uneven cobblestones. When he bumped into the old wooden shed, he felt the rest of the way with his fingers and opened the door. He flicked on the light switch.

It was a typical shed. Cobwebs hung from the ceiling and the gaps in between the wooden slats created draughts, but he loved it. It was his sanctuary. Barbara never understood what he liked about the old place. She'd been nagging him for years to clean it up, but he never did. He was guaranteed his own space as long as he shared it with spiders— Barbara was petrified of them.

He shuffled through to the back, past old paint cans and gardening tools, and through a doorway in a dividing wall.

The enclosed area was approximately two metres square. There were no windows, and no cobwebs or spiders. He cleaned this part often. Shelves along the back wall were piled high with car and gardening magazines. A single bulb hung down from the ceiling. He had to be careful to duck as he passed under it; he'd singed the top of his head on more than one occasion.

The small armchair, his destination, sat in the corner. He contemplated many things from this chair, with no interference from his beloved, but opinionated and annoying wife.

Once in the chair, he reached down, moving a heavy box of books from underneath the lowest shelf. He had to sit back and catch his breath for a couple seconds. His ever expanding waistline made bending difficult.

The second box was further back, but not as heavy, he slid it out.

He sat staring at the tatty cardboard box for a few moments. He stroked the faded print that showed it originally held jars of Marmite. However, Marmite had occupied the box for a short time. For the past thirty years it had held the true Brian, all his secrets and souvenirs.

He knew he would have to get rid of the contents. He even had nightmares about someone finding it. Yet he didn't know what to do with it. Several times he'd lit a fire in the backyard, telling

Barbara he was going to burn rubbish. Instead, he replaced the lid and stashed the box back into its hidey-hole under the shelf.

In the past few years, their friends had been dropping like flies, and he knew he wouldn't live forever. He also knew that if he died, Barbara or one of his children would find the box. That should have been enough reason to dispose of it, but he couldn't.

It was a sickness. He often felt sorry when he saw druggies and alcoholics on the street. He knew how strong the calling could be, regardless of what it was your body craved.

As he opened the lid, he felt the familiar stirring in his crotch. Once he had his hand on the first item, the pressure became too much, and he had to release himself from the restraints of his trousers.

His engorged penis flopped out of his opened zipper. He lifted handfuls of fabric from the box and arranged them onto the bare shelf in front of him. Bringing every second item to his face, he inhaled. His cock was leaping and bouncing unaided, as though it had a life of its own.

Once the shelf was full, he arranged several items on each knee. He took the last item from the box. It was wrapped in silky, ivory-coloured tissue paper and he unwrapped the contents.

He lifted the white cotton panties to his face and breathed deeply. These were the most recent ones he'd acquired, but the scent was fading fast. He knew once the smell had gone he'd need a new pair.

There was a shop in central London that sold them. However, it wasn't the same without knowing the girl who'd worn them. That was part of the fetish, visualising the wearer. He'd been lucky in his job. He had been able to feed his habit easily.

Opening up the panties, he sniffed at the inside of the crotch, his tongue darting out to lick the most intimate portion of the fabric.

He reached for a small pink pair adorned with yellow flowers and wrapped them around his huge cock then began to rub himself; the crotch of the panties encased the bulbous purple tip of his angry penis.

His breathing was getting heavier. Although he was excited, it wasn't enough. He needed something else. With his free hand, he reached into the side pocket of the armchair and pulled out a magazine. Young children, both boys and girls, adorned each page from cover to cover, all in various states of undress. He had piles of these magazines, bought from the same London supplier. Again, it was never quite enough. Nothing beat having pictures of children he knew and being able to recall the scent of each of the children in his photo collection.

Reaching the bottom of the box, he pulled out his photos. The first pile was of several small girls in the school gym. They wore nothing but navy blue knickers and white vests, all doing different activities. Some of the photos were new and others years old, long before gym-kits became the norm.

His favourite was of two young girls warming up on the mat. He had taken it through the window so the quality hadn't been the best from the start, but they were very dark now. He'd had them for such a long time.

The second pile was older still; they were the bikini-clad bodies of two young girls sunbathing on the beach. The heads were cut off in these photos. He was ashamed of these ones the most. The girls were his own daughters. Frantically pulling at his penis now—he was so close, but it still wasn't happening.

He knew why. It had been like this for months. The panties and the pictures were just not enough. He was scared of what he would have to do next.

Six months ago he'd taken the dog for a walk. It was a beautiful sunny day and the park was full of families. Some were having picnics, some ice-creams; all were having a wonderful time. He'd stopped for a while at the playground, watching some gorgeous kiddies. His hand in his pocket, he stroked his cock while he nonchalantly watched, and threw a stick to the dog with his other hand.

He'd been doing this for years and had mastered the art of seeming uninterested in what was happening around him. All the time he had one hand on his cock and his eyes on the little children.

That particular day he'd decided to walk towards the bowling green. It was no longer in use—the green and pavilion were unkempt.

Several times he'd masturbated there out in the open. The two paths leading to it were a good two-minute walk from either side of the green. He'd get plenty of warning if anybody approached.

As he reached the pavilion, he could hear voices but couldn't see anybody. Walking up the steps, he saw two little bare legs around the corner on the floor. He walked into the back of the pavilion without looking around and sat down, delighted to see two young girls around eight or nine years old.

The younger of the two jumped up and came running over to him. She had a mass of auburn curls and wore a pink top and short A-line purple flowery skirt.

"Aw, what's your doggie called?" She knelt on the floor in front of him, stroking the dog. She had one knee on the ground and the other bent giving him a perfect view up her skirt.

"Erm, Missy," he said and patted the poodle on the top of her head.

"Susan, come and stroke Missy, she's lovely," the little one called to her friend.

Missy was hopping about, licking the girl's face excitedly.

Brian couldn't believe his luck. His cock screamed to be released. He shifted its position so he was more comfortable.

Susan came over and sat next to her friend in front of him on the floor. She looked a little older than the first girl and had long black hair tied up with a yellow bobble. She wore lime green leggings and a yellow and green top.

"Are you here all alone?" he asked in a concerned-adult kind of way.

"Yeah," the first girl said. "We was wiv my sister, but she went off wiv her boyfriend," the younger girl said.

"Oh, that's not very nice of her to leave you alone like that." He smiled, all the time squeezing his penis through the fabric of his coat pocket. He'd undone the front of his trousers but was covered up by the coat. He'd made a hole in the lining of his pocket years ago.

Missy lay on her back. She loved the attention from the two girls, and they were besotted with her. This gave him a chance to watch them. If anybody came in there was nothing untoward going on. No one would be able to tell he was masturbating under his coat.

Susan was on her knees stroking the dog and Brian could see the outline of her panties through the sheer fabric.

He was close to an orgasm when Susan asked if Missy did any tricks.

"Yes, a few," he said, his jaw jutting at a funny angle and his breath coming out in short pants.

"Can you show us?" Susan said.

"They're a bit rude." He knew what he was about to do could get him locked up, but he was too far gone to stop now.

"Aw, show us," the younger girl said.

"Okay, if you promise not to tell anybody." He was going to come if he wasn't careful. He hadn't been this excited in years.

"We promise, don't we, Suse?"

"Yeah, promise," Susan nodded.

He called the dog over and made her sit in front of him.

"What do you want, Missy, hey? What do you want?" he said in the doggyfied voice she understood. They'd been practising this 'trick' alone for years.

She began snuffling into the front of his overcoat and the girls began to laugh.

"Hey, what's he doing, Mister?" Susan said.

"This is the trick. Are you sure you want to see it? I told you it's rude," he warned.

"Yeah," they both said, in unison. Two pairs of innocent eyes stared at him in anticipation.

Just then, he allowed his coat to separate, exposing his large, erect penis. Missy jumped up again, onto her hind legs, and snuffled and licked around in his crotch.

The girls gasped at first, then began to giggle. Wide-eyed, they stared at him and nudged each other. Still on the floor, they huddled together, the smaller one partially covering her eyes. He still had a view up her skirt. This was too much for him and he came almost immediately. Missy cleaned him up as she always did.

As soon as it was over, guilt overtook him.

"I'm sorry, girls, I shouldn't have shown that to you. You're not old enough yet."

"I'm old enough," Susan said. "I'm a big girl now."

The younger girl didn't say anything, which worried him the most.

"Remember, it was our secret?" he whispered as the enormity of what he'd just done and the potential consequences began to weigh on him. "If anybody finds out about what Missy does they'll put her to sleep forever."

The younger girl gasped again and tears filled her eyes. "Oh, no, poor Missy. We won't ever tell, will we, Susan? Never ever."

"Good, it's our secret then. Now, will you girls be okay if I leave you alone? Where will you meet your sister?" He stood up and put Missy back on her lead. He was itching to get out of there, to put as much distance between himself, the girls, the pavilion and the park as possible without drawing too much attention to himself.

"At the swings," said Susan.

"Then maybe you should head over there now—and don't talk to any strangers, will you?"

Ever since that day, he'd dreamed about going back but had managed to resist the urge. However, it was getting harder and harder to ignore.

The main reason he hadn't been back was that he no longer had poor Missy. He'd found her on the kitchen floor one morning, having continual fits. The vet couldn't do anything for her and she had to be put down.

There was no way a grown man could get away with walking through the park and pausing at the playground alone. He wasn't that daft. Parents were extra vigilant nowadays. Missy had given him the cover he needed.

He'd wanted to get a new dog, but Barbara wouldn't hear of it. She said Missy had made her breathing worse. He wanted to yell at her that the fucking cigarettes made her breathing worse—but he didn't.

Giving up, he folded his flaccid, bright-red penis back into his trousers, he knew he couldn't go on like this. He would have to do something, and soon.

Some of the panties had fallen to the floor, so he carefully picked them up and placed them back into the box. He folded the white cotton pair back into the tissue paper and put the photographs away.

He was disgusted with himself. He always felt the same, but he couldn't help it. It wasn't as if he hurt anybody. None of the children he looked at, apart from the latest two, were even aware of what he was doing. He was nothing like the others. Not like Dennis and Annie.

For years, he'd worked as a caretaker at the local school, and he always behaved appropriately. Unless, of course, you considered stealing underwear from the changing room inappropriate, but he'd never touched any kids.

Annie had also worked there as a teacher which was how they met. He wasn't even sure how the subject of kiddies had come up between then. However, it had happened, once they knew his weakness Annie and Dennis exploited it.

Five minutes later, he was back inside the house. He slammed the back door, calling through to Barbara that he was back, before putting the kettle on to boil.

Things always seemed better after a nice cup of tea.

He filled the teapot and put some digestive biscuits on a plate for his wife—they were her favourites. Then he carried the tray through to the living room. Barbara wasn't there.

"Babs, you up there?" he called up the stairs.

Nothing.

His stomach was turning somersaults. Maybe she'd been out to the shed.

He walked back through to the kitchen and paced the floor, his hands pressed either side of his head.

He opened the back door to the pitch-black night. There was no way Barbara would venture out there in the dark, he was certain of that.

Back inside, he checked the downstairs toilet.

Empty.

He began to panic.

Had she seen him?

Surely he'd have heard her if she'd come into the shed?

"Barbara!" He yelled, his voice rising.

He opened the front door. The wooden gate swung onto the path. He knew he'd closed it behind him earlier today, and nobody had been to the house since, as far as he knew.

Could Barbara have gone out?

He doubted it, considering her emphysema and how bitterly cold the night was.

He walked out to the gate and swung it shut, closing the temperamental latch as he did so. He leaned over the gate to get a view of the street, but there was nobody around. It was a total mystery.

Tiny prickles were beginning to form at the back of his neck, spreading down his spine.

Could this have anything to do with Dennis? He'd been waiting for something to happen since the first letter had arrived from Her Majesty's prison three months ago.

He ran back inside and straight up the stairs.

He searched the bathroom and their bedroom, not expecting to find anything, but he needed to check. Brian was already convinced that Dennis had done something to Barbara, just like he'd done to Annie.

***

As he stood at the gate waiting for the police, a feeling of dread enveloped him.

What could Dennis have done to her?

He wished he'd paid more attention to the news now. All he could remember was the reporter saying it was a 'gruesome scene'.

"Oh, Barbara. My sweet, sweet Barbie, what has he done to you?" he said, wringing his hands in front of him.

He didn't suppose it would take very long for the police to arrive. They'd seemed very interested at the mention of Dennis Kidd and Annie Duncan. They had told him to sit tight and wait for them.

Within ten minutes, an unmarked police car pulled up outside the house.

A short, blonde woman slowly uncurled herself from the driver's seat. She made it seem like very hard work indeed. Her grey trouser-suit looked at least two sizes too small. She pulled the jacket down over her black blouse. From behind, Brian could see where her bra strap and waistband squeezed her fat uncomfortably.

She stood upright as a second police car pulled up just behind her. This one was marked and held two uniformed officers.

"Mr Crosby?" The detective walked towards him, her hand outstretched. She had a very pronounced limp. "DI King."

Brian nodded, unable to utter a word. He ignored her hand and shuffled into the house. The officers followed.

He knew full well that he'd be in trouble now, but he couldn't live like this any longer. It was one thing having Dennis taunting and threatening him for years, but he couldn't allow him to hurt his family.

As they reached the living room DI King cleared her throat.

"Okay, Mr Crosby, maybe you should let us know the problem. PC Moore will make us all a nice cup of tea if that's all right?" She nodded at the younger officer, who had a ginger goatee that was more like bum fluff. He looked as though he should still be in school.

Brian nodded. His teeth were chattering and his breath escaped in short gasps. He made his way to his armchair and collapsed into it. The detective settled into Barbara's chair and it brought tears to his eyes.

"Okay, Mr Crosby. You said your wife was missing and you feel it has something to do with the dead woman."

He nodded again.

"Mr Crosby, we cannot begin to help you or your wife until you tell us what happened."

"I know," he whispered. Taking a deep breath, he sat up straight in his chair and cleared his throat. He removed his wire-rimmed glasses and rubbed his eyes. "I had a letter from Dennis. He's been writing to me on and off since going to prison. But in the last few letters he threatened me. I never thought he would be capable of murder though."

"I take it you mean Dennis Kidd? The convicted paedophile?"

Brian nodded and replaced his glasses.

"What did he have to threaten you about?" She squinted.

"Nothing, really. I mean, not what you're thinking anyway."

"And what am I thinking, Mr Crosby?" she said, eyebrows raised and a smug 'whatever' expression on her face.

"You know—like you said, he's a paedophile."

"So tell me, then, what *was* he threatening you for?"

"I knew him years ago. Annie too. I never touched any of them kids though. You've got to believe me. I'm not a sicko." His voice sounded high-pitched and unfamiliar to his ears.

"Okay, calm down, sir." She stood up and made her way over to the older uniformed officer and whispered something to him.

The officer nodded and then left the room and the detective limped back to the chair.

Brian wondered what she had done to her leg; she was obviously in a lot of pain.

"Tell us what happened tonight. Maybe we need to try and locate the whereabouts of your wife first."

PC Moore returned to the lounge with two cups of steaming hot tea and placed them on the coffee table between them. Brian reached for his and burnt his hands on the cup. He set it down again. Everyone was staring at him when he looked up.

"Oh, erm ..." He cleared his throat. "We were watching the news after dinner. That's when we found out about Annie." He rubbed the bridge of his nose—he had a migraine coming on.

"You knew her well then, sir?"

"I used to work with her at the school, years ago. I haven't seen her since, you know—since they were arrested. But I heard she was in a bad way with booze."

"So, what happened after the news?"

"I went out to the shed, to unwind. I left Barbara watching television. When I came back in she'd gone."

"Maybe she just popped out somewhere."

"No, you don't understand. She hasn't been at all well. She can barely walk. It takes her all her time to get upstairs to the bathroom with her emphysema. She would never go out without letting me know or needing my help."

"What did you do in the shed?"

"Eh?" Dennis screwed his face up. His eyes darted around the room.

"I said, what did you do in the shed?"

"Erm ... I read my gardening magazines."

The detective and PC Moore exchanged an odd glance.

"What makes you think your wife's disappearance is connected to Annie?" she asked.

"Dennis threatened me. He said I owed him and he would come to see me when he got out. I got another letter from him a couple of weeks ago. He said he would be around soon, but I never heard from him again. Now Annie's been murdered and my wife's missing." The last few words came out in a rush—all joined together. Brian buried his head in his hands.

"Why didn't you tell the police you were being threatened?"

"Because I thought he would just want a few quid and that would be the end of it. How was I supposed to know he meant violence?"

"What did he have over you, Mr Crosby? You may as well tell me—I *will* find out."

"Like I said, I used to know him. He said he would implicate me in some way, but it's a load of nonsense," Brian said as he slumped in his chair again. He stared down at his slippered feet.

"Mr Crosby, I think it would be better if you accompany us to the station. We need to take a full statement in order for us to try to find your wife."

As they were getting into the police car, the older uniformed officer called from the front door. "Ma'am ..." He tipped his head towards the house.

"Excuse me for a second, Mr Crosby."

His heart was beating like a big bass drum in his throat. They couldn't have found his box that quick, could they? They were only supposed to be securing the house.

Brian watched as the blonde detective limped up the path. He held his breath until he felt light-headed and let the air out in a huge sigh.

The detective listened to what the officer had to say. They both turned to look at him before they re-entered the house.

He was done for and he knew it. Why else would they have looked at him that way? His eyes were glued to the front door, his heart raced and his right leg twitched uncontrollably.

They came out. The officer remained by the front door and the detective limped back to the car and opened his door.

"Mr Crosby. PC Moore has made a discovery," she said, her tone flat.

Brian sat nodding his head, waiting for her to read him his rights. He couldn't meet her eyes.

"It's your wife, sir. She's dead."

Chapter 15

Adam

Once again, just as Adam's head hit the pillow, the phone rang.

As he jumped up, an image of Amanda flashed through his mind. "Stanley," he barked into the phone.

"It's Kate. Sorry to wake you, but I think you might want to come to the station."

"Give me twenty minutes." He hung up and raced to the bathroom. His first instinct had been to ask if Amanda was okay, but he hadn't wanted to appear too familiar. He knew it had to be something to do with the case though, or Kate wouldn't be ringing him. She was homicide and he missing persons, he wasn't usually her go-to guy.

He splashed his face and dressed in record time, his mind racing. He was annoyed with himself for not going back to Amanda's house to tell her about the prowler in her garden. But he hadn't wanted to freak her out any more than she was already.

What if it had been Dennis and he had returned? Adam felt sick at the thought.

He pulled up outside the station and glanced at his watch. It was just after midnight. God only knows what time he would get back to bed. He preferred the station at this time of the night—things were generally a lot quieter and less hectic.

"Evening," he nodded at the desk sergeant as he walked through reception.

"Hello again, sir. I thought you'd already left."

"So did I, Stevens. Is Kate around?"

"Yes, sir. She's in interview room two. Got a funny little man with her, she has."

He let himself through to the back corridor. Peering in through the window of the interview room, he could see Kate and a barrel-shaped, balding, older man. He tapped on the window.

Kate held one finger up to him before standing, leaning most of her weight on her good leg.

He'd overheard a conversation in the staff canteen about what had happened to her. She'd been taken hostage six months ago and had forced her abductor to crash the vehicle he was driving into a brick wall. He'd died on the spot. She survived, but suffered a fractured hip and pelvis and her leg had been broken in several places. It had taken months to recover, and although she had little more than a limp on some days, other days she was barely able to walk at all.

She stepped into the corridor.

"Hi, Stanley. Thanks for coming in. I thought you might want to sit in on this interview. Brian Crosby. He called us tonight after his wife had vanished. He was adamant her disappearance had something to do with Dennis Kidd." She raised her eyebrows and waited for this news to sink in. "Apparently Dennis had been threatening him for the past few months and told him two weeks ago he would be contacting him."

"What's he been threatening him with?"

"That's what I thought you might want to find out. He used to work with Annie at the school—he was caretaker there. What I want to know is why a known paedophile would have something on him? And if it's nothing, why not report the threats to the police in the first place?"

"And the wife?"

"A very sick lady. She'd gone missing from their home tonight, or so he thought when he called us. He said Dennis must have been around to give her a going over like he'd done to Annie."

"And you don't believe this by the sounds of things?"

She shook her head. "No. Mainly due to the fact that one of our officers found Mrs Crosby upstairs in the spare bedroom—dead as a doorknob. Looks like natural causes, according to the coroner, but we'll need a post-mortem to be sure.

Chapter 16

Brian

"Why am I still here? This is pointless. I've done nothing wrong!" Brian was dog-tired and distraught at the news of his beloved wife's death. He needed to go home.

"We have a few more questions, Mr Crosby. This is Detective Stanley," DI King said, nodding in the direction of the hulk of a guy who came in behind her.

"I don't get it—you've found Barbara. I made a mistake. She sometimes goes into the back room to get my attention when I'm outside. I didn't see her, that's all." He ran his hand through his hair, shaking his head. "That's the only window in the house that overlooks the shed. She doesn't like my shed. She hates—hated, spiders."

"I understand, Brian. However, we still have Annie's murder to solve and no leads, so we need your cooperation." She sat back down in front of him and Detective Stanley pulled up a chair next to her.

"I've told you everything I know, already." Brian felt claustrophobic. He reached for the glass in front of him, but his hand trembled so badly he spilled most of the water down the front of his rust coloured sweater.

"I don't believe that, Brian. Please tell Detective Stanley what you told me earlier?"

Brian sighed. "I ... I thought Dennis had come to my house and harmed my wife, like he's done to Annie. But I made a mistake, and now I need to go home."

"So—bear with me, Mr Crosby, but I'm finding this hard to understand. Your wife wasn't where you left her and straight away you think she's been murdered?" The male detective's deep Mancunian voice reverberated around the small room.

"Yes," Brian whispered, aware of how stupid he sounded.

"You didn't think to search the house before calling the police?"

"No, sir. I mean yes, sir. She was in the house, my poor, poor Barbie. In the spare bedroom. We never use that room and although I did look in there, I didn't see her. She'd fallen at the far side of the bed underneath the window." His voice shook and tears threatened to spill over.

"What made you suspect Dennis Kidd had something to do with her disappearance?"

Brian wiped his eyes with his sleeve. "He used to write to me, ask me to send him certain things. I even went to see him once. I know what he did to those kiddies was wrong but he always seemed okay to me." His hands shook so much the glass was making a racket on the table.

Kate King bent forward and took it from him. "Calm down, Brian. Take your time."

"Where are the letters?" Hulk said.

"I got rid of them. Barbara would have gone berserk if she'd known I'd been in touch with him."

"Then why do it?" Kate asked.

"I don't know. Because he wrote to me, I guess."

"Did it not bother you that people would think you were involved? Did that not occur to you at all?" she said.

The look of feigned bewilderment on DI King's face made him feel ridiculous. Brian sagged into his chair as though his bones had turned to jelly. "Of course it did, but what could I do? He was a dangerous man."

"You said he was okay until a few weeks ago. And anyway, he was in prison, he couldn't have harmed you if he'd wanted to. No, Mr Crosby, there's more to this and unless you're honest with us, you'll be going nowhere fast." DI King leaned forward again, her lips tight as she glared at him.

Brian tried to ignore the nagging voice in his head reminding him of the promises he'd made when he was praying for his wife to show up. He'd sworn to the heavens that he would confess all if she were found.

But once she had been found he couldn't bear to tell the truth, couldn't face everyone knowing his secret. He had to get home though, he needed to contact his children and arrange Barbara's funeral. Also, he intended to dispose of the box once and for all. But to do that he knew he'd have to give the police something before they'd consider letting him go.

"I found out about them, before everyone else did. I found out they were messing around with them kiddies," he blurted out. "Dennis warned me to keep my mouth shut—said he'd tell everyone I was involved. Everyone knows shit sticks whether it's true or not. I worked at the school with Annie. People love that sort of scandal."

"So, let me get this straight. You're saying you knew they molested young children yet you said nothing just to cover your own behind?" Hulk said, his top lip lifted, showing his teeth.

"Yes, sir. And then they got caught. At first I thought they would blame me for blabbing and send the police after me. The first letter came and I shit myself, but he only asked for cigarettes."

"So what changed?" Detective King said.

"I don't know," he shrugged. "I think because he was getting out and needed money and stuff. He thought I was a soft touch, 'cause I had been in the past, but I couldn't give him anything. I'm on a pension now. What would I tell Barbara? So, I ignored his demands. Then two weeks ago I received a hand-delivered note. He said he would collect what was owed to him—he threatened me. I wish I'd kept it now."

"Is that everything, Mr Crosby, because if we find out you're lying to us we'll come down on you like a sack of shit, you hear me?" The hulk's booming voice shook Brian to the core.

"Yes, I swear to you. When I saw the news tonight, I panicked. I realised he was capable of more than threats."

"So you think he's responsible for the murder of Annie Duncan?"

"I'd put my life on it, sir.

Chapter 17

Amanda

I turned over and stretched. Tired of trying to sleep. Tired of tossing and turning. Tired of being bone tired.

I'd got into Emma's bed in the end, creeped out that the police had been through my stuff. My bedroom looked like a crime scene. The drawers had been left wide open and the contents were in an untidy mess.

I cringed at the thought of nosy Mrs Corless across the street. She would have seen everything and been in her element. I'm sure the stories would be rife among the neighbours by now.

The way Michael had taken the children hurt like hell, but deep down I was relieved. At least this proved he was taking me seriously. I still felt sure that someone was watching me, and now, with Annie's murder, I didn't want my kids at risk.

I got out of bed. Emma's window-seat overlooked the small back garden. As I sat down a slight movement caught my eye and my heart lurched. A cheeky fox snuffled through the undergrowth. I steadied my breathing and laughed. "Hello, Mister Fox, you almost gave me a heart attack," I whispered, my breath fogging up the glass.

My mind was in turmoil. I'd been certain Dennis was responsible for Annie's murder but now I wasn't so sure. His prey had always been children—not adults. And although Annie had testified against him she'd been a willing partner and I was sure he'd never abused her. But then again, he was a stranger to me now, and prison had probably made him even more of a monster than he already was.

Annie had been a schoolteacher when she met my dad. I didn't know if she'd already had perverted tendencies, but my guess is that she was so in love she'd have done anything to please him.

The parties had started when we were very young. Dad and Annie would dress Andrew and me in skimpy outfits. We had to wait on the guests, fetching bottles from the fridge. Annie taught us how to pour them into a glass. Sometimes we were given money—not a lot, but Andrew and I would split whatever we were given between us at the end of the night. We had a wonderful time in those early days, being too young to realise what was actually going on.

That had been the start.

The men would sit us on their knees and bounce us up and down. We didn't know it was wrong. I remember one man who used to live down the street. He had what I now know to be a huge hard-on. I remember he joked that he had something for me down his trousers. Everybody laughed. I didn't understand then, but now I know why they all found it so funny—the sick bastards. At the time, I was puzzled and upset that I didn't get my present from him.

One night one of Dad's friends woke me. He spoke in hushed whispers, telling me to lie still.

This was the first time warning bells went off in my head. I was on the top bunk, Andrew underneath. I didn't want to wake him so I never made a sound.

The man pulled the bedcovers back and twisted me around so my head was wedged up against the wall, and my legs hung over the edge of the bed. He pulled off my pyjama bottoms and underwear and stood there looking at me.

After a series of grunts, he made a long, groaning sound and then hurriedly pushed me back into bed. He tucked my clothing under the pillow and whispered that I'd be in a lot of trouble if I told anybody what I'd done. He said he wouldn't tell on me if I was a good girl.

I was petrified.

I didn't want to be in trouble. I didn't even know what I'd done wrong.

I lay still for a few minutes and then pulled my pyjamas out from underneath my pillow. I couldn't find my panties. I needed to pee so I put the pyjamas on and climbed down the ladder as quietly as I could.

Out on the landing I saw down into the hallway. The man was standing by the front door with my dad. I was worried that he was going to tell him what I'd done and get me into trouble. They were speaking in whispers, but I heard him thank my dad. They shook hands and Dad patted him on the shoulder as he left.

Looking back, I realise that maybe if I'd caused a scene that night it might have gone no further. My silence and cooperation gave my dad and his sick mates the green light they wanted.

But I was only eight years old!

Emma's pink, fleece bedspread was half on the floor. As I bent to pick it up I noticed the sparkly seahorse fastened to the corner of it. I'd put in my jewellery box the day after the zoo—I didn't want to chance Emma losing it before we found out where she'd got it from—bloody Michael. He must have given it to her again.

I sat on the bed. Another wave of sadness came over me and I pulled the bedspread across my legs and buried my face in Emma's pillow to stifle the sobs.

Chapter 18

Brian

The house was eerily quiet.

Brian had been sitting in Barbara's armchair since getting home from the police station in the early hours.

He'd waited until he knew the girls would be awake before making the necessary calls. They both said they would come over as soon as they could.

He also called a couple of close friends and now he had no energy left. The rest would have to wait until later.

Telling his daughters their mother had died was the most terrible thing he'd ever had to do.

It hadn't come as a complete shock to them, however. Barbara's health had been getting worse for a long time, and although they didn't often visit, the girls spoke to her every week.

Pamela had taken it the worst. She hadn't been able to talk and in the end her partner, Clive, came on the phone. She called back a short while later and confirmed she'd come over as soon as she could arrange a child-minder for little Amy. I suggested she bring her too, but Pamela insisted it was no place for a sensitive four-year-old.

Alison had been much calmer, but she always was the cool one in a crisis. She said she would be there as soon as she could. She was coming from Manchester, which was a fair way off. He didn't expect to see either of them until later today or maybe even tomorrow.

His stomach growled. He'd not had a thing to eat since last night's frozen lasagne. So much had happened since then. His eyes pricked with tears once again.

Shuffling into the kitchen, he set about fixing a ham sandwich and a cup of tea—not his usual choice of breakfast but he'd had no sleep so it seemed more like supper.

Everything was a massive effort. He suddenly felt ancient and couldn't imagine life without Barbara—she'd been his rock for as far back as he could remember.

He took two cups from the sideboard and proceeded to brew a pot of tea for two. As he poured the amber liquid he realised his mistake and with an animal-like roar he snatched up the white china cup from the bench top and slammed it across the room to the wall. It shattered into thousands of tiny pieces. He let out another pained cry and put his head in his hands and sobbed.

He'd always been a very calm man. He'd never lost his temper with his wife or children, and he didn't see the point in wild displays of affection or grief. He was usually much more subtle than that. This outburst shocked him. He'd never experienced emotion this close to his soul and didn't know how to cope with the raw pain surging through him.

After a few minutes, he wiped his eyes on a teatowel and reached under the sink for the dustpan and brush. He began to clear up the fine shards of porcelain. The gaping, empty ache in his stomach was much worse than any physical pain he'd ever experienced.

He was on his hands and knees when there was a knock at the door. He glanced at the clock—barely eight o'clock. "Who can this be?" he mumbled to himself.

Knees creaking, he got to his feet and emptied the contents of the dustpan into the rubbish bin.

The knock came again, louder and more urgent this time.

"All right, all right, keep your hair on," he called, shuffling into the hallway.

As he reached the door, he lifted the security chain and as he was about to secure it he shook his head and let it drop instead.

A tall, well-dressed blond woman stood on the doorstep. She was familiar but for the life of him he couldn't place her.

"Hello. Can I help you?" he asked.

"Hi, Brian. Can I come in?" the woman asked as she shoved past him and stomped into the living room.

"Hey! Hey, hold on a minute. Who the heck are you?" He followed her.

She had sat in Barbara's chair and had her back to him as he tentatively shuffled into the room, his hands wringing together in fear. Why would this woman scare him so much?

"Ca-can I help you? Who are you? Please leave!" Brian cringed at the sound of his own whiny voice.

She turned to face him and another flash of recognition hit him but was gone as fast as it came.

"Surely you remember me, Brian?"

Her voice was husky and sexy, and no doubt if you were into that type she would be incredibly attractive.

"I-I can't play games with you. What do you want? I lost my dear wife last night, so I'm sure you'll understand that I'm not being rude by asking you to leave."

"Always the gentleman, hey, Brian. Ever so polite when really all you want to do is drag me kicking and screaming from your home." She smiled. "What a shame Barbara isn't here for your unveiling."

"I have no idea what you're talking about," he said, feeling light-headed. His breathing had become very shallow, barely reaching his lungs.

"I'm sure you do, Brian. Though I've got to hand it to you—you certainly pulled it off all these years. She didn't have a clue, did she?" She raised one well-groomed eyebrow as she awaited his response.

"You're talking in riddles," he said, his voice rising even higher. He wiped his sweaty palms on his trouser legs and then put his hands in his pockets.

"What's in your pocket, Bri? Is it the old trouser snake?"

He gasped and it was as though a couple of mousetraps had gone off in each pocket—he pulled his hands free and held them out in front of him in absolute horror. His blood ran icy cold.

"All those innocent little girls. Do you think the part you played was any less sick than all the others?" Once again, she raised a questioning eyebrow.

"I-I don't know what you're talking about," he said. Brian was aware of his rapid heartbeat and realised he hadn't taken his blood pressure pills. "I must insist you leave. I'm expecting my daughters any second now."

"Do you still ogle them, Brian? Little Pamela and Alison?" Her lips turned up at the corners, not quite a smile, and a glint of amusement in her eyes. "I bet they won't let you anywhere near their kids. They know what you are. You may have kept it from everyone else, but they have always known."

He couldn't stand any longer. He sat heavily on the sofa, tears pouring down his face. He made no effort to cover them up, and they flowed freely. He couldn't believe it, this stranger was killing him with her vicious words. How could she know so much?

"Aw, poor Brian, what a shame. There, there," she jibed.

"Who are you? Did Dennis send you? Is that what all this is about?" he whispered. "What does he want? He can have anything if I've got it to give. Please—please just stop this, I can't stand anymore."

She smiled, shaking her head. "Don't you remember me, Brian? How you bounced me on your knee when I was little? How you encouraged my dad to help you get your rocks off with his own kids? You even paid him for the pleasure, you sick fuck! You allowed the abuse to go on, Brian."

"But it was going on anyway! I didn't touch anyone—it was them, all them. I swear to you."

"Have you listened to yourself? Is this how you justified the part you played for all these years? By telling yourself you're innocent, because you didn't actually *touch* anybody? Well whoop-dee-doo—my mistake. If it's all so innocent then, you won't mind sharing your story with the police, will you?"

"What do you want from me?" Brian screamed, his voice was more like a squeal.

"What do you think?" The woman got up and stood over him.

He was petrified. Couldn't imagine what she was about to do. He cowered—covering his face with his raised arm, he peeked over the top of it.

She reached into the large grey bag she had slung over her shoulder, pulled out a blowtorch and pressed a couple of buttons. A tight blue flame blazed from the nozzle.

Brian was now glued to the seat with fear, his thoughts rioting through his mind. "What the ...?" He shook his head. His breathing was now noisy, short pants, and sounded like someone sawing a plank of wood.

"For all those children, Brian. I'm going to make sure you never look at another little girl *ever* again—not here or in hell."

She bent towards him. The intense heat of the controlled flame closed in on his face.

"No, please! I beg you," he cried. Moving much faster than he had in years, he pushed backwards and caused the sofa to tip. Then he rolled sideways, scrambling to his knees with more agility than a man half his age, and still crawling, headed for the front door.

Even though he'd picked up speed he knew it was pointless when halfway down the hall he heard the sound of her heels as she caught up with him.

He screamed as she grabbed his hair and yanked his head back. Then her high heeled leather boot stamped down on the back of his neck, pinning him to the floor.

The gurgling sounds that escaped him made him think he would die that way. He couldn't breathe at all. Her strength blew his mind. She pulled his head back in an unnatural angle, and his arms flailed uselessly at his sides.

He heard the tell-tale crackling, before he felt his hair singe. The incessant roar of the torch was driving him mad—there was no way to escape it.

The white-hot pain, when it arrived, was like nothing he'd ever experienced. The flame licked at his right eye, the tearing metal of the torch prodded his melting eyeball. The smell was unreal.

He felt his eyeball pop and heard the squelching sound as she pushed it into his brain.

Chapter 19

Amanda

The incessant ringing of the phone broke through to my dreams and I wished someone would answer it. I forced my heavy eyelids open. Sunlight poured into Emma's bedroom window and I remembered I was alone.

I ran down the stairs taking two at a time, praying it was Michael. I reached the phone just as the answering machine picked up.

"Hello, Michael?" my voice echoed from the kitchen followed by Michael's answer phone message. "Hold on a minute," I said.

I waited for the message to finish and the machine to beep. "I'm sorry—who's speaking, please?" My voice still boomed from the kitchen.

"Hello, Mrs Flynn?"

"Yes," I said.

"Jeff from PK Plumbing just confirming our appointment today in Kingsley."

"Oh, bloody hell, I forgot. What time?"

"I'm about finished here, so ... say, an hour?"

"Any chance we can make the appointment a bit later, or tomorrow? I don't have a car."

"Sorry, love. If you need to re-book, the earliest would be next week. We're chock-a-block."

Of course you are, I thought, sighing. "No, don't worry. I'll see you there in an hour."

My plans had been to ring DS Stanley and to get the car sorted out. Instead, I'd wasted almost three hours sleeping. The car would have to wait since the drains were far more important. I couldn't work with that terrible stench for any longer than necessary.

It's at times like these I regret not getting to know the neighbours. Being a loner suited me most of the time, but it left me with nobody to turn to in an emergency. I heard Dr Freda's voice in my head saying, "Yet another symptom, Amanda." I screwed up my face and blew a raspberry at the imaginary voice.

Next, I called a cab. The fact it would cost a small fortune was the least of my worries right now.

I threw on a tracksuit, stuck my hair up with a few clips and was ready to leave a few minutes later.

In usual London fashion, the journey took ages. When we pulled up outside the property, I could see the plumber sitting in his van on the other side of the road. I paid the cab driver and got out just as the plumber started up his van.

I ran across the road, jumping and waving my hands about like a mad woman. I reached the van as he was about to pull out into the road.

"Hey, hey, where are you going?" I cried.

The pounding on the bonnet startled the plumber. He slammed on his brakes and wound the window down. "Watch out, lady, you almost got flattened!"

"Where are you going?" I shrieked. "I've just had the cab ride from hell to get here and find you're about to leave."

"I've been waiting twenty minutes already. I told you I was busy!"

"Well, I'm here now and you're going nowhere until you fix my drains."

I stood my ground, my hands on my hips, trying to appear forceful. I was so angry I could have thumped him and I think he knew it.

Begrudgingly, he got out of the van, his mouth set in a firm line, and pulled a large toolbox out from the back of the van.

Running on ahead, I opened the front door and stepped into the hall. "See what I mean? It's terrible, eh?" I said and buried my face into the crook of my arm.

His head snapped back as though I'd slapped him. I showed him to the cellar door and he pulled the front of his sweater up over his mouth and nose and squinted his eyes before going down the steps.

I raced through to the kitchen and opened the windows and doors, filling my lungs with fresh air. I stood on the back step and waited.

Within a matter of minutes, the plumber was back upstairs.

"What made you think you had a plumbing problem?" he asked, his face screwed up as though he had shit on his top lip.

"Because of the stink. The house has been shut up for years and I thought it must be a blockage."

"You didn't see a blockage then?" His lips turned down at the corners and he gave a smug backwards nod.

I really didn't like this man's attitude, but I needed him to get the problem sorted. Keeping my voice as level as possible was an effort. "No, but how else do you explain it?"

"I've no idea, but as far as I can tell it's not your plumbing. I'll check outside but it all looks fine to me."

"I don't know how you can possibly think it's fine when you can't even breathe in here."

I followed him out into the garden and watched as he pulled up the manhole near the front gate. He got on his knees and peered down the hole, then replaced the cover.

He walked over to his van and without a word put his tools away and opened the driver's door.

"Hey," I yelled across the road. "Where the fuck are you going?" My patience had completely left me now, and I felt as though I was about to blow a gasket.

"I told you, miss, it isn't your plumbing," he said, jumping into the van and starting the ignition.

"You can't just go!" I ran into the street, but I was too late. I watched as his van sped away and turned the corner.

As I walked back over to the house, tears began to fall. I slid down onto the doorstep, and as the anger fizzled away, I was left feeling sorry for myself.

I had no choice, I'd have to go down to the cellar myself and find out where that god-awful smell was coming from.

The last time I'd been in a cellar I was ten years old. Poor Andrew had spent a lot of petrified nights down there but once was more than enough for me.

I hadn't misbehaved. All I was guilty of was refusing to cooperate while Dad and Annie were making one of their home videos. They were forcing Andrew to do things to me and it wasn't right. I'd been carted off to the cellar as punishment.

My most vivid memory of that night was listening to the rats scurrying about. I remember burying my head into the dingy foam mattress on the floor, my hands over my ears, trying to shut out the sound. It was damp and so, so cold. I cried the whole night and didn't get a wink of sleep.

I was relieved when my father unlocked the door and called me up into the warm kitchen where he had a mug of hot, sweet tea waiting for me. I was ready to agree to anything—and I had.

I zipped up my tracksuit top and pulled the front of it over my nose and mouth like I'd seen the plumber do. The icy, damp air hit me first. I felt around for the light switch and found a pull string.

There was one measly bulb that didn't light up much except for a circle in the centre of the room. It reminded me of a spotlight on a stage.

The cold chilled me to the bone. I shuddered and almost changed my mind, but instead I forced myself to step down each wooden rung until I reached the bottom.

The ground was a mixture of cobbles and dirt, plus a couple of concrete areas. It gave me the creeps. I wondered what was buried under there.

A huge boiler stood against the back wall next to the sink, and the door to a cupboard underneath was wide open—probably left that way by the plumber. It was empty except for an old plastic ice cream container plus a large spanner and screwdriver.

A hose pipe lay on the ground all tangled and knotted. And the large metal grid in the middle of the room was no doubt connected to the drains.

Bending over the grid, I sniffed to see if the stench was worse down there. I gagged and twirled round, making it to the sink before throwing up. I retched on nothing but the glass of water I'd had this morning. Wiping my mouth on my sleeve, I pulled my top over my mouth and nose again.

Yet the plumber had been right—the stink, although terrible, wasn't coming from the drain.

The furthest part of the room was very dark. I stood still for a few minutes, waiting for my eyes to adjust.

After a short while I could make out a built-in cupboard with a double door. I walked over and tried to open it, but it was shut tight and wouldn't budge.

I made my way back to the sink and got the tools I'd seen earlier. The flat head screwdriver fitted into the gap. I jimmied it, making the gap bigger and jammed the spanner in. Within a couple of seconds, the door gave.

I stepped backwards, my eyes searching into the cupboard. The smell, if possible, was now even worse.

Our eyes met.

I heard a blood-curdling scream just before he jumped out at me.

All the air left my lungs as Dennis knocked me backwards, landing on top of me. I was pinned to the cold, wet floor.

I began lashing out at him, the screams still assaulted my ears. The awful stench overloaded my senses. I couldn't think straight.

I managed to escape from underneath him somehow, but the screaming continued.

I needed to stop the screaming.

I lashed out. Blow after blow rained down on his head. His face was no longer familiar to me, but still that awful noise continued. My arms were covered in blood and fuck only knows what else.

The tools made wet, squelching sounds as they disappeared time after time into the grotesque mess.

I was exhausted, unable move another inch. The screams, although much quieter, still continued which puzzled me. There was no face now. How could he make that sound?

I realised, the screams were my own.

Chapter 20

Michael

"This won't work, Michael. They need to go back home to their mother," Toni said, kneeling on the floor at the side of the sofa, scrubbing at blackcurrant stains on the cream fabric and beige carpet.

He'd left her in this exact same position half an hour ago before he'd taken the kids to the day-care.

"This place isn't geared up for children. It's not their fault, I know but ..." she whined.

"You begged me to move in only two days ago, Toni. Now you're telling me to leave?"

"No, I want you to stay, but there's no room for your kids." She stopped what she was doing and lifted her head to look at him. "Honestly, Michael, I'm not being horrible but this is not what I meant when I suggested you move in."

"How can I send them back, Toni? Amanda's unstable." He sat down on the sofa and pulled her into his arms. "Come on, babe, it's not forever, I promise. They can go home as soon the police find Amanda's dad and I know the kids will be safe."

"What if they *never* find him? What then, hey? I'm not Mummy material, Michael. I'm sorry but if I'd wanted to share my home with a load of rugrats, I'd have had my own."

"A few more days, that's all. I'll sort it." He stroked the edges of her breasts with the flat of his hands. Her breath caught in her throat and her body relaxed against him.

Holding her chin he lifted her face to his, gazing into her fiery green eyes, he kissed her deeply. He teased his tongue in and out of her mouth with gentle flicks that he knew drove her crazy.

Toni pushed back from him, shrugging out of the white lace blouse, and then unclasped her wine-coloured bra. She took the lead as always, pulling him to her, and in a flash he was lying on the floor with her straddling him.

Her generous breasts swung to and fro. A mass of red curls hung down over her shoulders like fine tassels—threatening to conceal the delicious coral-coloured peaks, but not quite. He couldn't tear his eyes away—they were exquisite.

She undid his belt and pulled his penis out from the top of his briefs before moving to kneel on the floor beside him. Then she placed her mouth around his cock, sucking and slurping for all she was worth.

He turned her around so she was kneeling above him, once again giving him a perfect view of her tits, jiggling from side to side. With one hand, he groped at them, roughly pulling at her nipples with his thumb and forefinger. With his other hand, he lifted up her skirt, exposing her large, milky white buttocks. He was delighted to find she wasn't wearing any panties.

He stroked and kneaded the ample flesh, then raised his hand. He brought it back down with a sharp, stinging slap.

Toni squealed.

He felt her teeth graze along the length of his penis as she jumped from the contact. A large red handprint appeared before his eyes in the centre of her curvaceous rump.

He began stroking the raised welt tenderly before—WHAM! This time, his palm connected with her lower buttocks as well as the delicate, reddish pink folds of skin in-between.

Toni's cries were louder now, but she moved to make the contact easier for him. THWAAAP! His palm stung and his fingers throbbed and burned. Encouraged by her cries, his fingers parted the folds of skin and pushed deeply into her, twisting and thrusting.

He needed to regain control—wanted her to know he was in charge, so he flipped her onto her back and raised her legs, putting her ankles onto his shoulders. He positioned himself for maximum penetration before burying himself into her.

Spent, they lay on the rug in front of the gas fire. Toni wore his grey T-shirt and was curled on her side. He admired her shapely, porcelain-white legs that were much more voluptuous than Amanda's. Her behind, probably her best feature, had a lovely rosy tinge. He felt the stirrings of his erection again, and knew she would be game—she was amazing.
But he had to collect the children.
After a quick shower, he ran back through to the living room. "I'm going now, babe. I won't be long."
She still lay in the same position in front of the fire and she ignored him.
"Oh, for God's sake, Toni, what's wrong now?"
"I hate it when you go."
"I'll be back in a few minutes." He knelt down beside her. "Go and get some clothes on," he said, patting her firm, round and very pink bottom.
"Yes, I know, you'll be back that's the problem. You'll have those brats with you."
He sat back onto his haunches and grabbed her face, viciously turning her to look at him. "Don't you *ever* call them brats again," he said through gritted teeth.

Her eyes widened in panic as his fingers squeezed her cheeks so hard he could feel her teeth through the skin. "They are my children and we come as a package, so you either like it or fucking lump it. Now go and get dressed."

He let go of her face with a shove and she let out a cry as the back of her head hit the floor. He felt a twinge of guilt as silent tears ran down her cheeks. But he needed to start this on his terms. If he'd wanted an awkward, tetchy bitch he'd have stayed with Amanda.

Toni avoided him for the rest of the day which pissed Michael off all the more. He tried to include her with the children, but she wasn't interested.

She's too touchy for her own fucking good that one, he thought. It wasn't as if he'd hit her. Most men he knew would have given her a backhander for disrespecting his kids like that.

After dinner, he showered the children and got them ready for bed. They didn't cry at bedtime like they had the night before which was a relief. After reading them a story, he kissed them both goodnight.

He had no idea what he was going to do next. He'd made a mistake bringing them here, he knew that now. But he hadn't thought it would be a problem since he'd intended moving in with Toni anyway. She'd always been great with the kids whenever they'd met up in the park. How wrong he had been.

His thoughts turned to Amanda. He'd half expected her to turn up at day-care today and he'd even warned the staff not to allow her to take the children. Although he felt a bit of a shit for spreading rumours that she was involved in the death of the wino, what else could he do?

He walked into the kitchen and poured himself a glass of wine from the already opened bottle. Toni hadn't poured him one which proved she was still sulking.

Picking up the phone, he dialled his home number. It rang several times until the answer-machine picked up.

"Hi, Amanda, it's me ... Are you there? Pick up ..."

Toni walked into the kitchen, looking at him with narrowed eyes and shaking her head.

He turned his back to her and continued. "I thought I'd let you know the children are okay—missing you, of course, but okay. I was thinking, maybe I should move back home for a while until all this blows over. What do you think? Call me on my mobile." He hung up.

Toni opened her mouth as though to protest, but he put his finger onto her lips. "It's for the best, Toni. This isn't working out."

"So you're just going to run home to ... to her?" She was shaking her head in bewilderment.

"For now. I need what's best for the kids and you obviously need your own space."

"Not from you, Michael. I love you," she said, in the childlike voice he had always found adorable before.

"Anyway, she may not want me to, but the kids can tell there's something wrong with us. Plus they have to share a bed, which isn't ideal. I should have thought this through before taking them from their home."

"You can't take them there now. They're fast asleep."

"They can stay where they are for tonight. I'll get them out of your hair first thing in the morning."

It niggled at him that Amanda wasn't home. He thought that maybe she was at the Kingsley house. He tried her mobile number which went straight to voicemail. It suddenly occurred to him that she might have been charged. He felt awful for ratting on her to the police—he didn't really think Amanda had anything to do with the murder. He called the station.

They transferred Michael's call several times before he finally reached Detective Stanley.

"Hi, Detective, it's Michael, Amanda's h—"

"Yes, Michael, what can I do for you?" he interrupted.

Michael thought he detected a hostile tone to the Detective's voice, but he proceeded anyway. "I just wondered how my wife is. I haven't heard from her all day, and she's not answering her phone. Is she still in custody?"

"No, she was released last night. Her car broke down and I said I'd help her with it today, but I haven't heard from her. I'll call in on my way home tonight."

"I'm going over there now. What if he's got to her?" Michael said, running a jerky hand through his hair.

"Who?"

"Her fucking crazy father, that's who!" Michael snapped.

"You seemed convinced *she* was the crazy one yesterday Michael, and that her father was also dead."

"Maybe I was a bit hasty saying those things. I'll go to the house now and call you from there. Do you have a direct number I can get you on?"

Chapter 21

Adam

After hanging up the phone, Adam sat for a few minutes, pondering. He felt bad for not checking on Amanda earlier, but things had been hectic since last night.

Brian Crosby hadn't been much help. He was obviously keeping something from them, yet he'd refused to cooperate. They kept hold of him as long as they could, but in the end they had no choice but to release him.

He thought back to the person in Amanda's garden last night and jumped to his feet, grabbed his jacket from the back of the chair and ran out of the door.

Michael's car was half on, half off the pavement, at an angle. Lights blared throughout the house and the front door stood wide open.

Adam stepped inside. "Amanda?" he called. "Michael?"

Walking into the lounge, he heard a series of bangs. Then Michael came tearing down the stairs taking four steps at a time. "Oh, it's you. I thought ..."

"No, sorry—only me. I thought I'd better come over. She's not here then?" Adam asked.

"No. Everything seems in order though. Her mobile's in the kitchen, which explains why she's not answering. Maybe she's still at work."

"I checked her car before I left the station, and it's still in the same place."

Michael sat down on the arm of the sofa, rubbing his hands through his hair.

"There's something else you should know," Adam said. "When I dropped Amanda off last night, I saw a person hanging about in the garden."

"What if it was him? Her dad?" Michael said. "What if he's got her?"

"I had a patrol car driving up and down the street every hour or so. There were no sightings of anybody near the house all night."

Michael went through to the kitchen. Moments later Adam heard Amanda's voice, "I'm sorry about that, who's speaking please?"

It took a second for Adam to realise it was the answer-machine. He hurried into the kitchen and listened to the end of the message.

"So we know she went to meet the plumber—what time was that? Can you tell from the machine?" Adam asked.

"No, it's an old one. I've been meaning to upgrade it."

"Do you know the address of the house where she's working?"

"No."

"Where's your phonebook?"

"Hang on." Michael opened a drawer in the kitchen and handed him the yellow pages.

Adam found the number he was looking for and dialled. Thank God for the plumber, he thought.

The number went through to a voice mail message giving a mobile number for emergencies. He hung up and dialled again.

"Jeff speaking."

"Hi, Jeff. My name is Detective Inspector Stanley. I wonder if you could help me."

"If I can. What about?"

"You went to a Kingsley address today where you met Amanda Flynn?"

"Yes. What about it? If she's complained ..."

"No, nothing like that. We have reason to believe Mrs Flynn is in danger and we need the address."

"Hold on, I'll get my diary. I thought she was acting strange."

"In what way, sir?"

"There was an awful smell coming from the basement—she said it was the drains, but I couldn't find any problems. She screamed at me when I left. She's unhinged that one. A bloody nut job she is, mate. I couldn't wait to get out of there."

When they reached the Kingsley house, it was in darkness. Adam parked by the kerb.

"Can't see Amanda being in there—she's scared of the dark," Michael said.

"We may as well check. We're here now," Adam said as he got out of the car and walked towards the front of the house. It was a very dark night, but he had his police-issue torch.

He heard the passenger door open and close behind him. Michael had decided to follow.

Adam walked up the concrete steps and as he tapped at the front door, it swung open. A tingling started at the base of his skull and travelled down his spine.

Holding his breath against the stench wafting out, and raising his torch, he reached his hand inside and located the light switch. Bright lights flooded the hallway. He heard Michael gasp in surprise, but Adam wasn't sure if it was because of the light or the God-awful smell.

He pushed the door further open. A handbag sat on the phone stand by the door. Adam pointed. "Do you recognise that bag?"

Michael nodded. "Yeah, it's Amanda's."

They looked at each other. Adam banged on the door. "Amanda? Are you in there?"

Nothing.

He checked the two front rooms before walking towards the back of the house. Michael kept a good distance between them, his fingers pinching his nose.

"Police! Is there anybody there?" Adam called again. He was under no illusions what was causing the stink—something or somebody had died. He put his arm across his face. "Amanda?"

Nothing.

He reached the kitchen and switched on more lights. The back door and windows were also wide open.

"She must be here. Amanda would never leave the house open like this, and what the hell is that pong?" Michael stood at the back door, gasping for fresh air.

"I think you should wait here, Michael. I'll go upstairs."

"She'll be okay, won't she?"

"Just stay here," Adam said. His request was futile—not many men would stay put when a loved one was missing and possibly in danger. But Michael did as he was told.

As he left the kitchen, he noticed a door in the hallway and pushed it open with his foot, exposing a set of stairs leading downwards. "Amanda?" he called as he started down.

A feeble light hung from the centre of the cellar below him. It was barely better than no light at all. "Amanda, it's DS Stanley—are you down there?"

There was a sound coming from under the stairs and he proceeded to walk down slowly, almost gagging at the smell. It was much stronger down here.

Patting his pocket for his phone he remembered he'd left it in the car once again. He knew he should go and get it and call the station for backup, however, even though he didn't want to find the cause of the stench, he needed to find Amanda.

As he reached the bottom step, he realised he'd been holding his torch up above his head like a weapon. If somebody had jumped out on him, he would have clubbed them first and asked questions later. He lowered his arm.

The sight that awaited him made him run to the sink and bring up the jacket potato he'd eaten for dinner.

Looking back at the mess on the floor, he could see a body but there was no face, just twisted and mashed-up tissue. The blood beneath the body was congealed and contained in a small area, unlike any murder scene he'd been to before.

He heard another sound from underneath the stairs.

Lifting the torch above his head again, he made his way towards the sound. The breath caught in his throat and his stomach lurched when he pulled aside a cardboard box and came face to face with a crazy-eyed monster.

After his initial shock, Adam realised it was just a woman. She was covered in blood, her hair plastered to her head. Her face looked as though it was in the middle of a silent scream and her eyes stared straight through him.

"Amanda?" he said. "Amanda, it's me—Adam Stanley." He knelt down at the side of her and pulled her into his arms. She was shaking uncontrollably, holding a screwdriver and a spanner to her chest.

"Let me have these, Amanda. It's okay, I'll look after you." He removed the tools from her grip, placing them on the ground beside him.

She noticed him for the first time.

"I killed him," she whispered. "I killed him, I killed him, I killed him."

Adam grasped her hands as she began to struggle. She tried to tear herself from his grip.

"Hey, hey, calm down, Amanda, it's okay." He heard footsteps at the top of the stairs. "Michael, stay where you are," he called.

"Have you found her? Is she okay?"

"Yes, I've found her. Go out to my car and get my phone."

"Oh my God, is she all right? Amanda—Amanda, it's me, Michael." His voice sounded close to hysterical.

"*Michael!*" Adam yelled "*Phone. Now!*"

"I-I have mine here. Wh-who should I ring?"

"Call 999 and tell them there's been a murder and we need an ambulance too. Then go and sit in the car."

"But what about Amanda?" Although calmer, he still sounded close to tears.

"She's unhurt. I need you to make that call, Michael." The no-nonsense tone to his voice seemed to have the desired effect. A couple of seconds later he heard Michael talking on the phone; then he heard him leave.

Adam continued to coax Amanda out from under the stairs—she seemed to have gone back into a trance-like state.

Then he held her in his arms until the ambulance arrived.

Chapter 22

Michael

Sitting in DS Stanley's car, Michael watched dozens of vehicles come and go. It freaked him out.

Toni had gone mad when he'd told her he was going to check on Amanda. He'd left her looking after the children regardless of the abuse she hurled at him as he left.

He'd had a terrible feeling something was wrong. The cop said more or less the same thing—making him even more nervous. However, he'd never expected this.

Amanda was brought out on a stretcher and put into the ambulance. He hadn't recognised her at first. She looked like a mad woman with staring eyes and she was covered in something dark and greasy.

He should have gone to her, but he'd never been any good in a crisis. He just wanted to leave. To pick up the kids from Toni's and take them home.

He considered going back inside to find DS Stanley, but a police officer guarded the front gate and the property was surrounded with 'CRIME SCENE — DO NOT CROSS' tape. So he had no option but to stay put.

Eventually, Stanley came out. He stripped his jacket off and threw it into the boot of the car before sliding in the driver's seat. "Oh, Michael, I forgot about you. Didn't you want to go in the ambulance with Amanda?"

"No, I don't do hospitals. Can you take me home, please?"

"Not right now, sorry. I need to check on Amanda even if you don't want to. I promised her I wouldn't be far behind."

"What's wrong with her? Is she hurt?" Michael wrinkled his nose and moved as far away from the detective as possible. The stench from inside the house seemed to be all over him and it made Michael's eyes smart.

"Not physically, but she is in a real state."

"What the hell is that stink?"

Adam sniffed at his hands as though he couldn't smell it anymore. "Amanda found a dead body. He'd been there for a while, I'd say."

"Who is it?"

Adam shrugged as he started the engine.

"So, she found him? She didn't kill him?"

"She told me she'd killed him and she was covered in his DNA, but the body wasn't fresh. I'd bet he's been there at least a week, maybe two."

"How can that be? Do you think she could have done it before tonight?"

"I'm not sure. Anyway, I shouldn't be discussing this with you. Do you mind if I drop you off after the hospital? Otherwise, I'll get another officer to take you home."

"No, after is fine."

Chapter 23

Adam

At the hospital, Adam's first stop was the bathroom to scrub himself before finding Amanda's room. A uniformed police officer sat outside the door and there was another one inside. Handcuffs fastened Amanda to the bed.

"Is this necessary, Officer?" Adam pointed to the handcuffs.

"Just following orders, sir."

"Here's another order. Get them off! Now! Then get out while I talk to her."

"But, sir, I—"

"Never mind the buts—just do it!"

The officer didn't argue further; he removed the handcuffs and scurried into the corridor.

Adam pulled a chair up to the bed.

Amanda had been cleaned up and changed into a hospital gown. Her eyes were open, but she wasn't there. He remembered reading she'd been like this for weeks after giving birth when she was a teenager.

Adam didn't have weeks to waste. He needed to know what had gone on today.

He believed the body to be Dennis Kidd, Amanda's father. At least, the wallet on the body belonged to him. She hadn't killed him—not today, anyway. But she had attacked him, he presumed, with the screwdriver and spanner.

He also had the testimony of the plumber. The smell had been there before he'd arrived this morning. In fact, Amanda had called him regarding the smell several days ago. They would check out the owner of the property and anybody else with access, but he needed Amanda's help.

"Hey, Amanda," he said in a soft voice.

Nothing. She didn't even blink.

"I told you I would come, didn't I? It's Adam."

Still nothing.

"You're going to be okay, Amanda. Dennis is dead, remember? He can't hurt you anymore."

Not a murmur.

He wondered if she might respond to her useless, coward of a husband who was still sitting outside in the car. Adam had been shocked when the man had refused to come in. If she'd been Adam's wife, nothing would have kept him from her side.

Thinking about his own wife, Sarah, made his heart flutter. Not a very macho thing to admit, but true. His beautiful wife no more deserved to be where she was now than Amanda deserved to be in this hospital bed—of that he was certain. But on both counts he could do nothing to change it.

"Okay, Amanda. I have to go but if you need me just ask one of the officers to call and I'll be here right away."

Nothing.

***

"There's no way she's responsible, Kate. I just know. You didn't see her. She thought she'd just killed him."

Annie's autopsy report was back. She hadn't been bludgeoned to death as first thought. She had choked on something lodged in her throat—a dismembered penis with the testicles still attached.

This fitted with the body in the basement whose genitals had been removed and were missing. Now, unless there was another dick-less body out there waiting to be found, it was fair to assume they belonged to Dennis.

The body had Dennis' ID in his back pocket and had been dead for at least two weeks, which fell in with the period when Dennis vanished. They still had to wait for DNA confirmation, but they were pretty certain it was him.

Kate rubbed her face with both hands, focusing on the area around her eyes. "Adam, Adam," she said, sounding exasperated. "Amanda was found with the body, was covered in his blood. She has the motive. And she was the only one with access to the house!"

"Not entirely true, Kate, the owner also had access."

"But who is the owner? Until Amanda comes round, we won't know who gave her the instructions."

He pulled his pad out from his jacket pocket. "The house belongs to Mrs Judith Pitt and the address we have for her is in Chelmsford. I'm going to see her in the morning." He snapped the pad closed. "Wanna come?"

***

Sitting outside the Chinese takeaway, in his car, Adam's phone rang and he pulled it out of his pocket. Then groaned as he read the screen, he considered ignoring it but on the fourth ring he hit the green button.

"Hey—how's it going?" he said.

"Hey, buddy, I thought you were screening me call's," his best friend and ex-partner, Matt, drawled. It was comforting to hear the strong Mancunian accent he'd been brought up with.

Adam laughed. "As if. I've just been busy that's all. How's it?"

"Oh, you know—same old. How you liking the smoke?"

"It's okay. Pretty quiet, considering."

"You still play acting at being a cop?" Matt asked.

"I've been investigating a murder for your information," Adam said, good-naturedly.

"Really? Well, that's good, isn't it?"

Adam shrugged. "I guess," he said.

"You know it is. You're wasted running around the place looking for runaway's and you know it. You're a great detective. What happened with Sarah can never change that."

Adam's stomach flipped at the very mention of her name, he didn't want to get into this, he wasn't ready. "Anyway how's Carole and the girls?" he said, changing the subject.

"Great they said to say hi—they miss you."

"I miss them too, I'll come home for a visit soon, I promise."

"We'll hold you to that, buddy."

"Anyway, I've gotta go, Matt, thanks for calling."

Adam woke up in his lumpy armchair in front of the TV. The meal he'd bought for his supper had fallen to the floor uneaten, though the fried rice had dried and hadn't made too much of a mess on the already stained carpet.

He'd moved into the furnished rental when he arrived from Manchester. The small bedroom, kitchenette and lounge with a TV were all he needed for the time being.

Sarah would have been horrified to see where he was living. He knew she wouldn't have set foot in the place, preferring instead, to sleep in the car.

Once again, the thought of her made his chest contract—he struggled to breathe properly. He didn't think it would ever get easier.

He picked up the framed photograph that had slid down the arm of the chair. Tracing a finger across the lips of his beautiful wife, he held his breath, allowing the familiar pain to course through his body, and settle in the middle of his chest.

Half an hour later he and Kate were on their way out of Pinevale. The car's built-in GPS said they would arrive in Chelmsford just after nine.

Kate was very quiet during the journey. He glanced at her a couple of times, checking if she'd gone to sleep.

"What's on your mind?" he asked.

"Oh, I'm just taking this time to go over everything in my head." She reached for her handbag and took out a box of pills.

"Got a headache?"

"Always. Sometimes it's worse than others, but it's always there." She popped the pills into her mouth and swallowed without any problems.

Adam smiled to himself. She would have called him a wimp if she saw him taking pills. He struggled even with a jug of water to help him.

"What's so funny?"

"Oh, nothing really. I was admiring the way you took the pills without a drink. I can't do that.

"If you'd had as much practice as me you would."

"Is this from your accident, you mean?" he asked in a tentative voice. He'd never spoken to her about her personal life before and was unsure what her reaction would be.

"Yes, unfortunately. Although I only take a few now. I try to do without them if I can."

"I heard they said you wouldn't walk again. You must be one tough cookie."

"They're not always right, Adam," she said tetchily. "Have you called to let them know we're on our way?"

"No, I thought it best if we just turn up—catch them unawares, so to speak."

"I don't know what you're expecting to find. Everything's pointing to Amanda, and unless we find evidence to the contrary she'll be arrested as soon as she comes to."

He didn't want to get into another dispute with her so he said nothing the rest of the way.

The address was on the outskirts of Chelmsford, halfway between Bloomfield and Little Waltham. They pulled up outside the property. It was surrounded by a high fence, and electric gates crossed the driveway.

Adam let out a long, slow whistle.

"So much for catching them unawares," Kate said. "They'll have at least a ten-minute warning."

Adam ignored the amused tone in her voice and edged the car closer to the keypad.

A young girl's voice came over the speaker. "Hello? Who's there?"

"Good morning, Miss. I have a delivery for you."

"Wait a minute, please."

They waited for a couple of minutes, and just as he was about to press the intercom again the gates began to swing open. A smile played on his lips and his eyebrows rose cheekily as he looked at Kate.

"Smart arse!" she said with a grudging smile.

The driveway wasn't as long as they'd expected. As they rounded the first row of ancient oak trees, the house jumped out at them—a quaint cottage with several outbuildings forming a horseshoe shape.

They got out of the car and walked towards the cottage. A young girl with fine blond hair and a pale face opened the door as they reached the top of the steps. It was difficult to pinpoint her age.

The waif-like frame could belong to an eight or nine-year-old, but the knowing look in her eye said she was much older. She eyed them suspiciously.

"Good morning. Is Judith Pitt at home?"

"She told me to take it off you."

"Sorry? Oh, the delivery. I told a white lie, sorry. We need to talk to Mrs Pitt." Adam took out his badge and saw Kate doing the same. "My name is DS Stanley and this is DI King."

"But she's in bed." Her eyes darted from Adam to Kate and back again, two deep creases appearing on her forehead.

Adam glanced at his watch. "We've come a long way, miss, and it's urgent we see her—please let her know we're here."

The girl pursed her lips to the side of her face, sucking air between them noisily. She went inside, closing the door behind her.

"Is it school holidays?" Kate asked.

"Wouldn't have a clue." Adam shrugged.

The door opened again and the girl invited them in.

"My mum's sick in bed. You'll have to see her in her room."

"What's wrong with her?" Kate looked concerned. "Is it contagious?"

"Can't remember the name—but if you mean can you catch it, no."

They followed her down the hallway into a small, dark room on the ground floor. The girl walked towards the window and opened the curtains a touch. Enough light shone in for them to make out the bed against the wall and a shape under the blankets.

The girl went to the bed and folded back the sheets, before helping the woman upright and leaning her against the pillows. Adam felt terrible for the intrusion, this person was obviously very sick.

When the girl had her mother positioned, she motioned them to the side of the bed.

Judith Pitt was hunched in a semi-sitting position. One side of her face was twisted and the eye on that side was closed, but the good eye shocked and fascinated Adam. It was alive and sparkling.

"Hello, Officers, how can I help you?" The speech was slow and slurred but clear enough to be understood.

"Hello, Mrs Pitt. We're sorry to bother you, but we need to ask a few questions. My name is DS Stanley and this is DI King." He was aware he'd slowed his speech to match hers.

"What about?"

"Your property in Kingsley. We believe you appointed Amanda Flynn to see to some restoration work."

"Yes, that's right," she said.

"Can you tell me who else has access to the property?"

"Nobody. It's been shut up for years."

"I'm sorry to inform you, Mrs Pitt, but a murder was committed there sometime in the last two weeks. We need to be sure that nobody else has access."

"No one, only me." Her good eye had widened with shock and she shook her head. "Murdered? Who was murdered?"

"We still don't know yet. Could anybody else have got the details without you knowing?"

"I-I don't think so." She was becoming distressed. "Mary?" she whispered.

The girl moved over to the other side of the bed and wiped her mother's mouth with a tissue.

"Okay, we'll leave you in peace. Would it be okay to get a few more details from your daughter before we go?"

Mrs Pitt nodded.

Mary Pitt showed them into the lounge. It reminded Adam of his childhood visits to his grandma's house. Heavy beige drapes hung at the small windows. A pale-green, hand-knotted Chinese rug covered most of the floor. Occasional tables and tasselled lamps were placed around the room for optimum effect. A huge bookcase covered one wall and was crammed full with books.

"Please sit down. Do you want a cup of tea or coffee?" she asked.

Adam was again reminded how much older than her years she seemed. An old soul, his mum would say.

"Coffee would be nice," Adam said. Kate declined.

Once alone, Kate got up from the floral armchair and began snooping around the room.

"Hey, Adam, come and see this photo of Mrs Pitt. It was taken before she got sick, I'd say. I can't believe how much older she looks now. The daughter hasn't aged much so this picture must be quite recent. She can't be more than forty-something."

Adam stood up to take a look. No way could the old lady they'd just met be in her forties. Thinking about it though, Mary was around ten years old—twelve at the most, so Judy couldn't be as old as she seemed. He picked up the picture frame and walked towards the light of the window.

"It's her all right," he said. In the picture, Judith and Mary were sitting on a stone wall. A man sat between them with his arms around their shoulders. They were all smiling. "I wonder if this is the husband. Mary's the image of him." He put the picture back on the sideboard and sat down again. "You were very quiet in there, Kate."

"Certain situations unnerve me," she said, rubbing her temples, her eyes screwed up.

"Still bad?"

"Huh?"

"Your headache. Is it still bad?"

"Oh, yeah, sorry." Her mobile phone rang, but the ringing stopped as she pulled it out of her jacket pocket. "No signal, I'll go outside and call the station back."

She almost collided with Mary, who was bringing the coffee in on a tray. "Sorry, love," Kate said before limping outside.

"My colleague has to make a call. She couldn't get a signal in here," Adam explained.

"Yeah—I don't have a mobile but my dad does, and he keeps his in the kitchen to get a signal."

"Is that your dad?" he said pointing to the photograph before picking up his coffee.

"Yeah, we were on holiday in the Lake District last year." She looked at the picture for a couple of seconds. "This is the only one we've got with all three of us together, before Mum ... you know, before she got sick."

"It must be hard on you. Who looks after her?"

"Me and Dad. Dad home-schools me so it works out well. She's not always in bed—she sometimes sits in here with us. You just caught her on a bad day."

"Where is your dad now?"

"He had to go into town to collect a prescription and buy food. He's self-employed. He designs computer programs."

Adam raised his eyebrows and nodded. At least that explained how they paid for the properties,

Adam thought as he finished his coffee and put the cup back on the tray.

Mary was obviously a shrewd little girl, because she guessed what he was thinking. "Oh no, Dad didn't pay for all of this," she said, shaking her head. "It used to belong to Nana and Gramps before they died. Mum said dad doesn't need to work, but he says computers are his passion, so he does it anyway."

Kate knocked on the window and beckoned to him."

"Looks like I'd best be off, Mary. Thanks for the coffee. Would you ask your dad to call me, please?" He handed her his business card and rushed out to see what was so urgent.

Kate stood by the car. "Come on, we've got to go."

"Why, what's happened?"

"Brian Crosby's dead. Murdered."

"Shit!" he said as got in the behind the wheel. "Though at least we can rule out Amanda this time."

Kate glanced at him, her tight lips forming a straight line across her face.

When they reached the house, forensics were already installed and examining the crime scene. Adam and Kate put on the standard white hooded overalls and bootees before entering.

Brian's body lay face down in the hallway, his head twisted sideways. His eyes were gone, replaced with two gory holes.

Adam felt his gorge rise.

"Not much blood, considering," Kate said to the medical examiner.

"The wounds have been cauterised," he replied. "Something extremely hot did this damage and sealed the wounds on exit."

Adam couldn't stand looking at the body any longer. He walked in to the small house. No signs of a break-in and the only evidence of a struggle was in the lounge. The sofa had tipped backwards, and there was a broken cup in the kitchen rubbish bin. Everything else was very tidy.

"Has anybody spoken to the neighbours?" he asked a plain-clothed detective.

"Yeah—nobody saw a thing. His daughters found him this morning."

"Where are they now?"

"Next door at number twenty-nine."

"Time of death?" he asked, making his way back past the body towards the front door.

"Yesterday sometime. One of the daughters spoke to him at eight o'clock yesterday morning, so sometime after that."

He passed Kate, who was still bent down looking at the body. Adam couldn't stomach it—he still had the smell of Dennis up his nose.

Pamela Foxton was hysterical, and her wailing unbearable. She was curled up next to her sister on the sofa. Alison Jones, on the other hand, was calm—clearly upset, but calm.

"Take a seat, Detective," Alison said, indicating the chair opposite them.

"Thank you. I know this is difficult, but I need to ask you a few questions."

"We've already told the other officers everything." Her arms were wrapped around her body, giving herself a hug. Her hands rubbed her back and shoulders, as though soothing herself.

"I'm sorry, but I need to do this." They went through their statements once again. Pamela made it no easy task, wailing the whole time, but it was clear they knew nothing. Alison had arrived from Manchester late last night and stayed at Pamela's house. They found their dad when they arrived this morning. Alison had looked through the letterbox when he didn't answer the door, and made the gruesome discovery.

Adam needed to dig a little deeper to see what else they knew. "Did your dad tell you he'd been questioned by the police a couple of days ago?"

Pamela's head lifted up and her incessant noise stopped mid-wail while she listened.

"No!" Alison said, "What the hell for? He never said anything." She looked at Pamela for confirmation.

Pamela shook her head.

"He had been confused when he couldn't find your mother, and instead of searching the house he called us. He was convinced a man called Dennis Kidd had abducted her."

Pamela sat up now, gawking at Adam. "You mean that dirty pedo? Why would he abduct Mum? She's not a kid."

"We never got to the bottom of it. No crime had been committed so we had to let him go. But I'm sure this is connected." He let this information sink in for a few moments before continuing. "Did you know him? Dennis? He would have lived close by when you were growing up."

"Not me. I never met him. I met his missus though, she was a teacher at our school," Pamela said. "A wrong 'un if ever I met one."

"What makes you say that?" Adam leaned forward in his chair, not wanting to spoil things now he had the unstable Pamela chatting.

"She was just weird. Dad knew her though. I used to see them together at lunchtime in the stafroom. When they saw me, they would stop talking like they were trying to hide something. Maybe they were having an affair."

"Pamela!" Alison's voice was sharp and disapproving.

"What? I'm only telling the truth."

"How about you, Alison? Did you know them?" Adam asked.

Alison shook her head. "No." She chewed her bottom lip, her brow furrowed.

"Is there something else? You look as though you've just thought of something," he coaxed.

Alison turned to her sister and grabbed for her hand, her eyes searching Pamela's before turning back to face Adam. "Dad was just dad to us. We loved him. He was kind and gentle. But sometimes we would see him looking at our friends a bit funny. I often wondered if he had something to do with those two."

"You mean Dennis and his wife?" Adam said.

"Yeah. Mum used to tease him about it when they first got banged up. We would laugh with her, but deep down I had my suspicions."

"That's not fair, Ali—he's dead. What if it's not true? If this gets out, dad's good name is ruined," Pamela said.

"If they need the truth to catch whoever did this we have to be honest. And anyway, let's face it, we know it's true. You wouldn't even bring little Amy to see him. Mum never understood why but I knew."

Sitting quietly and taking all of this in, Adam was very thoughtful. So, Brian had something to hide after all. But since both Dennis and Annie were already dead, none of this information would be of any use to Adam and Kate unless they could find another lead.

Chapter 24

Michael

"Where's Mummy?" Emma demanded.
"She's had to go away for a few days, pumpkin. She'll be back soon, I promise."
This had been going on all morning and it was his own fault. He should have left them at Toni's last night instead of bringing them home.
As soon as Emma opened her eyes in her own bed this morning she called for her mummy, and when Amanda didn't appear she ran around the house searching.
"Where to?"
"She's working. You know you stay with me when Mummy's working."

"Pwease phone her," she begged. She looked so pathetic with her enormous eyes full of unshed tears.

He wondered how Amanda was this morning and thought of ringing the hospital to check, but he didn't want Emma any more upset. So he decided to call after he'd put the children down for their afternoon nap.

He checked his mobile for messages. Nothing. He thought he might have heard from Toni by now, but she was obviously still sulking.

He was a little sad about the way it had turned out. The sex with her had been incredible. Still, if she couldn't accept his children then it would never work out. He may have his faults, but his children were top of his list, full stop.

She'd been asleep when he arrived back last night. He got the kids' stuff together, then woke her to say goodbye before carrying the sleeping children to the car.

He'd left her sitting in the hallway sobbing, snot running down her face.

Not the prettiest sight.

***

There were no spaces in the hospital car-park. Michael had to park on the main road and walk back. He cursed himself for not bringing the pushchair. Jacob insisted on being carried and felt like a ton weight.

Emma walked nicely, excited to be going to visit her mummy. He'd called the hospital when the children were having their nap and spoke to her doctor. The doctor confirmed Amanda hadn't shown any signs of coming round, but thought it a good idea for the children to visit—that maybe they could get through to her.

Michael had refused at first and hung up the phone.

Then he'd got a call from Detective Stanley, telling Michael there'd been another murder and that he thought Amanda was in the clear.

He'd also suggested Michael take the children to see her, and once again Michael had refused. But when Emma woke up screaming again for her mummy he changed his mind. He hated seeing his daughter so upset.

He told them Amanda had been poorly and was asleep in the hospital. That she might not wake up for them, but they would be able to see her and give her a kiss. This cheered Emma up. Jacob, as usual, was oblivious to everything.

It startled Michael to see a policeman outside Amanda's room.

"Good afternoon." The officer nodded to them as they approached.

"Hi, we've come to visit my wife, Amanda. Is that okay?

"Certainly."

Emma was standing behind Michael, holding onto his legs and peeping out at the police officer. Normally a chatterbox, she didn't make a sound.

The officer stood up and opened the door for Michael. "Hey, Stu—fancy a cuppa?" he said to another policeman inside the room. Stu was sitting on a plastic chair reading a Woman's Day magazine, one foot resting on the metal at the end of the bed.

Stu jumped up immediately, as though he'd been caught sleeping on the job. "Oh, sorry—gets a bit boring sitting here for hours on end," he said, tucking the magazine under his arm.

"No, not at all." With Jacob still in his arms, Michael shuffled into the room, the tight hold Emma still had on his legs making it hard for him to walk.

Once the policemen left and the door closed behind them Emma ventured out. "Why was there powicemen?"

"They are looking after your mummy," Michael said as he glanced over to where Amanda lay.

"But that's what nurses do."

"And sometimes policemen, baby. Come on, let's see if she'll wake up." He placed Jacob on the bed next to Amanda, then moved the chair the policeman had vacated to the top of the bed and lifted Emma up to stand on it.

Jacob was getting excited and couldn't understand why Amanda wouldn't wake up.

"Shush, Jakey, Mummy's poorwy—isn't she, Daddy?" Emma whispered.

"She sure is, baby. We need to be very quiet," he whispered back. "Maybe if you tell Mummy what you've been doing she'll wake up."

Emma, leaning on the bed, now turned and sat down beside Amanda. "We've been to Toni's house, but she shouted at me and I cwied. I missed you, Mummy. I'm sorry I didn't let you bwush my hair."

"What made you say that, Em?" Michael asked.

"Cos I made Mummy sad and then she wented away."

"Oh, Emma, Mummy didn't go away for any reason other than she was sick. Once she's better she'll brush your hair again."

Michael hadn't noticed that Amanda had opened her eyes. The first he knew was when she lifted her hand and placed it on Jacob's arm.

"Mummy, you're waked!" Emma squealed.

Amanda still seemed a million miles away. After blinking several times she tried to sit up, which proved impossible with both children now almost on top of her.

"Hey, come on, guys. Let her get her breath for a minute." Michael lifted them both off the bed. Jacob was not impressed with this and proceeded to throw a tantrum on the floor. Michael ignored him and went to tell someone that Amanda had woken up.

Two nurses followed him back into the room and set about making Amanda more comfortable.

"I'll take the children out for a few minutes," he said to the short nurse he'd spoken to at the desk.

"We won't be long and then you can have your Mummy to yourselves again," she said to the children in a musical Irish accent.

Emma wasn't pleased to be made to leave. Michael coaxed, "Come on, I'll get you a can of Coke and a chocolate bar." This did the trick. They'd passed a couple of vending machines on the way in and he had a pocket full of change.

Michael got one can of drink and two chocolate bars. Then he found an empty lounge room, with faux leather chairs and an old-fashioned square TV in the corner.

Afterwards, they walked back to Amanda's room. She was sitting upright and looked more awake than she had. Michael lifted the children back onto the bed.

"What happened?" Her voice was feeble and croaky.

"Don't you remember?" He didn't want to do this in front of the children.

"No, nothing."

"I'm sure it will all come back to you. The police are waiting to talk to you so we'd best be off."

"The police? No, wait—please, Michael, don't take my babies yet." She held them both to her chest, close to tears.

"I'll bring them again tomorrow, I promise. Get some rest. I've brought your mobile and a change of clothes. They're in a bag in your locker."

"Thanks."

"Say bye-bye to mummy, Jacob." He unwrapped Amanda's arms from his son and picked him up off the bed, bending him towards her for a kiss.

"Baabaa." Jacob was smiling and waving.

Emma hugged Amanda and buried her head into her neck.

"Come on, Em, don't be silly. Mummy needs her rest."

"No! I want my mummy."

"Remember what we said? We mustn't upset her. Do you want to come again tomorrow?"

"Yes," she whispered.

"Do as your daddy says, baby," Amanda said, nuzzling her hair. "I'll be home soon."

Emma sat up and kissed Amanda. "Pwomise?"

"I promise."

"Michael, thanks for bringing them," Amanda said, her voice already fading with the effort of talking.

Chapter 25

Adam

It had been another chaotic day. Adam knew he wouldn't be in his bed this side of midnight—he still needed to get through a huge stack of paperwork before he could even think of knocking off.

The hospital had called to tell him Amanda was awake although she couldn't remember anything. He intended on visiting her before it got too late.

Nothing more had come to light with Brian Crosby's murder. His body was now with the medical examiner and they would do an autopsy in the morning, which Adam intended to be present for.

The only other thing was they'd found a pair of child's panties in Brian's cardigan pocket.

Adam wondered if someone had planted them or if Brian had acquired them himself. Either way it showed that his daughters might be correct. Perhaps Brian did have a sick interest in children too.

He'd left a team going through Brian's house and he was praying something would turn up. They were at a complete stop at the moment.

He poured himself a tar-like coffee from the percolator in the office and he drank it in two gulps. Realising he was starving, he hadn't had anything to eat or drink since breakfast. He glanced at his watch and was startled by the time, seven o'clock.

Grabbing his keys from the desk, he decided to head to the hospital before they locked the doors—he'd pick up a couple of burgers from the drive-through on the way.

Adam spoke to the officers when he arrived at Amanda's room. He made the decision to relieve one of them, keeping one officer to watch over Amanda as there was still a killer on the loose.

Amanda was sound asleep and looked just the same as yesterday, apart from her eyes now being closed. He sat on the plastic seat, looking through the glass door as the officers wandered off down the corridor.

"Amanda?" he said, barely more than a whisper.

Her eyes flickered but stayed closed.

"Amanda, it's me, Adam Stanley."

Once again, nothing. He stood up and walked to the window. He could see for miles, they were so high up.

"Adam."

He thought he'd imagined it at first. He went back to her side.

"Hey, there you are," he said. "I thought you were pretending to be asleep so you didn't have to talk to me."

"No." She smiled. "Can't keep my eyes open ... so tired."

She seemed so vulnerable that Adam was shocked and reached out his hand and almost grasped hers, pulling it back before she noticed.

"The doctor said that's to be expected—you've had a terrible shock," he said. In fact, the doctor had told him on no account should he interview her at all.

"I can't remember. What happened? I know the kids are all right—they were just here." She screwed up her eyes as though trying her hardest to remember something just out of reach.

"Take it easy for a couple of days and then we'll talk."

"No. I can't stand it. Please tell me," she whispered.

"Seriously, leave it for now. I'm under strict instructions not to distress you in any way," he said.

"This is distressing me. I need to know, Adam. Please?"

"Okay, tell me, what's the last thing you remember?"

"Making the bed at home." She closed her eyes and rubbed her temples.

"You don't remember getting a call from the plumber?"

She opened her eyes slowly. She was squinting. "Kind of. I mean, I do—but it's like a dream."

"Well, let's try to remember a bit more of the dream," he coaxed.

"I had to go over there in a taxi." She was looking straight ahead at the stark white wall as if seeing her *dream* playing out.

"Mmm-hmm. Anything else?"

"Yeah, he wouldn't do the job. I was angry with him."

"What did you do?"

"I can't remember," she cried.

The stocky Irish nurse came in, giving Adam a disapproving look. "That'll be all for tonight. Come on—out! This girl needs her rest," she said, bustling around Amanda and shooing him towards the door.

"Get a good night's sleep, Amanda. I'll come back tomorrow—maybe you'll remember a bit more by then."

"But-"

"Come on now, lovey," the nurse interrupted, her hands on her ample hips. "That's enough for one day." She shot Adam a ferocious glare.

"Goodnight, Amanda," he said as he backed out of the room.

"Goodnight." Her eyes were already closed before he reached the door. It was a funny thing, the brain. He understood that it would shut down to protect itself, but he couldn't work out why she would be so tired considering she'd been asleep for almost twenty-four hours.

He didn't look forward to telling her about her father. What if it caused another trauma? Hopefully, she would remember on her own

Chapter 26

Michael

Emma had been a nightmare since leaving the hospital. Michael tried to appease her by taking them to the jungle gym and then for a pizza, which worked for a short while, but it didn't take long before she was sulking again.

It was dark by the time they got home, way past the children's bedtime. Jacob had fallen asleep in the car. Michael carried him inside, still fast asleep.

As he opened the front door, something didn't feel right, but he couldn't put his finger on what. He took the children into the lounge and plonked Jacob in the middle of the sofa, telling Emma to keep an eye on him. He left them there, closing the door behind him.

A strong breeze was coming down the hallway. He looked around him for something to use as a weapon, but the only thing in the hallway was Amanda's flowery pink umbrella. He hefted it above his head and made his way to the kitchen.

The back door swung wide open. Michael knew the door had been locked because Amanda had the only key since he'd lost his key ring months ago. That very morning he'd had to walk around the house to hang the washing on the line.

Nothing else seemed out of place. He checked the lock and it all seemed okay—no damage as far as he could tell. He heard a sound coming from upstairs, a bump-bump-bump.

Picking up the phone, he dialled Adam's mobile number getting his voicemail. "It's Michael. There's somebody in the house," he said in a hoarse whisper. "Come quick."

He crept up the stairs, taking his time and keeping his back to the wall. Bump-bump-bump-bump-bump. What the hell could it be? The brolly was still raised—not that it would do much damage. He kicked himself for not getting a knife from the kitchen.

Jacob cried and Emma knocked on the lounge door, calling for him. Thank heavens the door handle was too high for her to reach.

At the top of the stairs, he was surprised how draughty it was. The sound came from the bathroom. He braced himself at the bathroom door, his heart pounding so hard he could hear it. He held on to the doorknob for several seconds before bursting in, the umbrella held above his head.

The window swung wide open and the lace curtain blew into the middle of the room. He attacked it with the umbrella before realising what it was. The sound was the window lever hanging loose and banging against the frame.

"What the hell!" Putting down the umbrella, he reached over the bath to lock the window.

Both bedroom windows at the back of the house were also open, though everything to the front was shut tight. He searched the house thoroughly before going back to see to the kids.

Jacob by this time was hysterical. His face was blood red and snot mixed with tears poured down his face.

Emma, crying too, didn't say a word. She just picked up her backpack and stomped up the stairs to her room.

"Your sister is as feisty as mummy," he said to Jacob. "I feel sorry for her husband when she grows up."

Chapter 27

Adam

Back at the car, Adam noticed his phone flashing on the dashboard—a voicemail message. With no signal, he couldn't retrieve it until he was almost at the station. After listening to Michael's hushed message, he did a speedy U-turn without even checking the road was clear—luckily it was.

Through the lounge window, he could see Michael sitting on the sofa as he approached the front door, maybe a false alarm. He tapped on the window.

"Oh, thank God you're here!" Michael stood back to let Adam through the door.

"I just got your message. What happened?"

"Someone's been in the house today. We stayed out until late and when I got home the back door and all the upstairs windows at the back of the house were wide open."

"Sorry to ask, but is there any chance you could have left them open?" Adam said as he walked into the lounge.

"No, I didn't leave them open. Besides, I don't have a key for the back door—Amanda's got the only one." He glared at Adam.

"Okay, I'm sorry. Did you check if the lock had been damaged?"

"Yeah, and it's fine."

"I told you about the guy I saw hanging around here the other night, didn't I?" Adam said.

"Yeah, you told me. What did he look like?"

"I didn't get a good look at him. He was in the shadows—the headlights from my car lit him up briefly. He wore dark clothes with a hood." Adam sat down on the chair opposite Michael and put his face in his hands, rubbing his eyes. "There has got to be something we're missing here. Was anything tampered with in the house?"

"Not that I can tell, just the windows and the door. It's as though somebody's playing games with me."

"If this is connected with the murders—and I guess we have to treat it as such—then we're dealing with a very dangerous and unhinged person. Make sure you double-lock all your doors, and ring me if you're at all concerned about anything. If you can't get me for any reason, call nine-nine-nine."

"Do you think they'll come back?" Michael said, alarmed.

"Hard to say. Whoever it is wants you to know he's been here. I've made sure Amanda is safe and I'll get a car parked out on the street tonight in case he does decide to come back."

"Thank you," Michael said.

Adam's phone was flashing again by the time he reached the car. Voicemail told him he had another new message.

"Ah, erm, hello. This is a message for Detective Inspector Stanley. I believe you came to my house this morning to speak to my wife and daughter. My name's DJ—DJ Pitt."

Adam returned the call.

Mr Pitt sounded younger than Adam had expected, probably because of the old-fashioned, cottagey feel of his house, but his daughter had explained that already.

"Good evening, Mr Pitt. Thank you for calling."

"That's okay, although I'm not sure how I can help you."

"Did your wife tell you what's happened at your Kingsley house?"

"Yes, and quite frankly, I'm appalled."

"Indeed, sir. Do you know who else might have had the key code to get in?"

"No, I don't even know it myself to be honest with you. Though I do know, Judith keeps it in her diary."

"Does anybody have access to her diary that you know of?"

"No—nobody comes here. We care for Judy ourselves, although for how much longer I'm not sure. As you saw this morning, she's quite sick."

"What is wrong with her? If you don't mind me asking."

"She has Acute Multiple Sclerosis. She's lost the sight in one of her eyes and has paralysis in various parts of her body. She still has good days, but they are becoming few and far between. We'll be getting some extra care brought in very soon."

"That's awful. I am sorry," Adam felt the griping twinge of grief in the centre of his body. He knew what it was like to lose a wife. Thankfully, his wife hadn't suffered.

"Thank you. If that's all, Detective, I should go."

"Of course, Mr Pitt. I'll keep you informed. The house is still a crime scene at the moment, so if you need to go there for any reason ..."

"We won't. Goodnight, detective." He hung up the phone.

Before driving away, Adam arranged for a squad car to spend the night outside the Flynn house.

Chapter 28

Amanda

I woke up in a strange room and it took several minutes for me to remember I was in the hospital.

Sweat dripped from me. The sheets were stuck to my sopping wet body.

Lying there half-asleep, listening to the sounds of the hospital going on around me. I closed my eyes and began to nod off again as a graphic image came to me. I screamed.

Within minutes, my room was filled with strangers and then Adam Stanley seemed to appear from nowhere.

"Hey, Amanda, it's okay—settle down."

His voice was so hypnotic and calmed me down instantly. All the while he held my hand, his chocolate eyes gazing into mine.

The doctor and nurse fussed around for a while, but before long there was just the two of us.

"I—I killed him. I killed my dad."

"No," Adam said.

"I *did*!" I sobbed. "I know what happened. He was waiting for me, hiding in the basement cupboard, and I killed him."

"No, Amanda. I know you think you did, but he was already dead, had been for a while. Maybe he fell out of the cupboard when you opened it, but I promise you—he was already dead."

"You mean I didn't do it?"

"No, I don't think so."

"But how did he get in there? Who else could have done it?"

"That's what we need to find out. Had you given anybody the key code? Any subcontractors? Anyone at all?"

"No." I buried my head back into the pillow. This was a nightmare.

"Do you know Brian Crosby?"

"Why?" I sat back up.

"He's been murdered too, and there are some links to your father."

"Yeah, I knew him, he worked at the school with Annie."

"Was he part of your dad's sick gang?"

"Yeah, but he never touched us, not really. He just looked."

"Who else knew? Apart from the adults involved in the abuse, who else knew about him?"

"Nobody, just me and Andrew."

"Amanda, look at me."

I turned to face him, looking into his eyes.

"I've just heard Brian was murdered on Monday morning—sometime between eight and nine. Where were you?"

"I don't know. I can't remember. I don't even know what day it is."

"It's Wednesday. Monday was the day you found Dennis."

"I left the house around nine. I got a taxi."

"So you have no alibi before nine am?"

"No. Do I need one?"

"Kate will want to talk to you."

Adam Stanley continued questioning me until I felt dizzy.

"Just a couple more things, Amanda, and we can call it a day. I know you're tired," he said, rubbing his eyes, not for the first time. "Where are your house keys?"

"My house keys?"

"Yeah."

"Should be in my bag." I swung my legs off the bed and bent to peer in the drawer of the cabinet. I pulled out a bunch of keys. "Here they are."

"Is the back door key on there?"

"Yes—this one," I said, holding up the large bronze key. "Why?"

"Michael said there's only the one key."

"Yeah, he lost his ages ago. What's this about?"

"Somebody was in your house yesterday and they opened that door. Have you any idea who could be responsible?"

"No, I've no idea. Did they steal anything?"

"That's the strange part—nothing seems to have been touched apart from a couple of windows being opened."

I couldn't understand it. Who would want to go into our house and open some windows? "I need to get out of here."

"It's not up to me, but I don't think it's a good idea."

"I don't care—I need to get out of here *now!*" I got off the bed again. My legs felt weak; they almost buckled underneath me. "Please help me—I need to be with my children."

Adam caught me and swivelled me around on the spot, sitting me down on the chair. "Wait there," he said.

He left the room, returning a moment later with a doctor.

"What seems to be the problem here?" The doctor didn't have a very soft speaking voice considering he was in a hospital. He was grating to say the least.

"I want to go home." I stood up and jutted out my chin in defiance.

"I recommend you don't go anywhere for another day or two at least."

I shook my head. "I've got to go."

"Mrs Flynn, I think you should reconsider, but it's your choice."

"I'm sorry, Doctor. I'm going home."

The doctor left the room, shaking his head.

I gradually became a little steadier on my feet and walked around the bed. In the bottom of the cabinet was a brown paper bag filled with the clothes Michael had brought in yesterday. I took it into the adjoining bathroom.

After a quick wash, I changed out of the hospital gown and brushed my hair. I felt much better. I was surprised to see Adam still in the same place, looking out of the window with his back to the room. "Any chance of a lift home?" I asked.

He turned around, his face unreadable.

"I can't lie here with a killer on the loose. They might hurt my children," I explained.

"If they'd intended to do that I'm sure we'd know by now. You, on the other hand, might not be so fortunate. At least while you're here you can be watched over."

"I don't care. I've got to go."

"Come on, then, let's get your stuff together."

"I've got no stuff." The police had taken my tracksuit as evidence and ever since then I'd been wearing a hospital gown. I had my handbag, that's all, and Adam tucked it under one arm, and me under the other, then slowly walked me out to the car.

"There's one more thing we need to discuss, Amanda." Adam's eyes didn't leave the road and I could tell he felt uncomfortable.

"What is it?" I asked.

"They've released your father's body. They need to know who to contact regarding the funeral."

"What?" I was horrified. "I can't arrange that!"

"I understand. Are there any other relatives? Any brothers or sisters?"

I shook my head. "No, there's only me, but I won't have anything to do with it. He can rot in hell as far as I'm concerned."

"Fair enough. I had to ask," Adam said,

"So what will happen?"

He shrugged. "Not sure. The funeral director will sort it, I guess. Anyway, don't concern yourself. I'll pass on your wishes."

As Adam parked the car, the front door opened with a bang, and Michael ran towards us.

Adam wound his window down.

"I was about to call you—he left a message." Michael's words left him in a rush.

"Who did?"

"Whoever broke in yesterday. They left a message on my computer. I just found it."

I got out of the car, and Michael seemed surprised. He obviously hadn't noticed me sitting there.

"Amanda, what are you—?"

I didn't hang around to make small talk. I raced to the house and found the children in the kitchen playing. They were both on top of me, squealing with joy, by the time Michael and Adam caught up.

Michael looked pale with purple circles under his eyes.

"Are you all right?" I asked him.

"Not really. Maybe we shouldn't talk about it in here?" He nodded at the children.

"No, course not. Hey, babies, Mummy needs to go talk with Daddy and the nice policeman. You play here for a few minutes."

I found Adam and Michael upstairs in the office, both staring at the computer screen. I couldn't make out what they were looking at until I got further into the room.

In bold, large red font, flashing in the centre of the screen, was:

You're next — CHEAT!

"What the ...?" Tiny lights began shooting in my peripheral vision. My legs threatened to give way. I groped for something—anything, to steady myself.

Chapter 29

Adam

Adam knew it had been a mistake for Amanda to discharge herself so soon. Luckily he'd moved fast enough to prevent her falling to the floor. He was supporting her by her upper arms but didn't know what to do with her in the cramped room.

"Why the hell did they allow her to come home so early?" Michael snatched the chair out from under the desk and held it steady while Adam eased Amanda down onto it.

Adam shrugged one shoulder. "They didn't. She insisted when I told her about your intruder."

"She needs to go back to the hospital."

"No. I'm okay," Amanda whispered.

"But Aman-"

"I'm okay!" she snapped. "Is it worth getting the fingerprint guys out again to dust the computer?" She was looking at Adam.

"I guess it's worth a shot. Although there have been no fingerprints left at any of the crime scenes, so it's doubtful we'll find anything."

"They're threatening my family—it's not safe to stay here." Amanda sat upright, colour returning to her pallid face.

"Are you feeling a bit better now?" Adam asked.

"I'm fine."

"Maybe Amanda's right and you should all stay somewhere else for the time being." Adam glanced at Michael, whose eyes had drifted back to the computer screen. "Michael?"

"Sorry, what did you say?" Michael said, his hands opening and closing into fists.

"I was just saying, maybe you should stay somewhere else?"

"I'm going nowhere. You can if you want to, 'Manda, but I'm staying put."

"I've got nowhere to go. Besides, they'll just follow us," Amanda sighed.

"It's not you they're threatening, though, is it? It's obviously aimed at me." Michael ranted.

"Okay, I'll get going and arrange for fingerprints and also a squad car," Adam said as he stepped onto the landing. "Michael, would you see me out, please?"

"What about my car?" Amanda called after him.

"It's at the mechanics. Michael's been sorting it out. If you need a lift to pick it up, let me know."

Michael followed Adam down the stairs, and once outside Adam turned to face him. "About the message on the screen—you know what it means?"

"I've been having an affair. That's the only thing I can think of."

"Who knew about it?"

"Nobody, really—except Amanda."

"Would Amanda have told anybody? A close friend, maybe?"

"I doubt it. Amanda's very private. She doesn't have any close friends."

After taking down the 'other' woman's details, Adam put a large hand on Michael's shoulder. "Thanks for your honesty, Michael, I'll be in touch but call me if anything ..."

"I will. Thank you, Detective."

Adam sat hunched over his desk. This case was giving him yet another headache. He rummaged about in his drawer for some aspirin but found an empty blister pack instead. He knew Kate would have a supply, but he didn't want to bother her. She'd already given him a blasting when he'd returned to the station earlier.

Kate was certain Amanda was involved in some way, even though it was practically impossible for her to have killed Brian Crosby and get back to the house before the plumber called. Then there was the break-in at her house. Amanda had still been in the hospital then. There must be something we're missing, he thought.

He checked through a list on his desk, picked up the phone and dialled.

"Hendricks," a raspy voice said after the first ring.

"Hey, Hendricks, DS Stanley here. A quick question about Tuesday—is there any chance Amanda Flynn could have left the hospital without you knowing?"

"Absolutely not!"

"Thought not. That's all, thanks, mate." He hung up, jotting the information down in anticipation of Kate King's questions.

He walked into the central office and studied the whiteboard. There were three columns: DENNIS KIDD, ANNIE DUNCAN, BRIAN CROSBY.

Annie was the main connection between the three of them, then the school and their interest in children.

On another line were Dennis's two children and Brian's two: AMANDA FLYNN, ANDREW KIDD, PAMELA FOXTON, ALISON JONES.

Amanda and Andrew were victims of abuse at the hands of Dennis and Annie, who had both served time for the repeated sexual assault, rape and prostitution of the children. However, Brian had managed to keep *his* secret from his family—or had he?

Amanda was connected to both Dennis and Annie on the board. She had expressed concerns that she was being followed. Could, whoever it was, have followed her to the Kingsley property? Could they have got close enough to see her punch the number into the keypad? Unlikely. He tapped the whiteboard marker on his teeth.

Amanda's daughter, Emma, followed her 'mother' at the zoo. The assistant also said she saw Emma leave with a woman dressed like Amanda.

The seahorse. Emma had asked for one and somebody provided it—not the actions of a madman intending her harm.

The break-in at Amanda and Michael's home. The intention had obviously been for Michael to know someone had been in the house. The threat on the computer screen was also aimed at Michael. Cheat! He had been having an affair, but nobody knew about it.

A woman fitting Amanda's description was seen with Annie the night she died. At the time, Amanda had been at the Kingsley house with no alibi.

The person skulking in Amanda's garden. Nobody else had been home that night—Michael had taken the children. Could he have come back?

Michael Flynn—maybe he found out about the abuse of his wife and took revenge? Adam didn't think he had it in him. He could have easily planted the seahorse though, he could also have left the message on the computer screen, and there was only his word about the break in. It made no sense though. Michael had admitted to having an affair. He could have been trying to frame his wife—but if that was the case, why would he stage the break-in at a time when Amanda had a watertight alibi?

Andrew Kidd was also on the board. Missing from home since the age of fifteen—twelve years ago. There had been an investigation at the time, but to no avail. In light of the abuse the children had suffered, it was concluded that he'd run away since there was no evidence that anything untoward had happened to him.

Adam walked back to his office and sat down at the desk. He rubbed at his temples, sighing deeply. It was so frustrating. In each case there was nothing to go on. No forensics and no witnesses—nobody saw or heard a thing.

Chapter 30

Amanda

Sitting at the kitchen bench, I picked up the phone for the umpteenth time in the last ten minutes. I replaced it once again. "Why is this so hard?" I said aloud. Even if she didn't want to know, I knew she'd be nice about it.

I took a deep breath, then quickly raised the handset and punched in the number before allowing myself to breathe again. My heart was doing the can-can in my chest.

After several rings, I realised she wasn't home. The answer machine cut in. Should I leave a message? Aargh—what to say?

"Hello, Sandra, it's Amanda. I ... erm ... Oh, I bloody hate these machines. Call me, same number. I hope you're okay." I hung up, aware of a weakness in my limbs I'd never felt before. Gosh, I hadn't even said please—just demanded, after all this time. Demanded she call me.

Michael and the children were sweeping up leaves outside. Or should I say, Michael was sweeping up leaves—the children were having a wonderful time redistributing them around the garden. I watched them through the window for a few minutes before tapping on the glass and waving to them.

I was due at Dr Freda's office in half an hour.

Monika was engrossed in something as I entered the reception area. Her head was tilted to one side, the tip of her tongue poking out of the corner of her mouth, and her specs were perched on the very tip of her nose. As I got to the counter, I could see she was trying to thread a needle.

"Such concentration." I smiled.

"Hello, Amanda, I didn't see you there." She took her glasses off.

"Do you need some help?" I nodded at the needle.

"Blasted thing. I've been trying for the best part of an hour." She handed me the needle and some black cotton.

I threaded it easily and passed it back.

"Oh, gosh, what I wouldn't do for a pair of young eyes. Thank you love, take a chocolate." She pushed a small silver tray laden with Quality Street chocolates towards me. "Although I must warn you—it was probably the chocolates that caused my button to ping off." She laughed.

Not deterred in the least, I chose the flat gold circle—caramel was my favourite. "Ooh, thanks."

"She won't be too long, Amanda. Can I get you a cuppa?"

"No, thanks, I've not long had one. Did you book your next holiday yet?"

"I daren't—I'd better wait for a while or else she'll have a fit." She cocked her eyes towards the office door.

I laughed. "You're too good at your job, Monika—she can't do without you."

"She's gonna have to. I retire next year. There'll be no stopping me then, I ..."

The door opened, and Dr Freda walked out of the office with a middle-aged woman. Monika turned her attention to the client.

"Same time next week, Mrs Bailey?"

Dr Freda beckoned to me and I followed her into her office.

Instead of going to her desk, she sat on one of the leather sofas, her hand palm-up suggesting I sit on the one opposite.

"How are you today, Amanda?" she asked, raising her eyebrows and peering over the top of her glasses.

"It's been quite a week, Doc. I really don't know where to begin."

"How about we start with you telling me how you felt after our last session?"

"Confused, and I suppose a bit worried. I've been thinking about all the unexplained things that have been happening. And wondering if they could have been my own doing."

"Have you had a chance to discuss it with anybody?"

"No. But it all makes sense now. Things going missing and turning up in stupid places, or not turning up at all—drawers miraculously cleaned out. The way I show barely no emotion to things that should have me devastated. I've known all along there was something wrong with me, but I couldn't put my finger on what the hell it was."

"So, I see you've been doing some research. I'm glad you're finally taking this seriously, Amanda. Do you want to tell me what's happened this week?"

"Okay." I took a deep breath and then began. "Remember I told you my dad had gone missing?"

She nodded.

"He was murdered, and so were his ex-wife, and another member of their group."

"Ah, I saw the news. I'm sorry. I didn't recognise the names."

"Somebody apparently saw me with Annie—walking her home right before she died. And my dad's body turned up at the Kingsley house I'm working on."

Dr Freda pulled her eyebrows together so tightly they looked like a mono-brow.

"He'd already been dead for almost two weeks when I found him in a cupboard in the cellar. I thought he jumped out at me and I attacked him with some tools I had in my hands. I blacked out and was in the hospital for a couple of days."

"So I guess you have an alibi for your stepmother's murder? Otherwise, you'd be in custody."

"No. But nobody could identify me in the line-up. I'm the only suspect, but they have nothing on me."

"Where were you at the time of the murder?"

"At the Kingsley property, working late."

"And your father?" She pinched her bottom lip between her finger and thumb and began wiggling it side to side, mono-brow still in place.

"I'm not certain. He'd been dead a while, like I said."

"And the third murder victim? Did you know him?"

"Years ago I did."

"Did he interfere with you?"

"He never touched me really, just looked." As I said the words, I remembered being in Emma's room and thinking about what Brian Crosby had done to me. And soon after that I'd fallen asleep on

Emma's bed—at around the same time Brian was murdered.

Dr Freda said something, but my mind was in chaos. Images flashed: Brian taking my panties off ... Annie standing in the doorway of the lounge, a smirk on her face as my dad forced Andrew on top of me ... the seahorse ... Brian taking my panties off and leering at me ... hoarse whispers ... the cellar ... Brian taking my panties off ... prying the cupboard doors open ... Dennis jumping out on me, a sick grin on his face ... screaming ... that scream ... stop the screaming.

Whoosh! Something brought me back in line in an instant. Dr Freda stood over me, her palm raised and her calm exterior replaced by a shaky imitation.

I was lying half on, half off the sofa. One of my navy court shoes sat upside down on top of the coffee table. My stomach was in knots; I thought I might throw up.

"What happened?" My voice was barely recognisable.

"I'm not too sure—you started screaming. Are you all right now?" Freda said, her voice trembling.

Remembering the images, I froze. Oh, fuck! I think I killed them.

I had to get out of there. I couldn't tell her what I was thinking. Yet if I had murdered three people surely I'd remember something?

I reached for my shoe, my hands shook so much that it took an age to put it back on. "I've got to go," I said, standing up.

"Not so fast, Amanda. Calm down first. I don't know what just happened, but you're not in any state to drive yet. Have a cup of tea and see how you feel then," she said. I don't remember ever seeing her so ruffled.

"I can't, but I'm fine. I promise."

She raised her glasses to the top of her head. Her face had lost every bit of colour, giving a glimpse of the human being under the perfect ice-queen exterior.

***

Back at home I let myself in the front door. I could hear voices coming from the kitchen. There was no sign of the children—I presumed they were having a nap. I slowly walked down the hall, trying to work out who it was.

When I opened the door, my breath caught in my throat and my eyes filled with tears. I couldn't speak.

Sandra stood up and walked towards me. Holding her arms out, she pulled me to her and I began to sob. Michael ducked out the back door into the garden.

After a few minutes, I had the tears under control. I stepped back slightly so I could look at her. She'd aged a little and her mousy brown hair had more grey sprinkled through it, but she looked fantastic.

"How come you're here?"

"I got your message and tried to call back but there was no answer, so I came around. Michael was in the garden—he didn't hear the phone."

"Thank you. I didn't think you'd want anything to do with me."

"You know how I feel about you, Amanda—how Pete and I both felt. We always wanted nothing but the best for you. I hoped you'd call." She held my hand and we sat down at the table.

"I don't deserve you. I've been cruel."

"You've been confused, that's all. I don't mind, as long as we can stay friends now. I've missed you."

"I've missed you too."

Michael had filled her in on most things. I told her my version, including what had just happened at Dr Freda's. She didn't comment; just let me pour everything out.

Afterwards, she said, "You can't possibly think you killed him."

I shrugged. "I dunno. But don't you think it's strange that I'd been thinking about him right before he was murdered?"

"Coincidence—it's got to be, love."

I hoped she was right.

She'd known I'd had family problems as a child—hence being in foster care—but I wasn't sure if she knew the extent of the abuse. I'd never discussed it with her. In fact, I'd never discussed it with a soul, apart from Doctor Freda. She stayed very quiet for a while. I wondered if she was hurt that I hadn't confided in her before now. We had been close once.

When the children woke up we all played in the garden. Sandra stayed for the rest of the day. After dinner, she helped put the children to bed and it was as though she'd always been a member of our family. The kids loved her. I promised to call her the next day.

Later that evening, I realised there was something else I needed to do. I rang DS Stanley.

"Stanley," Adam's voice sounded sleepy.

"Hi, it's Amanda. Sorry to trouble you, but I need a favour."

"Fire away."

"I've changed my mind about the funeral. I think somebody needs to be there. Could you find out who to contact, please?"

"I'll make a few calls, but do you mind me asking—why the change of heart?"

"My foster mother thinks it'll be good for me, closure and all that. And to be honest, I can't bear the thought of nobody being there. He was a monster, but he needs a funeral and I may regret it if I don't go."

"Well, if you're sure. I'll get back to you in the morning."

***

We pulled up outside a lovely little chapel. I was surprised how quickly we had arrived.

"You sure you're up to this, Amanda?" Sandra asked.

"I ... erm ... I think so. Can I have a few minutes, please?"

"Of course, love. I'll go inside and let the vicar know we're here."

She got out of the car and I watched her walk across the road, tottering on her new, inch-high heels. Her tailored linen suit showed off her shapely figure—one a woman half her age would be proud of. I was touched by the effort she'd made.

I, on the other hand, wore the same beige slacks and cream blouse I had worn yesterday. I might have decided to make an appearance, but I was damned if I would mourn his death.

Michael had looked at me as though I'd lost my mind when I told him I planned to attend. I wasn't able to explain to him the reason. I just couldn't bear to think of a person, regardless of who they were or what they'd done in their lives, having a funeral and not one person showing up.

Sandra came back towards the car and I got out to meet her.

"You ready?" she asked.

"I guess." I steadied myself on her arm and held on for dear life.

"I told the vicar not to worry about a speech, lovey, to just get on with it."

"Thank you, Sandra."

"He said he'll say a short prayer."

"Okay."

The chapel was draughty and dark. The stale, musty smell was overpowering and it took all my efforts to suppress the urge to retch.

The vicar was kneeling at the pulpit and stood up as we entered. Sandra and I sat at the back.

A simple pine coffin had been slotted in an alcove. I tried not to look at it. My stomach did a flip and I momentarily felt immense sadness for what should have been.

The vicar said a prayer, but I didn't hear it. The curtains around the coffin began to close and a sob escaped my lips. I realised with a surprise that my face was wet from silent tears.

Sandra, still linking my arm through hers, now hugged it against her. "Come on, love," she said.

We walked back outside.

"Are you okay?"

"Yep!" I sounded brighter than I felt and was relieved it was over.

"I need to powder my nose. Are you okay on your own for a minute or two?"

"Yes. Honestly, I'm fine. Take your time."

I walked towards the gardens. An old stone wall surrounded beautiful flowerbeds. The trees displayed stunning autumn tones.

There was a rustling at my side and I looked around, fully expecting to see a squirrel or a bird, but instead I stood staring into the eyes of a ghost.

Chapter 31

Amanda

He was gone as fast as he'd arrived and for a second I thought I'd imagined the whole thing. I headed towards the spot he had stood just moments ago, but there was no sign of him. I couldn't go any further without clambering over the stone wall, so I ran back in the direction I'd come.

Sandra appeared as I raced past the chapel steps. "Amanda?"

I could hear her footsteps following behind me. There was nobody in the road. Sandra's car was the only one parked up. I stopped dead in my tracks and Sandra collided in to me, huffing and puffing.

"Hey, what was that all about?"

"Nothing," I whispered.

"Are you sure? You're shaking like a leaf."

"Yeah. I thought I saw somebody, but I was mistaken. There is nobody here."

"Let's get you home."

I couldn't rid myself of the ghostly image from the cemetery. Sandra dropped me off at home and I hoped she put my quiet mood down to the fact we'd just attended my father's funeral.

Michael had taken the children to see his aunt, and wasn't due back for a couple of hours.

As I poured myself a glass of wine, a heaviness hung over me. I went through to the hallway and opened the door to the cupboard under the stairs. I found what I was looking for at the back, under copious amounts of junk. I managed to pull the large, dusty box out and dragged it into the lounge.

After taking a deep breath, I exhaled in a rapid sigh and raised the cardboard lid.

A knitted patchwork blanket covered the top of the box. I lifted it to my face. Maybe it was just my imagination, but I was sure I could smell my childhood bedroom. This blanket used to be very special to me. I didn't know where it came from, but I'd had it as far back as I could remember, well before the nasty stuff began.

I put the blanket on the floor and looked back inside the box. A pile of newspaper clippings was the next thing I laid my eyes on. They weren't as yellow as I imagined they'd be after almost twelve years, nowhere near as yellow as the ones behind the door of the Kingsley house.

I carefully unfolded the first one. The headlines jumped off the page at me.

Child Sex Slave Scandal

I didn't want to read any more, but my eyes disagreed with me and rapidly ran down the page.

A fourteen-year-old girl is to take the stand to describe the cruelty and sexual abuse she suffered at the hands of her natural father and his wife.

Dennis and Anne Kidd deny all charges and are being held in custody on remand.

The next three articles told me more or less the same, except that they included more details as they had come out. There were interviews with our old neighbours, school teachers and even one with a girl from my English class that I hardly knew. I refolded the clippings and placed them on top of the blanket.

Next I pulled out a peg doll that my school friend, Jackie, had given me when we were eight years old, on one of the rare occasions I'd been allowed to visit her house. Her mum had bought it from a gypsy who knocked at the door and Jackie hadn't wanted it.

Two books came next: The Lion, The Witch and The Wardrobe, and The Magic Faraway Tree. These had belonged to our mother from when she was a girl.

Finally, I found what I'd been looking for. It was originally a shoebox that Andrew had covered with white wallpaper, and then drawn and doodled all over it. The sight of his childish artwork made my heart contract. Tears pricked my eyes.

I removed the lid. So sad to think this was all I had to show my brother had ever existed.

A Transformers pillowcase covered the top of the box. Then an Action Man in well-loved, threadbare clothing, and a poster of Michael Jackson's Thriller. A portable radio-CD player was tucked in the bottom of the box. I held it to my chest, remembering the day Andrew brought it home from school. He'd found it in the bin and worked on it night after night for two weeks until it was as good as new. The last item was a small white envelope.

I pulled three photographs from it and laid them face up, side by side, on the carpet beside me. The first photograph was the only one I had of Andrew and me together, around eleven years old. We were both smiling and we looked so happy. The abuse had started years earlier but didn't get bad until around this time.

In the second one, a very young Andrew aged three or four, sat on our mother's knee. She was gazing at him adoringly, but how could she adore him when she left us both less than a year later?

The last one was Andrew aged fifteen and the one I needed to see. The face gazing back at me from the photo was the one I'd seen at the cemetery. I was certain of it now. He was older now; however, the shape of his face, slim features, steely pale-blue eyes and the full, shapely mouth, was definitely the same.

What I wasn't certain about was if it had been my imagination. My mind had played all sorts of tricks on me lately. What if I was going mad?

Once everything was back into the boxes, I placed them under the stairs—everything except the last photograph of Andrew, which I slid into my jeans pocket.

Was it possible that he could still be alive? After all these years, I'd convinced myself he must be dead. Otherwise, why hadn't he contacted me before now? I needed to know for certain, but I had no idea where to start looking.

Chapter 32

Adam

Adam stretched back in his seat, his eyes closed, his left hand placed on his face, lips puffing out slightly as he exhaled. Things couldn't get much worse. He'd known Kate had been struggling with her leg, but he'd just found out that she'd been rushed to the hospital, and was undergoing emergency surgery.

Now the whole sorry case had landed with a crash on his shoulders. Three dead paedophiles, a serial killer on the loose, and no leads whatsoever.

If he didn't know better, he would think it a conspiracy to force him back into homicide, instead of the quiet life that had been promised by his superiors in Manchester.

He looked at his watch and then jumped to his feet. He'd arranged to meet Mr Pitt at the Kingsley address. Forensics had finished there now and Adam wanted him to see if anything had been taken. Mr Pitt's wife was too ill to join him, and he was in a rush to get back to her and their daughter.

Then Adam intended to check on Amanda, and see how she was after the funeral.

JD Pitt wasn't at all what he'd imagined. Long hair pulled into a band at the nape of his neck, not one strand out of place, and even the light stubble on his face was groomed to perfection. He wore a chequered black-and-grey shirt with a white T-shirt underneath, faded denim jeans, and soft brown loafers on his feet. He invited Adam inside.

"Thanks for meeting me here, Mr Pitt."

"No problem. I had to come into town to collect something for my wife."

"How is she?"

"Not too good, I'm afraid. In fact, we've employed a full-time nurse to care for her now. She seems to be deteriorating rapidly."

"I'm very sorry to hear that. How about your daughter? Mary, isn't it? How's she doing?"

"Yes. Mary. She's coping."

"It must be hard for you?"

"I won't deny we've had an awful year, but I owe it to Judy to keep going. She's been a wonderful wife," he said, his eyes drooping, seeming to focus on nothing in particular.

Adam's stomach felt as though it was twisting in on itself. He knew only too well what this poor man had to come, and he found it difficult to maintain a professional persona. "I'm sorry to have to drag you away from her, Mr Pitt. Shall we get down to business and then you can get back home?"

Standing in the hallway, Mr Pitt confirmed neither he nor his wife knew who could have got the number to the door lock. "We've racked our brains, and apart from the security company who installed it, no-one's been here for a long time."

"When was it installed?"

"A few months ago, just before Judy decided she wanted to tidy the place up. She thought it would be easier than having to make the trip into town every time someone wanted access."

"Maybe you could give me the details of the company that fitted it and we can chase it up. Although it's unlikely to have anything to do with them," Adam said. "Did you get a chance to inspect the property? To see if everything else is in order?"

"To be honest, I've not been here for a long time. It used to be Judy's parents' house. Nobody's lived here for a number of years. In fact, after her mother died her dad refused to set foot in the place. He just shut the door and walked away. He's been dead for two years now. The old place holds a lot of memories for Judy. I only encouraged her to get it tidied up to keep her occupied while she lay in bed."

"There are a number of antiques around the place. I don't suppose your wife has a list of the valuables?"

"I'm not too sure. I can ask her. I'm sorry I can't be more help."

"That's okay, Mr Pitt. Thank you for your time." They shook hands and headed for their cars. Adam was opening his door when he noticed Mr Pitt trying to get his attention. He walked back around to the pavement.

"I was going to say, Detective, and I don't wish to insinuate you aren't doing your job properly, but did you check out who has access to the decorator's emails? She's the only one Judy gave the numbers to."

"Yes. I've thought about that but thanks. I'll double check. In the meantime, if you think of anything else, please call."

Less than twenty minutes later Adam pulled up outside Amanda's house. The light was fading and the streetlights were already glowing.

As he walked through the gate, the front door opened and Michael rushed out, closing the door behind him. He double locked it and was startled, as he swung around, to come face to face with Adam.

'Oh, I didn't see you there."

"I'm sorry. I was just checking on how Amanda is after today."

"She seems fine. She's bathing the children right now and said she's having an early night. Do you want to go in?" Michael pulled the keys from his pocket again and motioned towards the door.

"No, that's okay. Is everything else all right?"

"Yeah, I guess so."

"Oh, well, I'd best let you get on. Goodnight."

"Goodnight, Detective."

Sitting back in his car, Adam watched as Michael drove away. Glancing at the house before starting the engine, he wished he'd taken Michael up on his offer to see Amanda. He couldn't put his finger on the reason why, but he felt an overwhelming urgency to protect her.

He was becoming obsessed with solving this case. It meant much more to him than it should. All the doubts he had in himself as a cop hung in the balance here. He knew it would signify the end to his career if he couldn't crack it. Right or wrong—Adam hadn't been able to save his wife—but he had no choice but to save Amanda if he had any chance of saving himself.

Chapter 33

Amanda

The kids in bed and Michael out God knows where, I sat at the computer and trawled through my emails. Finding what I was looking for, I hit the 'Reply' button.

Dear Judy,
Please call me urgently! I need to arrange to meet with you.
Regards,
Amanda

I pulled the photograph out of my pocket and gazed into the beautiful eyes of my long-lost brother. A sound from my computer indicated I had an email. It was from Judy.

Gosh, that was fast!

Dear Amanda,
My mother is very sick at the moment. She is not up to visitors. She told me to ask, what is so urgent?
Mary

Dear Mary,
I'm very sorry she's sick, but I am at my wit's end. It is more than urgent I speak to her. Please let me have your address. I promise I won't stay too long.
A

The reply was as fast as the last.

Dear Amanda,
She said she will see you. The best time of the day for her is midmorning. Address is below.
Mary

At ten o'clock the next morning I pressed the button on the electric gates, and moments later a young girl's voice came through the tinny-sounding speakers. "Hello."

"Oh, hi, you must be Mary. I emailed you last night. It's Amanda."

"Come in."

The gates swung open and I followed the driveway around past several large oak trees to a cute stone cottage.

A girl stood at the front door. It surprised me how young she was. She was a pale little thing with huge blue eyes surrounded by dark circles. I'd always had dark circles under my eyes as a girl, probably because of my similarly pale skin. I never went anywhere any more without my concealer pen.

"Hi, Mary." I held out my hand and she placed her skinny hand in mine. She never said a word, all the time just looking at me with an odd expression on her face.

"Thank you for this," I said. "I know it's a difficult time for your family."

Mary seemed to pull herself together. "That's okay. Come in."

She led me down a dark hallway, past several doors to a room to the right of the staircase. The only light came from a small gap in the curtains and it took a while for my eyes to adjust.

Judy was sitting up in bed. Her hair had been brushed back off her face and tied. Her gaunt features and sunken eyes brought to mind a skeleton. I inhaled sharply as I saw that the left side of her face was twisted and the eye drooped.

"I-I'm sorry to bother you, Mrs Pitt."

"Judy, please," she said. Her voice was little more than a whisper.

"Okay, Judy."

"Take a seat." She nodded at a chair placed to the side of her. "Mary, please get our guest a cup of tea."

I'd forgotten Mary was in the room. I turned and watched her leave, then I turned back to the bed.

"I'll get straight to the point, Judy. I don't know if you can help me, but I've got nowhere else to turn. Strange things have been happening to me, starting with your first phone call."

"Go on," she nodded, her eyebrows wrinkling.

"I was at the zoo that day with my family. During my phone call with you, my daughter vanished."

Her breath hitched.

"Don't worry. We found her after a frantic search—though when we did she said she'd followed me out of the building."

"I'm sorry, but what does this have to do with me?" Her voice was quiet and raspy, but I managed to understand her very well.

"Maybe nothing at all. But then my estranged father went missing and turned up dead at your house. That's too much of a coincidence."

"Yes, I can see that, yet I'm still unsure how I can help you."

"I don't know, but this is my only hope. I was wondering who else had the key code for the house?"

I became aware of a commotion coming from another part of the house. A man was shouting.

Judy said, "I already told the police we didn't give the number to anybody else."

"The troubling thing is, more murders have been committed since then, and all of them link to me in some way. I'm worried about my children."

Mary came back into the room looking flustered. "I'm sorry, Amanda, you've got to leave. My father's angry that I allowed you in."

I jumped up. "Oh, I'm sorry. I hope I've not got you into any trouble."

"My husband is over-protective of me," Judy said. "He'll calm down."

Rummaging through my bag, I produced the photograph of Andrew. "Before I go—could you tell me if this person looks familiar to you?" I handed the faded image to Judy who glanced at it before shaking her head and handing it back.

"No, sorry. You'd better go."

"Of course. Oh, and needless to say, I won't be able to finish the job."

"I understand. Please send me an invoice for the work you've already done and I'll make sure you get paid."

"Thank you. Goodbye Judy." I pressed my hand on the back of hers.

"Goodbye and good luck with everything," she said.

Mary was even more pale by the time we reached the front door.

"Maybe I should talk to your father, apologise to him for my intrusion."

"No!" Mary snapped. "He's busy."

"Please tell him I'm sorry."

"Okay."

As I pulled away, I noticed the curtain moving in the upstairs window. Mary was still standing on the doorstep and was waving to me. She was a serious-looking little thing—she looked as though she had a lot on her mind. I couldn't begin to imagine what she was going through. The death of a parent was tough at any age, but for a young girl like her it must be devastating.

Chapter 34

Michael

Michael dialled Toni's landline as soon as Amanda left the house and it rang and rang. Usually, after several rings the machine would cut in. Her mobile was off too.

She had been pissed off at him for moving back home, however when he spoke to her on Sunday she'd seemed all right again. They'd arranged to meet last night, but her apartment had been in darkness when he got there. She might still be punishing him, but he didn't think so.

He planned to go back once he'd dropped the children off at the day-care.

Michael sat on the brick wall at the front of the building and dialled her number again. Still no one home. He couldn't hear the ringing inside, which he thought surprising.

Pulling himself to his feet, he walked back up the short path, but instead of turning to the right and going up to Toni's front door he turned to the left.

The adjoining apartment shared not only the front gate entrance but also the rear patio. He knocked at the door. Just as he'd given up he heard a shuffling from within.

A large, Jamaican man opened the door. He had a mass of dreadlocks tied in a colourful band on the top of his head. He eyed Michael with suspicion and stepped forward, scanning up and down the street before Michael had a chance to speak.

Michael cleared his throat and stood upright. "Hi mate. Sorry to bother you but I'm trying to get hold of Toni, your neighbour. Do you happen to have seen her at all?"

"Na, man." The words were pronounced clearly and slowly and were tinged with a strong accent. "Not seen her in a whi-ale."

Michael felt uneasy. He would give this guy a wide berth if he saw him on the street, but he hadn't got much choice right now. He was worried about Toni. "I wonder if I can ask you a favour."

The Jamaican man cocked his head to one side, squinting one eye.

"I know you share the back balcony with my friend. Could I come through so I can look in her window? I'm worried about her."

The man sucked his teeth slowly before stepping back into the hallway and gesturing for Michael to enter.

The apartments were the same layout except the opposite way around, like a mirror image. However, that's where the likeness stopped.

Toni, a self-confessed neat freak, had everything in its place. Pastel colours throughout created a sunny, warm home. This apartment was very gloomy.

Huge dark flags hung over the patio door instead of curtains. Stale smoke filled the air—and not cigarette smoke if his memory served him well. A half-naked white girl lay spark-out on the dingy sofa. Her matted, long brown hair looked as though it hadn't seen a brush in years.

Michael struggled with lifting the flag while trying to open the door. The guy helped him by unhooking the heavy blanket-like flag off the curtain rail. This allowed the sunlight to flood the room, causing the girl on the sofa to moan in annoyance.

Glancing around the room now, Michael realised his first impressions had been wrong. The apartment, although basic, was clean and tidy. A coffee table in the middle of the room confirmed his suspicions about the smoke—a huge spliff was perched on the edge of the ashtray. He saw the suspicious look pass over the guy's face again. Michael hastily turned back towards the door.

All the apartments in the block shared a balcony with one other. Toni's and the Jamaican man's were ground level, but the block went twelve storeys high. A tiny, makeshift picket fence was placed halfway across the balcony. Michael stepped over it.

A thick lace curtain covered the patio door. Toni never pulled the curtain across. She had a pair of heavy fabric curtains that she closed at night. Michael placed his hands to the glass to shade the sun. It took a couple of seconds for his eyes to adjust.

The glass coffee table had been shattered and glass covered the whole carpet. Then he noticed a large smear of blood on the door surround that led through to the hallway.

Michael let out a cry that came from the pit of his stomach. His breakfast followed it.

The neighbour ran out and screwed his face up in disgust as Michael vomited in Toni's pot plant.

Wiping his mouth, Michael sat back on his haunches to rummage through his pockets and pulled out his mobile phone.

Adam answered on the first ring. "DS Stanley."

"I ... it's Michael Flynn."

"Yes, Michael, how can I help you?" the detective said with a bored tone to his voice.

"Quick! You need to come over. I think it's happened again."

"Michael, calm down! Where are you?"

He gave Adam the address. "Please hurry. I think she's dead."

"Is it Amanda?"

"Wha ...? No, it's Toni. I'm going to break in."

"Michael, listen to me. Don't do a thing until we get there. Do you hear me? Michael, do you hear me?"

"Okay, but hurry."

Toni's neighbour turned a funny shade of green. His Jamaican accent had vanished and was replaced by a cockney one. His deep, slow drawl also was replaced by a higher pitched, faster-paced chatter. "Did you call the pigs' man?"

"I knew there was something wrong. There's blood."

"Did you call the fucking pigs, man?"

"Yeah—they're on their way."

"You're fucking kidding me, man!" The man ran indoors and began banging and clattering. He shouted at the girl, "Jess, get your lazy, fat arse up—the pigs are on their way."

Michael stepped back over the fence and walked into the room. "I'll wait outside for them."

The man ignored him and continued throwing stuff from a kitchen drawer into a Tesco carrier bag.

The girl was still in the same position on the sofa. Michael walked out of the front door and sat back on the wall to wait for Adam.

Uniformed police arrived first, followed by an ambulance.

Michael was in a daze. He had no idea how they gained access to the flat, but it took them a matter of seconds.

A gentle, young policewoman placed him in the back of a police car to wait for Adam.

Michael watched as they crawled all over the property like worker ants—heads down and focused. The policewoman was knocking on the neighbour's door though Michael knew it was a waste of time. The Rasta and the skinny, scraggy-haired girl had left seconds before the police arrived.

A dark-grey Mondeo pulled up. Adam jumped out and crossed the road in a couple of strides and entered Toni's flat. Michael had a strange feeling of déjà vu. Just over a week ago he'd been sat in another police car waiting for Adam to emerge from a murder scene.

Several minutes later Adam opened the car door and indicated for Michael to get out.

"Is she ..." Michael asked, terrified of the answer.

"I'm not sure. There's a lot of blood and evidence of a struggle, but we can't find a body. When did you last see Miss Sellers?"

"The other night—Monday, I think. I haven't seen her for more than a week. We had a fight because I'd gone back home, but I spoke to her on Sunday and arranged to come over last night. That's where I was going when you called at the house."

"You will have to come to the station—we need more details and a statement from you."

"I can't. I've got to collect the children from daycare soon."

"Could you ring Amanda? If she can't pick them up I'll arrange for an officer to collect them. It's urgent we get this done right away."

Michael dreaded Amanda's reaction when she found out he'd left the children alone. Well, not alone exactly—there were lots of staff and parents to keep an eye on them, but Amanda would still go berserk. He reached into his pocket for his phone.

Chapter 35

Amanda

Something niggled at me, but I couldn't put my finger on what it was. Meeting Judy had shaken me up. I knew she'd been ill, but I hadn't been prepared for how ill she actually was. Just a few weeks ago, when she asked me to fix up her parents' place, she'd said she hoped to move into it soon.

But without some kind of miracle, I didn't see how she would go anywhere ever again, except maybe to the hospital.

The ringing of my phone on the passenger seat brought me out of my daydream. I hit the loudspeaker button. "What do you want, Michael? I'm driving."

"Amanda—any chance you can collect the children from day-care?"

"What do you mean? Did you leave them there?" My voice had raised an octave.

"I had to. It's Toni. I think she's dead—they need me at the police station."

I hung up and glanced at the clock and realised the kids should have been collected ten minutes ago. I wasn't too far away, I put my foot down.

My mind raced, wondering what had happened to Toni. I remembered something Judy said and it made me feel sick. She'd questioned who else had access to my emails, and Michael was the only other person. Now, the connection that linked Toni to my family was also Michael.

It didn't make sense. Michael couldn't have had anything to do with the murders. He never knew of my past. Unless, of course, he'd found the newspaper clippings under the stairs.

Or maybe this latest death was a coincidence and had nothing to do with the other murders at all.

As I parked, I noticed several groups of people emerging from the day-care and hurried in to collect my babies.

There was no way I could face going home. The murderer no longer seemed fussy who he bumped off. I feared we would be next on the hit list.

After buying a selection of sandwiches and cakes from a small bakery, I drove to the other side of Pinevale.

Sandra seemed pleased to see us. "What a lovely surprise," she said as she showed us through to the kitchen.

"I'm sorry for just turning up at your door, Sandra. I had nowhere else to go."

"Don't be silly. I told you the other day—I'm here for you. Stay as long as you need to."

She sat the children on a rug in front of the television, setting out a picnic-style lunch from the paper bags I'd brought from the bakery. A few minutes later, she and I were sitting opposite each other at the breakfast bar, a pot of tea in between us.

"Michael just called me. He said that Toni has been murdered."

Chapter 36

Adam

Adam screwed up his face as he looked at the snivelling mess in front of him. He wouldn't have minded except that he hadn't even got started yet.

"When did you last see Miss Sellers?" he asked.

"I told you. It was last Monday, after Dennis' body was found. She got angry with me for moving back home. We were meant to meet up last night, but she didn't show." Michael said, and another bout of sobbing followed.

"Harden up, man!" Adam snapped. The more time he spent with Michael, the more irritated he got. He found it hard to understand what Amanda ever saw in him.

"How long have you been seeing her?"

Michael shrugged. "Four months or so."

"When did Amanda find out?"

"A few weeks ago. Why? Do you think she ...?"

"This is the second time you've accused your wife of murder, Michael. Do you honestly think she's capable of it?"

Michael shrugged again. "She hasn't been herself lately, you know that."

'Yes, I do, but I also know she has good reason for that—don't you think?" Adam was now standing in front of the desk. He put both hands down in front of Michael, bent forwards and glared at him, a sneer lifting the corner of his mouth.

Michael sat back on his chair trying to get as far away from Adam as possible. His eyes were wide and wary.

Adam asked, "What did Amanda say about the affair?" Did she ever threaten Toni?"

"Yes, once when she was around at our house. Amanda went berserk and threw her out."

"Again understandable, wouldn't you say?

"Yes."

"Do you love your wife, Michael?"

"I ... er ... I don't see what that has to do with anything."

"Answer the question, please."

"I used to."

"So in other words you don't love her anymore?"

"No."

"When did you stop loving her?"

"After I found out about her past. She kept it from me all this time. Disgusting."

"How can you say that? It wasn't her fault."

"No, but it makes me fucking sick, thinking of her having sex with her own dad."

"He raped her when she was only a child." Adam shook his head, baffled by the mentality of this ignorant arsehole. "How did you find out about her past?"

"She told me the night you came to the house looking for Dennis."

"So you were already having the affair? Not the actions of a loving and devoted husband."

Michael bent his head, staring at the table.

"How did you feel when you first found out?"

"I told you—it knocked me sick."

"Were you angry?"

"I guess."

"Angry enough to commit murder?"

"Hey—back up a bit. What are you saying?"

"I'm saying, Michael, that I think you found out about Amanda's past earlier than you're letting on, and that you took revenge on Dennis, Annie and Brian."

"Don't be so stupid! How could I know? Why would I want revenge anyway? It wasn't me they messed with."

"Do you have access to your wife's emails?"

"Yes. We share an email address. What does that have to do with anything?"

"Whoever has access to the emails also had access to the key code for the house in Kingsley. The house where Dennis' body was found."

"I think I need to call my solicitor."

"Good idea."

Adam knew he wouldn't be able to keep him for much longer without charging him. He also knew Michael didn't have the balls to commit murder. But Adam had to look as though he was doing something, and why not have a bit of fun at Michael's expense before releasing him?

After a thorough search on Miss Sellers' apartment, it seemed as though someone had smashed the lamp through the glass coffee table, cutting themselves in the process. The blood, although a lot, was in only a couple of places, nothing frenzied. In fact, the place was looking less and less like a crime scene. They found her mobile phone in the apartment, and the land-line had been unplugged from the wall. No sign of her handbag, coat or car.

Nothing turned up at Brian's house, not one fingerprint or stray hair—which didn't surprise him. No doubt they were dealing with a professional. Never in all his time as a homicide detective, had Adam seen such vicious attacks executed with such meticulousness. It was as though two people were involved—one responsible for all the planning and another to carry out the actual attacks.

They'd found a large stash of child-based porn in Brian's shed as well as a collection of girls' underwear. Part of Adam couldn't help but feel grateful to this killer or killers, for getting these worthless and revolting creatures off the streets.

As his mobile phone rang, he sighed and sat down at his desk. "Hi Mum."

"Oh Adam, I'm glad I caught you. Auntie Betty's birthday is coming up and they've asked me to go and stay for a few days."

"You should, it'll do you good," he said.

"Do you think? But I'll miss all my programmes. Our Betty doesn't watch the TV."

Adam laughed. "Oh, Mother, you're funny. I'm sure it won't kill you to miss a few episodes of Coronation Street."

"I know it's not important to you, Adam, but I don't have much else in my life you know. Since my one and only son has moved to the other end of the country."

"I know, Mum." He sighed. "I tell you what—if you want to go for the day I can take you. I just need to know the dates. I promised Matt I'd come for a visit anyway."

"Oh, would you? It would be lovely to see you, thanks, darling. I couldn't imagine having to go all that way on the train—not with me bunions."

"I've got to go, Mum. I'm working. Speak soon."
He hung up, the last thing he needed was a full on blow by blow account of her bunions.

He felt better. Though she drove him to distraction, a couple of minute's conversation with his old mum had him grounded and feeling lighter than he had in a while. He chuckled as the phone rang again.

A stunning, voluptuous redhead, waited for him in reception. Her angry green eyes fired daggers at him.

He held his hand towards her. "Detective Stanley. Can I help you, Miss ...?

"Sellers, Toni Sellers. Now if you don't mind, could you please tell me what the hell's been happening in my apartment?"

Chapter 37

Amanda

The children were tucked up in bed and I finally had a few minutes to myself. I rang DS Stanley and he confirmed he was about to release Michael. Toni had turned up safe and well. She'd been to stay with her sister for a few days—after she smashed the coffee table in a temper and had cut herself, which explained the blood.

I was relieved. She wasn't one of my favourite people in the world, but I didn't want her harmed—well, not too harmed anyway.

I told DS Stanley where I was staying, but asked him not to say anything to Michael. I still needed some space to get my head straight. Although I worried that by staying here, we were putting Sandra in danger too, but I had nowhere else to go.

Back in the lounge, I glanced over at Sandra. "I need to tell you something."

Sandra tipped her head to one side as if to say, *now what?*

"I saw my brother at the cemetery yesterday."

"Oh, my God, Amanda, you need to tell the police. Are you sure?"

"No. That's why I didn't say anything. I thought I might have imagined it."

"So much of this doesn't add up. You should write everything down. Do a timeline." Sandra was always the queen of lists.

"I don't know how a list would help."

"Not a list, a timeline. It can't hurt."

"I guess not."

I ended up sitting on the lounge rug with the coffee table shoved to one side. Sandra gave me an old roll of wallpaper that was ideal and I rolled it out.

"Right, lovey, I'll leave you alone and walk this poor pooch before he bursts."

Monty jumped up from his basket as soon Sandra picked up his lead, and he began pirouetting mid-air. The scruffy, little brown dog had been in hiding all day. Jacob adored him and had terrorized him at every opportunity. Once the children were in bed Monty ventured back to his basket.

"Wrap up well. It's bloody freezing out there," I said.

Using a magic marker, I wrote down as many details as I could. I had to check some dates out on my email, using Sandra's computer.

Early September
- Feeling of being watched
- Saturday 13th October — The Zoo
- Call from Judy.
- Emma vanished.
- Zoo assistant saw her leave with a woman dressed like me?
- Emma said she followed me?
- Seahorse found in Emma's backpack.

Sunday 14th October
- Request from Judy for quote
- Key code and address emailed
- Arranged initial inspection for following day.

Monday 15th October
- Inspected property and sent quote through.
- Between 12th & 17th October
- Dennis killed.

Friday 26th October
- Visit from DS Stanley — missing person's enquiry.
- Email from Judy confirming the job was mine.

Monday 29th October
- Started work on Kingsley house.
- Bad smell noticed and plumber called.

Wednesday 31st October
- Annie killed.
- No alibi — stayed late working.

Friday 2nd November
- Annie's body found.
- Visit to police after I heard about it.

Saturday 3rd November
- Met with homicide — Kate King.

- Questioned and kept in overnight.
- Witness statements describe me as the person who walked Annie home. Another witness identifies me as buying the vodka left at Annie's place.
- Michael moved to Toni's with the kids.

Sunday 4th November
- Released without charge.
- Car wouldn't start; DS Stanley drove me home.
- He spotted a prowler in my garden.

Monday 5th November
- Plumber rang to confirm appointment.
- Took taxi to Kingsley.
- Discovered Dennis' body.
- I was found by Michael and DS Stanley, and taken to hospital.
- Michael returned home with the kids.

Tuesday 6th November
- Brian Crosby found dead.
- I woke up in hospital.
- Somebody broke into our house.

Wednesday 7th November
- Left hospital.
- Found message on computer screen threatening Michael.

Monday 12th November
- Dennis' funeral.
- Saw Andrew in cemetery?
- Toni goes missing.
- Tuesday 13th November (today)
- Visited Judy
- Michael arrested

Once I reached the end of the timeline I was none the wiser.

The back door opened and Sandra appeared, looking seriously windswept.

"Shall I make us a nice cuppa?" I said, jumping to my feet.

"I think we can find something a little more exciting," she said. "Have a look in the fridge—there should be a couple of bottles of white."

I poured us both a glass of chardonnay and carried them through to the lounge. Sandra was sitting staring at the list in a world of her own.

"Penny for them?" I said as I passed her a glass.

"Oh—sorry, love, I'm trying to get my head around everything."

"Yeah, I'm surprised you're not dizzy. There's a lot to take in."

"It's just ... something is puzzling me."

"What is?" I set my glass down on the coffee table in front of us.

"According to this, your father went missing before you'd even started work on the house."

"Aha."

"So whoever it was gained access, killed him, and left his body there for you to find—and all this before you even got the job."

"I hadn't thought about that." Sandra was very astute—even Adam had never mentioned this contradiction. "Which takes us back to Judy," I whispered.

"Do you think another visit is in order?"

***

Sandra offered to look after the children for me while I went to see Judy. I decided not to take them to the day-care. I'd been shocked to find out Michael had been leaving them alone there.

As I gathered up my bag, my phone rang for what seemed like the thousandth time this morning. The following beep indicated yet another message. I'd already cleared several from Michael, but more kept coming through. He had been released and was now in search of the children, but I wasn't in the mood to speak to him.

I perched on the edge of the bed and dialled my voicemail again. Six messages in half an hour for heaven's sake. The first three were more from Michael—ranting and raving, demanding all sorts. The next two were silent apart from some heavy breathing.

The last one was the same, more breathing, and I was about to hang up when I heard a faint voice. "Amanda, I need to see you. Please call me as soon as you can."

Judy was the last person I would have expected to hear from. I'd been stressing about how she was going to react to me turning up unannounced. I called her back, and Mary answered.

"Hi, Mary, it's Amanda Flynn. I missed a call from your mum. Can I talk to her, please?"

"She can't come to the phone right now—the nurse is in with her. She said to tell you to come over. She has something she needs to discuss with you, but it has to be between ten and twelve today."

I glanced at my watch—8.50am. I would need to get my skates on. "Tell her I'll be there."

I found Sandra and the children having breakfast at the dining table. Jacob was sitting in a booster seat attached to a chair.

"Oh, that's a good contraption. Where did you find it?"

"I've had it for years from my fostering days. I'd forgotten all about it."

"Sandra," I said, lowering my voice. "I need to go sooner than expected. Judy called and needs to see me."

"Judy called *you*?"

"Yeah—coincidence or what?"

"Are you sure you'll be okay?"

"I'll be fine. Maybe she's remembered something."

"Call me as soon as you're out of there."

I wasn't used to having somebody care about me, and it brought tears to my eyes.

"I will. I promise. Thank you, Sandra. You're a true friend."

"Oh, get on with ya." She pretended to shove me away. "Just keep yourself safe, you hear?

Chapter 38

Adam

Adam felt as if he'd been bamboozled into an awkward position.

Since Sarah died, he didn't want anything to do with homicide or death in any way, shape or form.

During his years in homicide, he'd investigated and solved several high-profile murders. He'd seen everything, or so he thought. That was until that fateful Wednesday morning.

Sarah had been an early childhood teacher and ten years younger than him. Neither of them had ever been in a serious relationship before they met, but once they did, it was as though his life suddenly made sense.

He'd already been with the police for nine years by then, and had been promoted to the homicide division. Sarah was the younger sister of a colleague—his ex-partner, Matt, to be exact. They met at Matt's birthday party.

She was so beautiful that he never imagined she'd look twice in his direction. However, Matt couldn't wait to tell him of the half-hour quizzing she'd put her brother through.

With Matt playing matchmaker, Adam and Sarah arranged to meet the following weekend, and from that day on they'd been inseparable.

They'd planned to have at least three children, and even though they weren't ready to start a family, it hadn't stopped them practising at every opportunity. They had more than sex in common, though. It was as if their minds were fused together and they functioned as one, often finishing each other's sentences.

That morning started out no different than many others, apart from the alarm clock failing to go off, which made him late for work. He'd rushed around getting ready, before racing back to the bedroom for a goodbye kiss.

Sarah lay on her stomach, one gorgeous, shapely leg and her bottom uncovered. Adam grabbed her foot and began nibbling from her ankle up, growling like an animal, before reaching her buttocks. Sarah squealed and wriggled to escape, but he held on tight. With a swift movement, he flipped her over, pinning her on her back. He kissed her sexy full lips passionately, then he jumped from the bed leaving her panting for more.

"Aw, no! Adam. Come back here this minute!"

"Can't—sorry, baby, I'm late. Take it as a taster of what to expect later." He winked at her.

"Just a few minutes, plee-ease?" she begged.

"Nah, gotta go. I love you."

The amount of times he'd gone over that day in his head, wondering if anything would have altered if he spent an extra half-hour with her instead of rushing off to work.

He first knew something was wrong was when Matt came to his office looking as though he'd had the fright of his life.

Adam's stomach hit the floor.

Sarah had been in an accident.

They had been taking a group of children to the local jungle gym as they did every Wednesday morning. One of the children, a little girl called Molly, ran into the road. Sarah had managed to push the child to safety before a car struck Sarah head on.

Witnesses said she died instantly. She never uttered any last words of true love like they do in the movies. The driver had slowed, before slamming down the accelerator and fleeing the scene.

The driver hadn't been found to this day.

That had been the hardest thing to deal with. Knowing the person that killed his wife was still out there getting on with their life as if nothing had happened. Adam's life, on the other hand, was devastated beyond recognition. The fact that he couldn't find the person responsible ate away at him the way a parasite.

The reality that it hadn't been the driver's fault made no difference at all. The witnesses said there was no way the car could have avoided her—it had happened too fast—but Adam had been like a man obsessed. So much so that when he couldn't find them, he'd doubted himself as a policeman.

After a long absence, he handed in his notice, but his sergeant wouldn't accept it. Instead, he'd convinced Adam to transfer to another area on light duties, hence Missing Persons in the London borough of Pinevale.

Yet now here he was, up to his eyeballs in dead bodies and with no idea who was responsible.

He glanced at the thick file on the kitchen bench. He intended going through it until something made sense. It was meant to be his day off, but he knew he wouldn't be able to rest with all this going around and round in his head.

After making a large pot of coffee, he sat down for what he expected could be a very long day.

Chapter 39

Amanda

The gates stood open as I arrived at Judy's house, so I drove straight in and parked in front of the steps. I wrapped my scarf around my neck and darted to the front door to get out of the rain.

After the third knock had gone unanswered, I tried the doorknob and was surprised when it opened.

"Hello ..." My voice was little more than a whisper. I cleared my throat before trying again. "Hello."

I pushed the door wide and stepped into the hallway, wondering where everybody could be. I closed the door behind me, feeling like an intruder and didn't want to go any further without an invitation.

"Hello, Judy? Anybody?"

I heard a faint sound coming from the end of the hallway, Judy's bedroom. Seeing her door was ajar, I eased it open fully and saw Judy sitting upright in bed. The curtains were pulled and although it was a cold, dark day the light made the room look much brighter and more welcoming than it had the day before.

"Oh, hi, Judy. I'm sorry to barge in on you. I did knock."

Judy beckoned me into the room with her frail hand. "I know. I asked...the nurse to leave...the door unlocked. I...sent her away so...we can—talk." Her words were little more than a hoarse whisper, but I could understand her.

"Where's Mary? Are you alone?"

"Her father...took her to music class. That's why it...was important...you come at this time." She gripped one arm of the chair at the side of the bed and nodded towards it.

I sat down. "How are you feeling?"

"To be bru...tally honest, I don't...have much...longer. My husband...doesn't like me talking like...this but I don't...see the...point pretending."

"I'm so sorry." She seemed much worse even than yesterday.

Judy shrugged. "Just...one of those...things, I'm afraid. There's some...thing I need to...see to, though. That's...what I need...to talk to you...about."

"I was going to call you myself this morning. It seems we both have unfinished business, so maybe we can help each other?"

"Maybe—" A fit of coughing interrupted her. She bent forward, one hand holding her chest and the other pointing at the box of tissues.

I reached for them, handing her several. My hand brushed hers and it shocked me how cold she was. I stood close to her and rubbed her back as her frail body was racked with wet-sounding coughs.

Judy spat into the tissues and wiped her mouth. She seemed to have calmed down, but I was worried it might happen again.

I handed her the wastepaper basket and she dropped the bloody tissues into it.

"Are you okay now?" I asked. "You scared me."

"Pneumonia," she rasped between gasps. "This is...what will finish...me off."

I handed her some more tissues before putting the box back on the side table.

"Is there nothing they can do for you?"

"Nothing they...haven't...already tried. Besides...will be much...easier for everyone...this way."

"Oh, Judy, how awful."

Her eyes closed. After a few minutes, I thought she must be asleep. I got up and walked to the door, wanting to check if the nurse was anywhere to be found.

"Don't go." It was no more than a whisper.

"I'm not going anywhere, Judy—at least not until somebody else turns up. But you're tiring yourself out. Have a little rest."

"No, I need...to talk to you...now. It's impor...tant."

"Okay," I said, sitting back down.

"Promise me..." She gave another little cough. "Promise me...you'll look after...Mary when I'm...gone."

"I don't understand. What do you mean?"

"You will. I'm too...tired to tell you...now. Just...promise me."

A phone was ringing in another part of the house; it went unanswered and after a short pause began again.

I didn't want to add to her stress, but I wasn't about to promise I'd do anything of the sort. "Judy, I don't understand. I'm sorry, but why are you asking me this?"

"She's not...safe. My husband...been...behaving...strangely."

"Surely that's understandable considering what you're all going through?"

"I know, but...it's not...that." She took a deep breath and exhaled loudly before continuing. "You've got to under...stand, my hus...band is not...a bad—man, he's the most car...ing and cons...ider...ate person I've ev...er known." Each word was coming out on the end of a pant.

"Then why is Mary in danger?"

"He...gets...very...angry."

I thought back to yesterday's raised voice. "Judy, I know you're concerned about this, but your husband is going through an awful time. To watch you suffer like this must make him very angry—angry with you—angry at the illness—angry at everyone, probably."

She grasped hold of my hand and I was amazed by the strength in her scrawny fingers. One watery blue eye was like a saucer as she looked at me pleadingly, though the other one was drooping and closed.

The phone was still ringing. I felt as though I should locate it and put the caller out of their misery, but I didn't want to leave Judy alone.

"Please...take...her...home...with you."

"Oh, Judy, you need to rest. You're not making any sense." She was obviously delirious. I was mad at the nurse for leaving her for this long.

"No!" Judy spat, the frail and timid voice gone for a second before returning even weaker than before.

"I...need...you...to...promise...keep...her...safe."

"I'm sorry, Judy, I cannot take her home—and even if I wanted to, I'm sure her father would have something to say about it."

"She's ... not ... safe... with ... him. He ... looks ... at her ... like ... your father ... looked...at...you."

If it had been anybody else, I'd have given them a mouthful. She'd obviously seen the story in the newspaper and put two and two together because I'd never been named. Though, of course I'd told her yesterday that it was my father who had been killed in her house, so I guess it hadn't been that difficult to work out. I was shocked that she knew, but more so that she felt she could discuss it with me. I felt my face redden, suddenly very annoyed.

"Yes, Judy, my father looked at me in an unnatural way, but he was a monster who sexually molested me for years. Is that what you're saying your husband is doing to Mary?" I glared at her.

"No. I don't...think...so. But ... when ... I saw ... you ... yester ... day ...it all ... made ... sense."

"What on earth do you mean?" My voice was becoming louder. I didn't want to treat a dying woman this way, but the whole conversation was exhausting me. God only knows what it was doing to her. She had slumped down in the bed and was bending over sideways, looking very uncomfortable. I became worried she might topple.

"Here, let me help you sit up a bit." I put one hand under her nearest armpit and lifted her straight. With my free hand, I pulled the pillow back up behind her head. I heard a sound in another part of the house and prayed it was the nurse.

I finished straightening her blankets and she looked much more comfortable. "There you go.

That's better," I said, then was startled by the horrified look on her face as she stared over my shoulder.

"Oh, and isn't this cosy," said a male voice, coming from right behind me.

My stomach flipped as I realised it must be Judy's husband, but I tried not to show how flustered I was. I turned around with a smile on my face and my hand outstretched to introduce myself. But there was no need for an introduction.

Frozen to the spot, I tried to make sense of the situation. I looked from him to Judy and back to him, unable to work out was happening. I felt confused and dizzy.

Judy was speaking. Her breathing was even worse now and her speech very hard to understand. "Am-an-da hhh-as que-est-tion-s." She looked petrified and was blinking continually.

My eyes went from one to the other. I could not utter a word.

"Judith, you can barely talk yet you can still find the energy to lie to me, so just keep quiet," her husband snapped.

"I ...I ..." She was obviously searching for something to say.

"*I said, be quiet!*" he yelled.

His voice was so loud that both of my feet left the floor. Palpitations thundered in my chest and I had a whooshing sound in my ears.

He turned to me and smiled. "Well, I must say I hadn't expected this—what a nice surprise.
Good to see you, sis."

Chapter 40

Adam

Adam scraped his fingers through his hair, then stood up and stretched. He'd been hunched over for hours and still nothing. He'd wasted his day off on a pointless exercise. Now he fancied a beer, but he wanted his mind clear until he finished.

Heading for the fridge, he gave in to temptation. One wouldn't hurt. He almost emptied the bottle of Corona in a couple of swigs. Then his stomach growled and he realised he hadn't eaten in a while.

Piling all the papers back into the file, he decided to stop for now and contemplated going for a walk, but it was teeming down outside.

He picked up the manila folder from the table. He stopped dead in his tracks, the bottle almost at his lips, head tilted to one side, eyes glued to the photograph in front of him.

Grabbing his phone, he dialled Amanda's number.

"Hello," said a woman's voice he didn't recognise.

"Hello, I'm looking for Amanda."

"Oh, um, yes—she left her phone here. Can I take a message?"

"This is Detective Stanley. Do you know where she is? It's important."

"Yes, of course. She's gone to visit Judy, the owner of the house, you know? She left the children here. She should ..."

Adam heard no more. He hung the phone up, grabbed his keys and ran from the house.

He prayed there were no police around to slow him down as he was still new to the area. He would need to explain who he was and his reasons for flying up the motorway at breakneck speed with no siren or lights.

He need not have worried. The traffic more or less came to a standstill a couple of miles up the road and proceeded to crawl along. Adam scooted up the hard shoulder until he could go no further, blocked by a large 4x4 that had landed on its side after almost flattening a Mini Metro. The ambulance and police were already at the scene.

Adam jumped from the car and ran towards the uniformed policeman, saying a prayer of thanks when he saw a cop he knew.

Within a few minutes, they'd helped manoeuvre his car past the roadblocks and he had his foot down to the floor once again.

Chapter 41

Amanda

Words still wouldn't form in my mouth. I felt light-headed and wondered if I was close to another breakdown, becoming certain of it when laughter started to bubble up from my stomach. It took all my energy to keep it at bay.

"Dee-jay, where's Ma-ry?"

"Where do you think she is, Judy?"

Dee-jay? I was puzzled, who was Dee-jay?

Andrew's voice was different again, now calm and polite. It occurred to me that he'd lost his marbles.

"I...d-don-'t kn-know."

"Of course you do. She's been going every Wednesday for the past three years."

"Mu...sic."

"Bingo, got it in one. Now don't tire yourself, sweetheart—let me help you. Your next question is probably, why I am here, is that right?"

Judy gave a small nod.

"Because I knew something was going on. Mary can't lie to save herself. Then when I rang, and nobody answered, I knew you were up to something. Did you send the nurse away?" He paused. *"Well?"* he snapped. His smiling face had changed in an instant, his eyebrows now knitted together over glaring, hostile eyes.

"Y-e-s." Judy pulled herself further into her pillows as he stepped towards her.

Watching Andrew's face, I was certain he was unhinged. I now understood why Judy had asked me to take Mary—she was my niece.

"Andrew," I whispered.

Smiling again, he turned back towards me.

"Where have you been? I thought you were dead." I pushed a stray hair back from my face with a trembling hand.

"No—not me, sis. No doubt I would be if I'd stayed, but I got out."

"Why didn't you come back for me?" A slight twitch that had started in my right eye now made me feel as though I were winking at him. I rubbed the socket to try to stop it but to no effect.

"I planned to, but you were doing quite all right with your new family, I made sure of that. I decided you were better off where you were."

"But I missed you. I prayed every day for you to be found."

"I came back when it counted, didn't I?"

"I don't understand what you mean?" I reached for the chair behind me and sat down before my legs gave up on me.

"When they released that fucking pervert I sorted it. I did that for you and your kids."

"You mean you ... you ...?"

"Give the girl a medal." One side of his mouth lifted in a half-smile that didn't get anywhere near his eyes.

"Why are you so angry with me?"

He didn't answer. Instead, he curled his lip into a sneer, folded his arms and raised his chin. Looking down his nose, he sighed loudly.

"I understand it's a tough time for you at the moment." I glanced at Judy. Her eyes were closed and her breathing seemed a bit easier. I felt envious that she didn't have to deal with this crazy situation.

"You have no idea, sweetheart."

"What did you mean a minute ago? You said you came back for me."

"I think you understood what I meant, Amanda, for Christ's sake— you know me better than anyone."

"No, you're wrong. I don't know you at all. Not anymore. Did you kill all those people?"

"They weren't people! They were vermin, the scourge of the earth. They preyed on innocent children. But in answer to your question—yes, I did! Somebody needed to sort them out."

"Why did you make the police think it was me?"

"Just a joke of mine." He laughed. "Remember like we used to do? When we were kids?" His movements were sporadic, his eyes wild and scary.

I glanced at Judy again. Her breathing was very shallow and I could hear a rattling sound coming from her throat.

"Judy—oh my God! Judy, are you all right? Andrew, look at her!"

He ran around to the opposite side of the bed and lowered the back of the mattress until she lay flat. He was saying her name over and over.

Judy's eyes flickered open. "Ti-re-ed," she whispered, closing her eyes again.

Andrew sat with her for a few minutes and stroked her hair before jumping up again. "Where's that fucking nurse?" he snarled, irate once more.

Maybe this wasn't the right time to notice the way the colour of his eyes had changed from a pale grey-green when he was annoyed, to a lovely, soft blue when he spoke tenderly to his wife. I wondered if mine did the same. We were very alike. Both of us had our mother's looks and colouring, and though I hated it on myself, I admired it on everyone else.

The rattling noise was back again. Andrew began pacing the room.

I decided to go and see if the nurse was anywhere in sight. Judy had deteriorated a lot since I'd arrived, but she'd taken a rapid decline in the past ten minutes. The rattling noise was freaking me out. I got to the door, but Andrew stopped me in my tracks.

"Where do you think you're going?"

"I-I just thought I'd—"

"Sit down!" he boomed.

Shuddering, I did as he said—I didn't see any point in making him any more angry than he already was. Never in a million years would I have imagined a reunion with my long-lost brother to be like this. The mere presence of him in my personal space made my skin prickle.

"What happened to you, Andrew? You were such a gentle boy," I dared to ask.

His eyes softened for a split second before glaring at me once again.

"I'd have thought you of all people wouldn't have to ask that. Don't you remember what they did to us? What they forced us to do?"

"Of course I do, but ..."

"You can't have forgotten the things they made me do to you! Or the way they forced me to suck off strange men while they filmed it. I don't know about you, Amanda, but I think that might have something to do with the reason I'm so fucked up!" He yelled the last part and his eyes looked as though they might pop out of his head.

"I know what they did—don't forget it happened to me too—but I would never turn on my own family."

This accusation seemed to knock all the anger out of him and he slumped down onto the end of the bed. "I've never turned on them. I love them. Did Judy say that?"

I wasn't sure what to say while he was calm like this; I was scared of setting him off again.

"I noticed how petrified she is when you get angry," I said.

The door opened and a dark-haired young woman wearing a blue uniform edged her way into the room.

"Where were you? I told you never to leave her alone," Andrew said, his voice still calm.

"I'm sorry, Mr Pitt—your wife insisted I sit in my car along the road until her visitor left. I was getting a bit worried, though, so I came back."

Andrew shrugged. The fight seemed to have left him.

The nurse busied herself with Judy.

"Is she okay? She's been making some terrible noises." Andrew picked up Judy's hand and enclosed it in both of his.

"She's sleeping right now but we may need to get her throat suctioned—her saliva is pooling. I need to put the bed back up, I'm afraid."

Andrew helped get Judy back into a sitting position and her breathing seemed to ease a little.

I looked at my watch, surprised to find it was almost twelve-thirty. I'd been there for more than two hours.

"Andrew, I need to get home to the children."

His head snapped towards me. "I don't think so. Come with me."

He stood up and took my hand, leading me from the room. We walked back down the hallway towards the front door and into the first room on the right.

The lounge was very old-fashioned. If the circumstances had been different, I would have a field day with all the original features the quaint cottage held.

"Can I get you a drink or anything, Mindy?" Andrew seemed to be back in full control. The use of the childhood name brought tears to my eyes.

"No. Thank you." I sat on the floral, two-seater sofa.

Andrew sat in an armchair to the left of me and bent forward, putting his head in his hands. "What have I done? This is such a mess."

"I understand your reasons, Andrew. I might have done the same if I'd had the nerve. In fact, I was beginning to think that maybe it was me."

"I know. I heard you telling your friend," he said.

I was puzzled. I'd only told Sandra and we'd been alone in my kitchen at the time. "I don't understand. You couldn't have."

He smiled. "You'd be surprised what I've been party to over the years, Mindy."

"You spied on me?" As I said it, lots of things slotted into place. All the unexplained things that had happened—the missing or moved items in the house that Michael and I had blamed each other for. Had it been Andrew all along?

"Spying seems a bit harsh. More like looking out for you. Your husband is lucky he didn't end up on the list of victims, the way he's treated you—especially recently."

"You left the message on the computer screen?"

He nodded, a slight smile playing at his lips. "And the texts."

"How? How did you get in the house?"

"I own a full set of keys, courtesy of Michael. He can be careless sometimes. I was surprised you didn't change your locks though, knowing how paranoid you are."

"We didn't have the money and Michael swore they were still in the house somewhere. Anyway, if I am paranoid it's down to you." I shook my head, thinking about all the times I'd thought I was cracking up. "I don't understand why you tried to frame me for the murders."

"I told you, just a bit of fun. I wouldn't have let them charge you, which is why I went to your house while you were in the hospital. I wanted to confuse everybody."

"I guess it was you who took Emma at the zoo."

He nodded. "It was a test. I knew if I could convince your own daughter then I'd be able to convince anybody. I didn't hurt her—I'd never do that, Mindy. You believe me, don't you?"

I nodded, but my mind flashed to what Judy had said—Mary was in danger and he'd been looking at her inappropriately.

"There's something else I need to tell you." Andrew took a deep breath. "It's about Mary."

"What about her? Have you hurt her, Andrew?" My words came out in a rush.

"No! I would never hurt her." He shook his head.

Seeing the pained expression on his face and desperation in his eyes I felt like a huge hand had grabbed at my heart and squeezed it tight.

He said, "I know what you're thinking, but I'd never do that to her. I'd kill myself first. But sometimes ... sometimes my body betrays me. She looks so much like you did at her age and ... I'm frightened. I hated what Dad made me do to you, made us do to each other. Yet my body responded the way he wanted it to." Tears flowed down his face.

"What does that say about me? What if I'm the same as ... as him?"

"The difference is massive, Andrew. You know it's wrong for starters. He didn't. Or if he did, he didn't care. I'm sure you can get help for this sort of thing. I'll bet you never had any counselling did you? I had years of it and still do. If I didn't, I don't know where I'd be right now."

"Nah, all that mind-bending stuff's not for me." He shook his head. "I do need to tell you something though, and you'll be shocked."

"You mean more shocked than I already am, finding out my long-lost brother has been under my nose this whole time? Never mind all the other things you've done."

"It's Mary."

"So you said—what about her? What the hell does Mary have to do with me?"

"She's yours."

"Mine? My what?"

"Your daughter."

Chapter 42

Amanda

My head spun. "I don ...I don't understand."

"Your baby—our baby. I took her from her new family," he said.

I'd never found out who fathered the child. Maybe it had been Andrew, but it could have been my dad or any of the other men they forced on me. I think the police did tests, but nobody ever told me the results. I didn't see the point in mentioning this right now. Instead, I concentrated on the main point.

"I don't believe you. I'd have known. Nobody ever told me the baby had been kidnapped."

"You were in a foster home. The police interviewed the social worker. She assured them you weren't involved, and considering your mental state thought you shouldn't be told."

"How do you know all this?" I whispered, shaking my head.

"I made it my business."

"What about Judy?"

"What about her?"

"Does she know everything?"

"No. Though she knows some and has guessed some more in the past few days.

"Tell me how you did it—why they never found you."

"When I first left I got on a ferry to France. We'd been learning French in school and I'd dreamed of going. I hitched a ride to Dover with a group of guys I met in the motorway services. They were going on a booze run. I needed to get as far away from Dad as possible. I knew he'd kill me if he got his hands on me. The beatings had been getting harder to walk away from. You know, he filmed that last beating—I think he got off on them."

"Why didn't you go to the police?"

"Why didn't you?" he snapped, and then admitted, "Because I was scared. Ashamed."

"I'm sorry. Go on."

"Once I was in France, I travelled around, doing labouring jobs for food and lodgings. I met another traveller, Steve, who was much older than me and on his way to join the French Foreign Legion. He never told me what he was running from, but I knew it must have been bad. Although I looked older, I was only fifteen, but he helped me get fake documents. Drew Joseph Pitt emerged that day in France—Joseph was the name of the farmer we were working for, and Pitt—well, that's what we were digging. An offal pit. DJ I became known as.

A week or so later we both joined the Legion. I'd always been into electronics and was lucky enough to get in with the right people. I specialised in communications."

He stood up and walked towards the window. "I spent three years and four months there, including training. I gained a lot of computer knowledge, both legal and illegal. That's where I learned about hacking. I managed to hack the adoption records to find out where Mary was and I twinned your social worker's computer and mobile phone. I knew you were settled. Your foster parents loved you."

He turned to me, a faraway look in his eyes. "I intended to come for you at first, but you seemed so happy."

"You should have. I missed you so much," I cried.

"Do you remember when you all went to the Christmas market at the Millennium Dome and then ice skating?"

I nodded.

"I was never more than six feet away from you that night. You had your first mulled wine, a treat you begged your foster parents for, and a huge German sausage. After a few laps around the rink, you had to go and throw up."

I was in total shock. How could I not have noticed him if he was that close? But it was as he said—I had knocked myself sick. I still couldn't drink mulled wine to this day. "Why didn't you say something? I wasn't a kid anymore. I must have been seventeen? Eighteen?"

"I had no intention of disrupting your life. Mary, on the other hand ... her new parents had split up and Mary lived with her mother. The woman would leave her with anybody while she went out partying, often bringing the party back home. Allowing strange men around a three-year-old girl—no way could I allow it. I took Mary, Bella as she was called then, during one of those parties. Do you know, they never reported her missing until the next afternoon? By then we were already in France."

Hundreds of questions whizzed through my mind, but I had no idea where to begin. I found it hard to believe it was possible to kidnap a child in this day and age and never get caught. "What did Mary say? She must have been distraught."

"You'd think so, wouldn't you? However, she was used to being passed around and she never batted an eyelid. She made one comment about her

'Mummy' after a couple of weeks then nothing else, and that's the truth."

I tried to imagine someone taking Emma. They'd probably bring her back after five minutes—she could be very vocal if her screams at the zoo were anything to go by.

Andrew continued, shocking me out of my daydream. "After about a year in France we came back. The media hype had settled, and since there'd been no recent photographs taken of Mary, prior to her going missing, no one ever recognised her.

We both had valid documents—illegal ones, but as real as you can get. Getting those kinds of documents is easy if you have the right connections and deep enough pockets.

I rented a basement flat in Tottenham and set up a technology company, working from home. With the training, I'd had and the job I was doing, there was no reason I'd ever get found.

I met Judy when Mary was almost five. She was a client, the editor at her parents' small newspaper, and we hit it off. I told her Mary was born in France and that her mum was an old girlfriend who'd left us over there. Mary had the cutest French accent and birth certificate to match and so she never had any reason to doubt me. Once we were married she took Mary on as her own."

Still standing at the window, Andrew put his hands shoulder-width apart on the glass above his head and leaned his body onto them, and his forehead touched the window. Pushing himself back, he spun away from the window and began pacing the floor.

"We never had any problems. Judy realised you and I had to be related when you arrived here yesterday. Mary did too. But neither of them knows the full story. Nobody does, except you."

"How the fuck could you do this to me, Andrew?" The enormity of his confession began sinking in. "I detested that baby. Detested everything about it. The months it grew inside me were the worst of my life." I glared at him, unable to control the words spewing from my mouth as I relived the memories of that awful time. "Whenever I felt it move I would be physically sick."

I noticed that I was digging my fingernails into my arms hard enough to draw blood. "Towards the end my whole stomach would move in the most obscene way. I often imagined a horrible alien would burst through my skin." I shuddered. My lungs felt as though they were filled with rocks, with no room left for air.

"She's not an alien, Mindy. Just an innocent little girl—so like you were at her age. She's not to blame for the awful abuse. She was just a by-product that's all."

I'd never allowed myself to think about the baby I'd given up. I'd never craved to hold it in my arms or gazed longingly at babies in the street. I'd blocked all those feelings.

I never even remembered her birthday.

I felt light-headed. If I'd been standing, I would definitely have toppled over. I lay backwards on the sofa, trying to calm my raging pulse. Suddenly, the vision of a timid, slight little thing with dark smudges under her eyes popped into my head and made my heart flutter. Mary was my daughter.

I couldn't take much more. The walls zoomed in and out at me and it felt as though my heart was stomping on my ribs.

Andrew was still standing at the window and turned to face me. "Are you all right, Mindy? You look terrible."

I glanced at him. The concern in his face made me melt. I'd dreamed of a loving reunion for years. Longed for him to turn up and look out for me as he used to. At nine and a half months older, he was my big brother and he'd always tried his best to protect me. Most of the beatings he'd received had been for defending me.

"I prayed for you to come home, but if I'm honest, I never imagined you would. The police even dug up the garden once, searching for you. I always feared the worst."

Sobs racked my body. How would we ever get over this? Although I understood the reasons for what he'd done, my brother was a murderer.

The tears began to slow. I glanced at Andrew, who had his back to me again. We had always looked very similar, often being mistaken for twins, which was a fact our dad had played on for the sick videos he'd produced.

Although he was a couple of inches taller than me now, he didn't have a big build, and I understood how he managed to convince everyone he was me. His shapely, lean body filled out his skinny jeans and tee-shirt, the way most women only dreamed of doing. Blond hair tied at the nape of his neck was shorter than mine, but not by much. His hands were manicured and his eyebrows waxed. Add a bit of makeup and lose the stubble and I could have been looking at myself.

"Why did you do it? After all this time, why now?"

"When Dennis got out I watched him and I wondered if he'd actually changed at all. I bugged his room at the hostel and soon discovered he hadn't. Watching him trawl the internet for young girls knocked me sick and brought back all the old feelings. I easily lured him to me in a chat room. Once I got rid of him, though, I couldn't stop until our darling stepmother had paid too. Three stinking years she'd served for the part she played. It was a fucking joke!"

"What about Brian? Of all the people involved back then, he had been the least abusive. He hardly did anything."

"Just a fluke. The night you got home from the police station I'd just arrived and noticed the light on in your bedroom window, but your car wasn't there. The next thing I knew that detective bloke arrived and ended up chasing me through the garden. I doubled back and followed him home. I wasn't sure what to do about him. Nobody else had seen me and it kinda spoiled my plans. I sat outside his house and after a few minutes he rushed out again. I followed him to the station. You can imagine my surprise when Brian sauntered out as large as life a few hours later. I couldn't resist following him. He was the only other person I actually knew back then, and although he wasn't as bad as the others, he'd still got away with everything."

"So you killed him, just like that?" I clicked my fingers.

He nodded. "What will happen to me now, do you think?"

I shrugged. "If you turn yourself in, they'll go easier on you. Most people will understand why you did it. We had a horrendous childhood. I can vouch for that. We'll stick together, Andrew, like we should have done all along, and we'll get through this."

"What about Mary? I need to make sure she's cared for. I can't bear the thought of our beautiful daughter going into care."

"I'll do what I can, of course I will. I won't lie to you though, Andrew, I'm still in shock. But I'll do all I can. I promise."

Andrew turned to face me. Tears poured down his cheeks and he held his arms out towards me.

Standing up, I slowly stepped into them. I don't know how long we stayed that way. Maybe minutes, maybe hours; time didn't matter.

We started as the nurse called from the hallway. "Mr Pitt, come quick."

Andrew raced from the room. I followed close behind and got as far as Judy's bedroom door before I heard Andrew's stricken wail. "No, Judy. No! Wake up, my darling, wake up."

He had partially lifted Judy's lifeless body into his arms and buried his face in her hair. The sounds of his pain were too much for me to bear.

I walked out of the room and closed the door.

I couldn't get my head around everything I'd learned in the past few hours. Finding my brother after all these years was enough to blow my mind, but learning his daughter was, in fact, my daughter felt too much for my brain to compute.

I glanced at my watch and realised I'd been sitting here for almost an hour, curled up in the armchair and going over and over what Andrew told me.

I thought I should check in with Sandra, but couldn't find my phone. I must have left it behind. I knew the kids would be okay, although Michael was probably doing his nut.

I hadn't noticed much activity going on in the rest of the house since leaving Andrew with Judy. Now I heard a buzzing coming from the hallway and I got up to investigate.

A white plastic box at the side of the front door had a small screen with a red light flashing in conjunction with the buzzing. I guessed it was the gate. The black-and-white image on the screen was very grainy because of the rain, but I could make out a vehicle. I pressed the most obvious button.

"Hello?"

"Doctor Kessler." A deep voice boomed from the speaker.

"Oh, erm, hang on ..." I stuttered, pressing the only other button. The car moved out of view so I guessed the button had worked. I opened the front door.

Doctor Kessler was a tall Indian man in his twenties who splashed from the car with his briefcase held above his head. His cheap grey suit looked as though it had seen better days. He introduced himself to me, and I led him to Judy's room. I knocked before opening the door.

The nurse sat on the floor next to the sideboard packing away medical supplies from the bottom drawer into a red plastic box.

Judy lay on the bed. Her hair had been brushed and now framed her face. Her lips had a dark tinge to them and her skin a waxy sheen. Other than that she could have been asleep.

There was no sign of Andrew.

"Oh, Doctor, come in, come in." The nurse jumped up from her position on the floor.

The doctor began examining Judy.

"Do you know where Andrew is?" I asked the nurse.

"Who?"

"Andr— er. DJ."

"Mr Pitt left. He said to ask you to pick his daughter up from her friends. He said he'd left the address on his desk upstairs."

"No! He can't have left." My voice was louder than I'd intended and the doctor stopped to look around at me. "How long ago?" I asked.

"Fifteen-twenty minutes, I guess," she said, glancing at the clock at the side of the bed.

I took the stairs two at a time, my heart racing and my head throbbing. I couldn't believe Andrew would leave without speaking to me.

The first room I came to was obviously Mary's bedroom. The walls and bedding were all different shades of pink. Cuddly toys covered the bed, making me wonder how she managed to get in and out of it.

The next door was the master bedroom. A huge, solid-oak, antique bed took up most of the room.

Quaint, Queen Anne bedside tables and two oak wardrobes, the only other furniture, were all neat and tidy except that the wardrobe door was wide open. Andrew must have gone through it in a hurry because I realised all his clothes were gone.

Through the last door on the landing I found the office. Compared to the rest of the antiquated cottage, this room blew me away. State-of-the-art equipment covered every wall. On the wall above the desk, I saw two flat-screen monitors and my stomach lurched. I stared at images of my kitchen and lounge.

I thought they were photographs at first, until I heard a familiar sound, and Michael walked into the kitchen. I watched as he dug his phone from his pocket and dialled a number. "Amanda, this is getting stupid now. You've made your point—call me." His voice was as clear as if I were standing in the room with him.

I was relieved in a way that my instincts had served me well, although I had thought the watching was happening outside, not inside my own home.

I wondered how long Andrew had been spying on us. I presumed he normally locked this door. He must have intended for me to see this today—otherwise he'd have switched the monitors off.

There was a walk-in-wardrobe on the back wall and I opened the door to see a line-up of familiar-looking women's clothing, the first garment, a red, collarless jacket. Confused, I pulled it towards me. Next came a blue shirt, then a Pink blouse, a navy skirt, pale-blue jeans, beige dress, midnight-blue velour dress, black trousers and a silver blouse. The list went on and on. My mouth dropped open. I could have been looking in my own wardrobe at home. Everything was exactly the same. He'd obviously been able to check out via the monitors what I wore on any particular day, and then dress accordingly.

An envelope leaned against the computer with my name on the front. Beside it was a notepad with an address and a scribbled message asking me to collect Mary. I folded the envelope, shoving it into the back pocket of my jeans, and tore the front page off the pad.

Back downstairs, the doctor was finishing off and came through to the kitchen to wash his hands. He placed a sheet of paper on the table. "You can contact the funeral directors now," he said.

"Okay, thanks." I don't know why I didn't tell him it was nothing to do with me; instead I smiled and walked him to the front door.

As the doctor's car left, another car sped into the driveway. Adam bolted from the vehicle and reached me at the front door in a couple of strides.

"Amanda, are you all right?" he said as two more police cars with their sirens blaring screeched to a stop behind Adam's.

"I—I'm okay."

"It's just ... Andrew, your brother. I think he's the killer."

"I know, he told me." I stepped back and Adam followed me into the hall.

"What do you mean?" He grabbed me by the shoulders. "You need to stand outside. It's dangerous. Are Mrs Pitt and the girl inside?"

"Judy died. She's in the back room with the nurse. The doctor just left—Mary isn't here."

Adam barked some instructions to four uniformed officers. They ran up the front steps towards us before pushing their way into the house. They scanned the lounge, then two of them took the stairs while the other two ran towards the back of the house.

"Where is he, Amanda?" Adam turned back to me.

"He's gone."

"Gone where exactly?"

I shrugged. "I've got no idea."

Two of the officers reappeared in the hallway, shaking their heads at Adam, who barked more orders at them: "We need to search this property from top to bottom, including the grounds."

"There's no point, Adam," I said. "He's already gone. You're too late."

Chapter 43

Amanda

"Are you sure you don't want me to come with you, sweetheart?" Sandra said.

"No, honestly. It's a big help if you just collect the children after day-care, I don't know how long we'll be."

"Course I will, love," Sandra said as she loaded the breakfast dishes into the dishwasher.

As I swigged the last of my coffee, I wondered how I ever got by without this wonderful woman in my life.

Handing Sandra my cup, I rushed through to the hallway. "Mary, are you almost ready?" I called up the stairs.

"Won't be a minute," she replied in her quiet voice.

She'd been staying with us for the past two months and today we hoped to make her a fixture in our home by being granted a Permanent Residence Order.

I was, after all, her only living relative apart from her fugitive father. I hadn't told anybody about the confession Andrew made to me about Mary's past. She was just another victim in all this and I wanted to protect her from any more suffering.

Besides, what good would come of everybody knowing she was, as Andrew called it, the by-product of sexual abuse? To find out her father is her uncle, or maybe even her grandfather? No—as far as anybody needed to know, I was her aunt, end of story.

The doorbell rang and Emma came charging through from the kitchen.

"Calm down, Miss Em," I said. "I'll get it. You go and brush your teeth then help Grandma get Jacob ready for day-care."

"Aw," she said and huffed up the stairs.

I opened the door and was surprised to find Adam Stanley. He was dressed in jeans and a brown leather jacket.

My stomach gave a little twirl.

"Oh hello," I said and smiled. "This is a nice surprise. Come on in."

"No, it's okay. I know you're probably running around like a headless chicken. I just wanted to wish you luck for today–not that I think you need it, mind."

"How nice of you to remember. Thanks, Adam, it means a lot, I said. "Are you sure I can't tempt you to a cuppa? I have time."

"Thanks, but no. I might call in later though, to see how it went if that's alright?"

Adam had been calling in to see us every few days. At first I thought he was making sure Andrew wasn't about, but now I wasn't so sure.

"That would be lovely, Adam. Maybe we can open a bottle of sparkly grape juice to celebrate with the kids?"

"It's a date then, I'll bring the bubbles." He laughed.

I watched as he walked down the path towards his car. The same animal attraction I'd first felt towards him hadn't faded, I don't know how I'd resisted him for so long.

The fact that Andrew hadn't been caught made it awkward between us though. He'd vanished off the face of the earth, or so it seemed. He left no trace for the police to follow, having withdrawn five hundred thousand pounds in cash in the weeks leading up to his disappearance.

I knew he was close by. He was an expert at being invisible—he'd done it for long enough in the past. Now, without a young child to consider, it must be so much easier.

I still felt I was being watched from time to time, but instead of feeling scared and vulnerable, I felt safe and protected.

The letter he'd left for me explained everything that we'd discussed that day. He must have had it ready to give to me once Judy died. I was glad about that. At least I know he intended for me to find out he was alive. He said he didn't regret what he'd done. "Getting the scum off the streets" was how he described it.

I'd not had the cameras removed. I hoped he still checked in on us. And sometimes, when I was alone, I'd talk to him—tell him how Mary was doing and how much we missed him. There was no way of knowing if he heard me, but the chance he might was enough of a comfort.

It turned out that Andrew had planned everything down to the last detail. Judy had changed her will in the days before she died, her solicitor having made a special trip to the house.

The country residence had been left in trust for Mary, as well as a substantial amount of money. She would be financially independent once she reached eighteen.

The rest Judy had signed over to Andrew, who in turn, had gifted it to me. I would inherit the house in Kingsley, a property I never intended to set foot in as long as I lived, and also an obscene amount of money that I intended to invest. Things would take a while to be finalised, but I was in no hurry.

Michael had got a job and moved to the city. He came back to see the children on the weekends. He and Toni hadn't lasted very long. Apparently, he'd caught her in bed with her Jamaican neighbour. This, I must admit, cheered me up whenever I was feeling low.

We couldn't file for a divorce just yet, although we agreed I would buy him out of the house and keep all the furniture. He'd taken his personal belongings, and as far as I was concerned the house was a much happier place without him.

We made a few changes at home to fit in our new family member. The computer desk now lived in my bedroom and Jacob moved into the former study, which freed up a decent-sized room for Mary. We were in current negotiations about its décor. She had very definite ideas about what she wanted—something she had undoubtedly inherited from me.

The children adapted well to all the changes. They adored their new cousin and she loved them to bits.

I, on the other hand, no longer felt the dread I'd come to believe was part of being a parent. I could allow the children space to grow without feeling I had to supervise every move they made. I'd enrolled them both into full-time day-care and now enjoyed the quality time I got to spend with Mary.

Walking away from the court, I felt lighter than I had in ages. All the weight I'd carried over the years had somehow lifted.

I glanced downward and a gaunt little face looked back up at me. "Shall we get an ice-cream, honey?" I asked.

"Yes, please, Auntie," Mary replied.

"We should celebrate. You are happy about this, aren't you?"

Mary nodded, the small smile on her lips not reaching her eyes.

"Maybe happy is the wrong word under the circumstances, but you know what I mean, don't you? They said you can live with us forever. That is what you want, isn't it?"

"Yes. I love being with you and my cousins."

She did seem to be coming to terms with her new life. However, I knew it would take her a long time to fully accept the loss of her mum. She still had no idea why her dad had left or about the murders. I knew she would have to know one day, but not yet.

As Mary and I reached the car park, my phone tinkled in my bag. I stopped walking and dug around for it.

You have 1 new message

Congratulations! Big hugs to my two favourite girls — A :)

I hugged the phone to my chest. My eyes filled with tears as I turned on the spot, scanning the area.

"What's wrong? Why are you crying, Auntie?"

"Nothing, sweetheart, nothing at all." I dropped to my knees and pulled her into my arms.

"I'm just happy, that's all. Really, really happy."

The End

ABOUT THE AUTHOR

Netta Newbound, originally from Manchester, England, now lives in New Zealand with her husband, Paul and their boxer dog Alfie. She has three grown-up children and two delicious grandchildren.

For more information or just to touch base with Netta you will find her at:
www.nettanewbound.com
Facebook
Twitter

Acknowledgements

Massive thanks to my family—especially my husband Paul for all your support and encouragement.

To my wonderful critique partners Sandra Toornstra, Linda Dawley, Serena Amadis and Jono Newbound—you're the best.

To my Editor, proof reader and friend Sandra Toornstra. You're amazing.

And finally, to the BOCHOK Babes – my go-to group for anything from critiquing to formatting or just a good old moan. Where would I be without you?

Printed in Great Britain
by Amazon